THE
PRISONER
OF
ORCHARD BEND

a novel by
Patrick Lemieux

Published by
Across The Board Books™
Toronto, Ontario, Canada

ISBN: 978-1-926462-05-9

First Trade Paperback Edition: May, 2017

Cover Art:
"The Prisoner Of Orchard Bend"
Acrylic on canvas
12" x 16"
© Patrick Lemieux, 2016

Title Page Sketches:
Pencil on paper
© Patrick Lemieux, 2016

End Page Art:
"The Place Of Lost Souls"
Acrylic on canvas
9" x 12"
© Patrick Lemieux, 2016

About The Author Page Sketch:
Pencil on paper
© Patrick Lemieux, 2016

To Judith Ann Sparrow
For always being there

Also by Patrick Lemieux

Fiction:
   Revenge Of The Dark Witch Of Oz:
            The Illustrated Screenplay

   Horizon Line, Vol. 1 (A Comic Book Collection)

Non-Fiction :
   The Queen Chronology:
            The Recording & Release History of the Band
            (Co-written with Adam Unger)

   The Mike Oldfield Chronology:
            The Recording & Release History

   The Barenaked Ladies Chronology:
            The Recording & Release History of the Band

   The Rush Chronology:
            The Recording & Release History of the Band

   Play Of Light: The Art of Patrick Lemieux

Acknowledgments

I'd like to thank the following people for their support as this book came to be:

Michael Wiley – You edited the book for me, so you get thanked first!

Heidi Loney – For invaluable advice, encouragement and regular discussions of the craft.

Mary-Margaret Scrimger – For not compromising. The book is better for it.

Ashley Sirianni – For inspiration and motivation.

Tim, Mel, Emmet, Jill, Dave, Jack, Josephine, Mark and Liv – I look forward to the times we're together.

Mom and Dad – Always.

1

May 3, 1879
Orchard Bend

The night of the storm a stranger arrived, but none of us knew it right then. I listened to the wind all night. It gusted and slammed our tiny home, but my Da' said, "Sweetheart, nothing short of a twister is going topple over our home."

But the wind sure did blow fierce. Down the road Mr Staid lost his barn when the big old oak in his yard came crashing down on it. Mr Staid was in Yellow Brook at his nephew's wedding, so his team of horses was not inside the barn when it was crushed. The chickens weren't so lucky.

It was Sam O'Toole who found the barn in ruins the next day. Sam was my age, 11 going on 12, and he was getting a penny for feeding Mr Staid's livestock while Mr and Mrs Staid attended the wedding. Since the feed was in the barn and the barn was just as gone as gone could be, Sam ran home to tell his father.

Now, you'd think an act of God against a barn would be the most interesting thing to happen to a boy that Saturday morning (or most any Saturday morning, for that matter), but you'd be mistaken. No, something much more interesting than a devastated barn and dead chickens was about to happen to Sam O'Toole.

Running home, Sam had to cross the bridge west of town. It's still there today, the original stone and timber, even after all these years; the ravine of trees and flowers is still just as pretty as they were that spring morning.

Sam was anxious to tell his father about what that storm had done to the Staid farm. In his haste Sam didn't see the three riders at the bridge until he was halfway down the hill.

"Where you headed, son?" asked the big man in lead.

"Home, mister."

The man nodded and the other two looked around.

Now, I wasn't there, but Sam told me the story a few times and his telling never changed, so I know it was the truth.

"Where's the nearest town?" asked the shortest man.

"'Bout three miles that way," Sam said, pointing in the direction of Orchard Bend.

The men looked at each other and that's when Sam saw the guns on their hips. At first he thought maybe they were the law or a posse, but the cut of their clothes, dishevelled, you see, also made him think they were something worse.

And he was right.

But wouldn't you know it, right then young Miss Rose Adelaide, Sam's school teacher, comes round the bend toward the very bridge the four were occupying. Miss Adelaide was on her way to have tea with the Slaytons, but she rode up in her small buggy and must have known something was amiss. She stopped at the top of the hill overlooking the bridge and called to Sam in her best stern schoolhouse voice, "Sam O'Toole, come here."

Sam says he got three steps before the first shot took Miss Adelaide to the ground. The shot he felt pass an inch from his ear. He turned back to the three men. He told me later he didn't have time to think if he was about to be shot dead, it all happened so fast. Sam turned in time to see the lead man with his gun pointed straight at him.

That's when the stranger intervened.

Oh, there was such a commotion that poor Sam didn't know what in blazes had befallen him now. The shot meant for the boy struck the tree behind him, missing its mark by virtue of a well-aimed stone striking the big man's gun hand. I once saw Lightening Jim Sawyer pitch a game of ball in Carson Town and he could bull's-eye a bumblebee at sixty feet, as I live and breath, and I reckon the stranger's aim was akin to Lightening Jim's.

Now, this next part ain't for the light of constitution, ya hear? They tend to omit this detail from the stories they tell the young'uns about what happened that day. I'm gonna tell you all of it as Sam used to tell me, so it's all on the record, as they say.

The outlaw's hand was broken and the gun hadn't even hit the ground before the stranger was upon them. Sam said all he could make out at first was a flurry of black and steel, followed by red. A blade opened the second man's neck as the dark shape of the stranger darn near climbed up on the saddle with him. The man's horse nearly rolled and I declare the stranger would've been crushed by that stag, but again that speed... oh, what they said about the stranger's quickness!

"Man Jesus!" said the third outlaw as his companion's body dropped from his horse. The stranger was standing still as a marble statue. Sam stood much like a statue himself, taking in the scene. He said later he thought the stranger was the Angel of Death come to take them all. The outlaw drew his shooting iron and the stranger flinched. Or Sam thought the stranger flinched, until he saw the knife handle in the man's chest and the surprised look on his face. He regarded the knife like a man might look at the food he accidentally spilled on his shirt.

Not many people are good with both hands. We all have a favourite and all have a fool hand that just can't seem to catch up. The big outlaw with the broken right hand, the man who started the shooting to begin with, whether he was truly good with his stupid left hand, we'll never know. You see, he was packing on both hips.

He drew that second gun of his and cocked it at the same time. Sam says the big man cursed the stranger as he drew, just as the knife was doing its job of making his friend dead. The oath he uttered was so foul, Sam went to his death bed never wanting to repeat it aloud to another living soul. Sam also wondered if the curse didn't give him away. No sooner had the foul language left his mouth than the stranger's other blade flashed in the morning sunlight. Knives had ended the other two outlaws, but this other weapon was something Sam had only ever read about in stories and history books.

The stranger's quickness spooked the outlaw's horse and it reared back. You might be inclined to cry foul at injuring the

3

animal to get to the rider, but if you've had a spooked horse inches from your head, with the man atop it trying to put you in the ground, you ain't got time to fret over the finer points of the situation.

The stranger brought the horse down with a sword. The outlaw hit the ground, losing his second gun in the process, but wouldn't you know it, his first gun, dropped when the stone broke his hand, was within grabbing distance. The stranger, though, wasn't having any of it. The sword took off his left hand and was driven into the man's heart without so much as a pause.

When the big outlaw's horse fell, the other two bolted. The outlaw with the knife in his heart dropped to the ground in a heap.

No one was timing the scene and you can forgive Sam if he was wrong on this count, but he swears the stranger took about the count of ten to put down those three men. What brought young Mr O'Toole back into his right senses wasn't the carnage or the pained whinnying of the felled horse, but a cry of pain from behind him.

Miss Adelaide was shot, but she wasn't ready to meet her maker just yet, you see. Sam was at her side jackrabbit quick and saw the outlaw's bullet had left a bloody hole in her shoulder. Sam would never look at blood the same way after that. The slightest scratch made him think of the day he was saved by that stranger.

"Miss Adelaide!"

"Sam," Miss Adelaide said through so much pain, "need... Doctor... Shaw."

She was trying to get up, but shock was setting in and the school teacher fell unconscious.

Poor young Sam thought she was dead and had seen more in that morning than most do in their lifetime. Despite being times that tend to harden boys into men, this was all just too much for Sam and he broke, letting those tears take him.

"NO! Miss Adelaide!" he cried.

A hand touched his shoulder and he jerked away with a fright.

4

The stranger, head still beneath the hood of the cloak, was at his side. The voice that spoke was stern and calming.

"She's alive. I can dress the wound but she needs a doctor, kid! Where is the nearest one!"

The stranger was working fast, tearing a swath from Miss Adelaide's dress. Sam didn't answer at first. You see, he was still trying to get it through his rattled mind that the person talking to him, this stranger who he thought seconds ago was the Angel of Death, was a woman.

She pulled back her hood, barely pausing in her ministration of the wounded Miss Adelaide. She gave the boy a look so forceful it rivalled the ones his parents would give him when he done wrong and was facing a whuppin'! It was more than enough to wake Sam from his addled state and he spoke at last.

"Doc Shaw's not far, ma'am."

"Can you drive this buggy?"

"I expect I can."

The stranger discovered that the bullet that hit Miss Adelaide caused not one bloody hole, but two, having gone right through.

It must be said that it was a good thing Miss Adelaide decided to wear her Sunday best on a Saturday; it gave the stranger tending her wounds more cloth to bandage her up with.

There wasn't a thing Sam could do as he watched this woman work. Seamus O'Toole hadn't raised a dullard for a son and Sam had enough sense to watch and stay clear as she worked. He also held his peace on the questions coming into his head, like "Who are you?" and "Where did you come from?"

"That's all I can do," the stranger said, "help me get her up. We have to hurry."

Now, when the designers of that buggy put their heads together, I'm sure not a-one of them supposed it would be used in this fashion, a fact that became clear to Sam pretty quick like. There was no way it would hold all three of them.

"Do you know the way to the doctor?" the stranger asked Sam. "I can't go with you, but I'll try to follow."

Sam felt that curse of panic welling up again. He started to protest, "But—!"

"Kid, there's no time! Get her to the doctor right the hell now!"

Sam, steeled again, brought the buggy around and broke for town.

Racing back to Orchard Bend, Sam realized that the road's twists and turns had never seemed to take so long, even on foot, as when someone else's life was at stake.

Well now, when Sam O'Toole came crashing into town riding Miss Adelaide's buggy (and riding it harder and faster than I expect it was built for), you can be sure people came looking! Sam got Miss Adelaide to Doctor Shaw and while the man worked on saving her life, Sam told his story to the gathering crowd about happened out at the bridge. The Sheriff formed a posse and the men rode out to investigate.

Miss Adelaide did indeed survive and no one doubts the fact that the stranger's dressin' of the wound probably made all the difference under the sun, as they say.

The stranger's name as you already know was Emery Dale and that was the day she arrived in Orchard Bend.

2

May 14, 1953
Blue Creek

Cal Watson's head felt split in half.

After a moment of spiralling incoherence, he supposed it almost had been. He was lying on the grass, soaked by rain. It was dark as he blinked his eyes open. Shapes came into focus around him. A bright light shone not far away, silhouetting the familiar front porch of his house.

He started to get up and sharp pain replaced the throbbing coming from the back of his head.

Someone clocked me good, Cal thought. He looked around. A soggy paper bag with some soda bottles lay spilled on the grass near him. He remembered going to the store, a quick errand before the storm hit. His girlfriend, Debbie, liked cream soda, while Cal preferred Cott cola. He planned to tell her the store didn't have any. She'd pout and Cal would pull out the bottle and surprise her. He knew he'd get a punch in the arm and a kiss for that.

Cal came back from the store, walked up the driveway... then blackness and waking up in the rain. Someone had definitely hit him from behind.

He tried to stand up, but his knees threatened to give out from under him. Cal swayed and his hand found the car in the driveway. He shook the cobwebs from his brain. Lightning flashed above him in the storm's full gale. Cal stumbled forward. A body lay half draped on the hood of the car.

"Dad?" Cal said, rushing towards him.

Blood from his father's cut throat washed away in the rain. Cal couldn't even begin to process it. In his father's hand was a double-barrelled shotgun, the same one he used when taking Cal hunting up north each autumn. Cal took it, feeling numbness wash over him like the rain drenching his clothes.

This is a dream, Cal thought, *that's all, I'll wake up in just a second.*

A rusty crash and a scream made him turn to the back of the house. Cal knew that sound, the creak of the screen door leading to the backyard. But that scream, like something out of a bad horror movie? Only Debbie screamed like that and only when the movie went from fun to terrifying.

The pain in his head faded in the rush of adrenaline and panic. Cal rounded the corner of the house and stopped, dumbfounded by the scene before him.

A dark shape moved up and down on the ground. Cal made out arms and a face, a man in a black suit and tie, kneeling over the red and white shape of Debbie on the ground. He had recognition without emotion or any real comprehension. Debbie's blood mixed with the mud and rain as her killer continued stabbing her, tearing through her new blouse. Her muddy legs twitched under her light blue skirt.

The man stopped and she didn't move. The man looked up at Cal and smiled.

"Howdy, neighbour," he said.

"Mr Bullock?" Cal said.

Mr Bullock laughed. He stood up from Debbie's body and ran a bloody hand through his greying hair. Cal raised the shotgun, acting not out of any rational thought, but through thin, sharp survival instinct. He saw the knife in Mr Bullock's hand rinsed clean by the rain. Mr Bullock stepped over Debbie's body toward Cal and Cal didn't even think if the shotgun was loaded when he pulled the trigger.

Fortunately, it was.

The seasons of hunting up north with his father had been well-spent and Cal's aim was true. Mr Bullock's chest erupted in a spray of red and he fell back onto Debbie's body.

Time seemed to stop for Cal. After a while he heard sirens in the distance and still he kept the shotgun trained on Mr Bullock's dead body. The sirens got louder and then there were voices behind him, barking orders he couldn't quite process. He kept the shotgun trained on Mr Bullock. Hands were grabbing him and someone pulled the shotgun from his grip. Words started to make sense again. One finally allowed him to relax, "Police."

The police are here, Cal thought, *maybe now I can wake up.*

As the hands pulled him to the ground, Cal passed out.

3

May 16, 1953
Orchard Bend

The unpaved, one lane road was a test for the car's aging shocks. Each time it hit a depression in the ground (or a stone or a dead tree limb), the vehicle shuddered and bounced. This went on for several jaw-rattling miles. Behind the wheel, Detective Tom Reed cast a glance every few seconds to the trees' low-hanging canopy above him. He was waiting for a stiff spring breeze to bring one of the larger damaged branches down in front of him.

Or with my luck, right down on the car, Reed thought. *It would probably kill me.*

It had been a few days since the storm. The town had cleared the streets and yards of the ruined trees and branches after they caused some minor devastation, but out here in the less-traveled corners of Orchard Bend, the battered foliage still littered the ground. Above the road, Reed could see the damaged branches seeming to wait for another sharp gust of wind to break them loose. And no sooner had he thought that than the trees swayed in the breeze. He tensed up, but nothing came down on him.

Reed pulled into the clearing of the Hansen property and got out of the car. A gust of air caught his tie and sent it over his shoulder. Reed straightened it and did up the jacket of his suit to keep it in place. The fresh air brought in from the heavy rain two nights before was gone now, replaced with an oppressive thickness. The air was moving, though, but it wasn't helping much. The growing heat made Reed's shirt stick to him under the jacket.

Will Hansen stood on the porch, a beer in his hand at 9:42 in the morning. His heavy work shirt was faded, but it was clean apart of the growing sweat marks under his arms. In the small patch of sunlight across the shady yard, the family's clothes swayed on the line to dry. From around the other side of the house, Reed could hear the Hansen children laughing and playing. Hansen waved to the detective and Reed waved back. A patchwork of muddy puddles covered the yard, so Reed gingerly made his way to his trunk, popped it open, sat against the bumper and swapped his dress shoes for a pair of old work boots.

Closing the trunk, he saw Hansen approaching. The man up-ended the bottle and downed the rest of the beer.

"Morning, Tommy," Hansen said, then let out a satisfied belch.

"Good morning, Will."

"Hell of thing, ain't it?" Hansen looked out towards the woods at the far end of the clearing. The detective tried not to think about what he was going to see out there.

"Mind showing me, Will?" Reed asked, nodding in the direction of the trees.

"You and I been out here a million damn times, ain't we? Playing Cowboys and Indians and all that stuff. Remember that?" Hansen asked as they navigated around the larger patches of mud.

"Sure do," Reed said, "Your dad sitting on the porch, telling us not to go out of sight of the house."

"Damn straight. I tell my kids the same thing. 'If I can't see you, you gone too far.'" Hansen then noticed he still held the empty beer bottle and without breaking his stride, tossed it over his shoulder. Reed heard the bottle plop in the mud. "I'll grab it on the way back, don't let me forget."

Reed laughed. At the tree line, Reed glanced back at the house. The view was familiar from those long ago hot summer days. As boys Tom and Will pretended to kill each other with toy guns for hours on end. Sometimes Will's dad, the heavy drinking Mr Hansen, would be parked on the porch nursing a bottle. The days ended when Mr Hansen called to Will that dinner was on unless the boy wanted to starve.

Stepping into the underbrush, Reed and Hansen made their way into the thin woods. Despite the shade, the air seemed hotter and more stagnant, no longer moving. Reed undid his jacket and loosened his tie as they continued on.

"Jason and Allie said they were chasing a rabbit. That's why they went past the tree line. They know well enough they're not supposed to go out this far," Will explained. Jason and Allie were Will Hansen's kids, whom Reed heard playing when he arrived. Hansen sighed, "I'm guessing it'll be a long damn time before they want to play around these trees again."

They were well into the woods now and Reed looked back, unable to see the house. They kept walking a few more minutes and Reed asked, "They came this far?"

"Yup," Hansen said. "See it yet?"

"See what?"

"Up ahead," Will Hansen nodded. The detective squinted and scanned through the woods, seeing nothing out of the ordinary. "Let's keep walking, you'll see it."

A moment later, Tom Reed saw it.

Bunker-like, the small wood structure sat half buried in the ground.

"Well, I'll be..." Reed said, coming to a stop.

"Yeah, that's it," nodded Hansen.

"It's in there?"

Hansen nodded again and Reed looked around as if to spot more such bunker-like buildings. He could hear the stream babbling at the edge of the Hansen property.

"We're still on your land, right?" Reed asked.

"We are," Hansen replied, "there's a little bridge a ways back up the stream, closer to the house. There's a fence on the other side, about fifty feet from the stream, that's the edge of the property."

"We're going to have to bring people in here, take out what's in there, have a look around. You didn't touch anything, did you?" Reed asked.

"No, I didn't. I figured you'd all want to do something like that, so I left well enough alone," Hansen said.

"Okay then," Reed said. "Best I take a look."

* * *

Hansen stood watching as Reed approached the bunker. Moss grew in clumps, and dead leaves and needles covered the low, deformed roof. A misshapen door frame sat hollow where the bunker appeared to grow out of the ground. Beneath the moss, the walls were made of thick timber. Reed pulled his flashlight out of his jacket pocket. A breeze came through the trees and somewhere in the distance came a cracking sound and a crash. A damaged branch had finally come down.

Hopefully not on the road, Reed thought.

He stood at the doorway and looked for any distinguishing features. He turned to Hansen and called back, "Did you know this building was here?"

"I did, but I ain't never gone near it. Swear to God, Tommy," Reed believed him. He wondered if Hansen's father had ever gone inside. Maybe that's why he didn't want the boys playing too far in the trees all those years ago. On second thought, that didn't quite add up. When he drank, Mr Hansen got angry and violent, but sober he wasn't stupid enough to leave something like this out here. And there were plenty of times Tom saw Mr Hansen sober, like in town running errands, working part time as a mailman and part time at the printers behind the Orchard Herald. Some days when Tommy Reed came over to play with Will, Mr Hansen would have the ball game on the radio on the front porch. Instead of a cold beer, he'd have a pitcher of lemonade and a sandwich in the sunshine.

As if on cue, a cloud rolled away from the sun. The woods lit up around them with shafts of bright warm light. A bird chirped nearby and Reed turned on his flashlight. He expected to see it immediately, but instead saw only a small dirty footprint on the wood floor. Jason had found it, ignoring Allie's pleas not to go in, according to what the children would tell him later. Stepping down into the sunken recess of ground, Reed noted the broken door on the floorboards, another victim of the storm. Holding his breath against what he knew he'd find, Reed panned the flashlight around the interior, which seemed somehow larger inside than it appeared outside. In the far corner, an old cast iron wood stove sat unused for Lord knew how long. A chair lay on its side, two of its legs broken. There, Reed saw the first skeleton.

* * *

The remains lay covered in rags, clearly a human body at one time, but lacking a head and one arm. Reed felt no shock or fright at seeing it and that came as a relief.

He panned his flashlight and saw the other one, a complete skeleton, looking as though it had just sat down on the floor against the wall. On its ragged lap rested its skull on a thick leather belt.

A leather gun belt.

No, make that two *gunbelts, crisscrossing the hips gunslinger-style. Playing Cowboys and Indians, were we?* Reed thought with an uncharacteristic ghoulish snicker, happy to simply not be having the creepy-crawlies while looking at a pair of skeletons on his friend's property. And the gun belts still held shooting irons in the holsters and bullets unused in their loops.

"Now, how long have you two been out here?" Reed asked, shaking his head at the curious, morbid sight.

Next to the gunslinger's skeleton, a torn bit of the shirt lay on the ground. The badge pinned to it almost looked fake, like the one Reed himself used to wear when pretending to be Wyatt Earp or Bat Masterson. The patina on it, however, came from genuine age. Reed craned his neck and took a step forward to read the name.

Dale.

At first it meant nothing, then it came loud and clear in his memory.

"Oh shit," Reed said.

This has to be fake, he thought. Reed stepped out of the bunker and saw Hansen standing where he'd left him, hands in his pockets. Reed walked to him, thoughts spinning.

"Tell me the truth now, Will, and this ends here and now!" Reed said.

"What? What are talking about?"

"Did you stage that? Did you set that up as a practical joke or something?" Reed reached his friend and got right up in his face. He could smell the morning's beer on Hansen's breath.

"No. Hell no. Swear to God, Tommy. My kids found it and nobody touched a thing in there!" Hansen said. "Why? What the hell is in there? I just saw the skeletons and called you guys."

Reed looked into Hansen's eyes. He'd known the man since they were seven years old and Will's eyes spoke the truth.

"I ain't lying, Tom," Hansen said.

Tom Reed turned back to the bunker, hands on his hips, knowing what this meant.

"Shit," Reed said under his breath.

"Tom," Hansen said (and he never called him "Tom" unless things got serious), "What's going on, besides two skeletons in there?"

"One of them is her, Will."

"*Her* who?" Hansen asked.

Reed ran a hand through his hair, took a deep breath and let it out. He turned back to his friend and said, "Emery Dale. One of the skeletons is Emery Dale."

* * *

Tom Reed had practically sprinted through the woods back to Will Hansen's house to use his phone. Pausing to take off his muddy work boots before crossing the messy living room to the kitchen, he paused again debating which number to call first. Against the excitement and dread of the moment, he called the Sheriff's Office to send the coroner to pick up the remains from the bunker. Not wanting to start the rumour mill going, he didn't tell the secretary, Shelly Dickson, the name he suspected belonged to one of the skeletons.

Reed knew he had to work fast before the rest of Orchard Bend's police department arrived. Before that, he'd have to cordon off the area and start making notes while he had some peace and quiet at the crime scene, so he knew his next call had to be fast.

He tapped his pencil impatiently on the wall next to the phone, listening to the ring tone on the other end. At last, a male voice answered.

"Orchard Bend Historical Society," the voice said.

"Peter, it's Tom Reed."

"Oh, hey, Tom. What can I do for you?" Peter asked.

Tom paused, uncertain how to discuss this.

"Well, um. I need you to do me a favour and tell nobody about this call, at least for the time being. Police business, you understand. It's part of an investigation and I can't have any leaks."

"Yeah, alright. My lips are sealed."

"Good," said Reed. He paused again to consider how best to ask, but decided that he'd just have to be direct. "Peter, I need you to gather up everything you have on Emery Dale."

There came a pause on the other end of the line.

"Peter?" Reed asked.

"I'm here, just wondering if I heard you right," Peter sounded sceptical.

"You heard me right. *Emery Dale*. Anything and everything you've got. I'll call you tomorrow to set up a time to meet, but I need you to promise me you won't say anything to anyone." Reed was emphatic.

"I promise," Peter sounded uncertain, but Reed knew he could trust him. Peter probably thought him nuts, but Reed didn't care as long he kept his mouth shut and got him the records he needed.

Reed thanked Peter and almost hang up when a thought occurred to him, "Oh, and Peter, if by some chance someone *else* besides me comes knocking on your door looking for that information, stall them, tell them you lost it, I don't care. I need to see whatever you have before anyone else does, understand?"

"Um, not really, Tom."

"Just don't give anything about her to anyone before you give it to me. Can you do that?" Reed asked.

"Yes, of course. Police business. I got it," Peter sounded strange at the end, a mix of confusion and something else. Excitement maybe? Reed wasn't sure, but he said goodbye and hung up.

* * *

Hansen helped Reed with the police tape, stringing it from tree to tree in a wide berth around the bunker. Reed didn't believe any evidence outside the bunker would be preserved after all this time. If he was right, this crime scene dated to fifty or sixty years ago.

After taping off the area, Reed starting making notes, jotting down on his little pad everything he could remember hearing about Emery Dale. He wasn't sure half of it was correct, but that's where Peter Howard came in. The Orchard Bend Historical Society belied Peter's modest office and cramped museum space in the back of the Town Hall, what had previously been called the Town Archives before Peter took over the job a few years previous. Tom had gotten to know Peter Howard when Tom had started hanging out in the school library. That's where Maggie Cooper was doing an extra credit placement helping the librarian. Tom would watch Maggie and try to work up the courage to ask her out in between chatting with Peter and trying to get some actual studying done. Nowadays, with the Sheriff's Office adjacent to the Town Hall, Tom occasionally ran into Peter. While not close friends, Reed knew he could trust Peter to keep this Emery Dale business hushed up for now.

"You really think it's her?" Hansen asked as Reed paused in his note-making. "This woman from back then?"

"Yeah, I'm pretty sure," Reed answered. "Look, Will, I'm sorry about before."

"It's fine, Tommy. Relax."

"It's going to get really busy here soon and I'm going to try to keep a lid on this thing as best I can, but people talk and there's one person I don't want getting near this just yet, not till we're sure its her in there."

Will Hansen seemed to read his mind and nodded.

Reed continued, "This is your land, so you're within your rights to give him the ol' heave-ho if you see him snooping around."

"Can I shoot him?"

"Only as a last resort," Reed chuckled.

* * *

Reed left the crime scene last, climbing into his car as the sun sank below the tree line. Photos had been taken in and around the scene, many inside the bunker (probably an old hunting cabin, according the coroner, Jim Field. Reed still thought of it as a bunker, though). Every scrap of leftover clothing and practically everything inside had come out, including the heavy cast iron stove. Reed told everyone there to keep quiet about what they saw. He personally collected the badge with her name on it to avoid anyone else seeing, but he couldn't chance anyone talking too much about the specifics of what lay in the bunker.

Reed closed his eyes and rubbed them with the heels of his palms, letting out a long sigh. He wanted to get back into town and see Peter, start putting together the pieces and—

A tap at the window. Will Hansen stood there smiling.

"Tommy, we're looking to fix dinner, you're welcome to join us. Got a cold brew with your name on it," Hansen said. Reed smiled and rolled down the window.

"Actually, Will, can I use your phone again?"

* * *

Peter answered on the first ring.

"Peter, it's Tom again. Did you get everything I asked for?"

18

"I did, yes. And no one's come by poking around, if you were wondering," Peter said.

"No, huh? That's good to know," Reed said.

"I'm looking to lock up for the night, unless you're on your way over. In that case, I can wait for you. Anything I can do to help a police investigation, you know!" Peter said.

"No, it's okay, I'll call you in the morning. Thanks again," Reed said.

"I'm at your service. Have a good night," Peter said.

"You, too, Peter."

Reed hung up. Hansen sat at the table, a frosty beer in front of him. His wife, Ann, took a roast out of the oven. Hansen gave Reed a look that said, *Well?*

Reed smiled, saying, "I'll stay for dinner if the offer is still good."

4

May 17, 1953
Orchard Bend

In the basement of Orchard Bend Hospital was a little-used room that showed its age not in any sense of neglect, since it was clean and in good repair, but in the distinct lack of updating its décor. Posters dating from the Second World War still implored young ladies to join the US Cadet Nurse Corps and for men to to become field medics.

Reed waited for Dr Jim Field, the coroner, to finish writing his notes. Field was seated at the solitary desk at the far corner of the room, leaving the detective free to examine the evidence taken from the bunker.

The leather of the gun belts had cracked and moulded away in places decades ago. The buckles remained, as did some cracked hide with bullet loops and the holsters themselves. The pair of Colt .45 single action revolvers, the company's famed "Peacemaker" models, sat next to them. Unused bullets from the gun belts stood in a neat line. Along side the individual weapons, the spent shells of three rounds, two from the right hand gun and one from the left, sat next to the unfired bullets from each gun.

She got off three rounds, Reed thought.

A pair of Bowie knifes sat near the guns. The polish of the cherrywood handles had long since faded, but Reed could still make out the pink tint in the wood and knew that when these knives were first made, they must have looked brilliant.

The doctor grunted and got up from the desk, holding a clipboard with his notes. He shuffled across the room and stood between the two skeletons, each on an examination table. His

20

white hair glowed like a halo under the bright lights. The search of the area the day before turned up no sign of the skull and arm missing from the first skeleton. It lay incomplete on the cold metal table.

"Who do you want to start with, Detective?" Dr Field asked.

"The complete one," Reed said without hesitation.

"Okay then," started Dr Field. "Complete skeleton of an adult female—"

"You're one hundred percent sure it's a woman?" Reed interrupted.

"A first year medical student could tell you that, Detective Reed, it's basic morphology. Just by looking at the pelvis, her rib cage..."

"Sorry, Doctor, I just want to be certain."

Field nodded, grunted and continued.

"She was an adult female, 45 to 50 years of age, in excellent physical shape, you can tell by the impressions on the bones," the doctor pointed to the limbs with his pencil. "Well nourished throughout her life. No teeth missing, no obvious dental work. A few small fractures on her hands. I'd hazard a guess she threw the odd punch. Took some, too. There are a couple healed ribs fractures. Approximate height: 5 foot, 9 inches. Blonde and grey hair found around the skull is consistent with the approximate age."

"Cause of death?" Reed asked.

"It would appear she was stabbed in the neck and died of excessive blood loss," Dr Field pointed to one of the neck bones, "There's a mark consistent with a bladed weapon right here."

Reed looked from the bones to the stains on the tattered shirt next to the skeleton. Dr Field seemed to have come to the same conclusion when he said, "That would appear to have been her blood. I expect she died in a few seconds, though I can't be certain. There was a bloody bandana in her left hand, so she might have tried to stop the bleeding. There's a dagger on the table which I believe is your murder weapon"

That's how you died, huh? Stabbed in the neck in a forgotten hunter's cabin in a back corner of the Hansen homestead, Reed mused. He shook his head.

"What about the other remains?" Reed asked.

"An adult male. Skull and right arm missing," said Dr Field. "Approximate age: 35 to 40. Approximate height: 5 foot, 11 inches, though without the skull I could be off a bit. This man suffered numerous injuries throughout his life. A healed spiral fracture of the humerus bone of the left arm, sustain during childhood. Five healed ribs..."

"He took a few beatings in his life," Reed muttered.

"And gave a few," Dr Field added. "There are healed fractures in his hand, more-so than our lady friend here. You see these sorts of wounds in a professional fighter."

"What was his cause of death?" Reed asked.

"Not having the skull, which may contain evidence to the contrary, I'm hazarding the assumption that it was this gunshot wound to his chest. Taken at close range, too, judging by the remains of the shirt he was wearing," Dr Field pointed to the blue/brown rags. "See that hole? It's from the bullet that caused this damage to his breast plate."

Reed saw the very definite hole to the left side of the man's chest, shattering some of the ribs there. Dr Field gently picked up the rib cage and turned it over, saying, "And the exit wound is here. I believe the bullet was retrieved from the wall of the cabin. It's there on your right."

Reed saw it, a mushroomed slug. He would have it and the pair of Colt .45s sent for ballistic comparison, but he had no doubt one of these weapons shot the man on the table.

"One curious thing I found, Detective," Dr Field said, "Or rather what I didn't find... There's no evidence of wildlife disturbing these bodies."

"Really?"

"These aren't the first old bones I've examined that were found in the wilderness, but they are the first where I'm not finding bite marks or breaks from any wild animal deciding to have a free meal. These bones don't appear to have been found in that cabin by any dogs or foxes or anything else," Dr Field tapped his pencil to his lips as he stood looking at the bones.

"How unlikely is that?" Reed asked.

"Well, if the door was shut and they had no way in, rather likely the bodies would be left alone, Detective," Dr Field said, now looking closely at the incomplete skeleton.

"But the arm and head of the man are missing. I kind of figured an animal had gotten a hold of it," Reed said.

"It's possible. Maybe the Hansen children weren't the first to find that cabin and someone wanted a souvenir," said Dr Field.

Reed nodded and jotted some of this in his note pad.

"Detective, I'm going to go out on a limb and assume you've come to the same conclusion about who this woman was," said Dr Field. Reed turned to face him, fixing his gaze and sizing the doctor up.

"Emery Dale," Reed said. The doctor nodded.

"The badge there, the blonde hair, all of it," Dr Field said.

"Her last stand," said Reed.

"A lot of people are going to be interested in this case, Detective," Dr Field said, taking his glasses off his thin nose. "Emery Dale and this town... She's pretty close to being a legend."

"I know," Reed said. "And I know some quarters of this town would like to forget she was ever here."

Reed stood looking at the pair of Colt .45s now, the metal dark with patina, but little rust. The bunker, the hunting cabin, whatever it was, had preserved them and a great deal else inside.

"They've been dusted. Put on a pair of gloves and you can pick them up, Detective," said Dr Field behind him, "I expect they'll end up in the Orchard Bend Museum after this case closes. Now's your chance."

Reed smiled in spite of the gravity of the case. He took a pair of rubber gloves from the dispenser and snapped them on. He closed the chamber and picked up the right-handed revolver. It seemed heavier than it looked, heavier than his .38 Police Special service revolver. Reed wondered if some of that weight was just in his mind. This was one of Emery Dale's guns, after all.

* * *

Blue Creek Frontiersman Newspaper
Vol. 63, Issue 20
May 18, 1953

LOCAL MAN MURDERS NEIGHBOURS
by Audrey Dalton, Sr. Staff Reporter

On the evening of May 14, local man Anthony Bullock of 39 Brook St. W., recently divorced from his wife Nancy (nee Carpenter), broke into the home of Clifford and Lily Watson of 42 Brook St. W. Visiting the Watsons was Ms Debbie Elliot of 68 Shepherd Ln, aged 16. Bullock murdered Mrs Watson in the living room, Mr Watson in the driveway, Ms Elliot in the backyard, and was shot dead by the Watson's 17 year old son, Calvin.

Debbie Elliot, a long-time family friend of the Watsons, was visiting when Calvin left the residence to walk to the end of the block, to the Overland Market, to purchase groceries. Calvin was assaulted by Bullock upon returning to his home, was knocked unconscious and awoke to find his parents and Ms Elliot murdered. It is believed Mr Watson, before his death, was armed with a shotgun in self-defence and it was with this weapon that Calvin shot Bullock after regaining consciousness.

Inside the home, numerous signs of a struggle suggest both Mrs Watson and Ms Elliot attempted to defend themselves prior to their deaths.

Neighbours later said they heard nothing untoward at first, likely due to high winds and rain from the tremendous storm which blanketed the region that evening. Eventually Mrs Edith Wallop of 40 Brook St. W. heard screaming from the Watson's backyard, followed by a shotgun discharging. From her bedroom window, Mrs Wallop saw Calvin Watson standing motionless with a shotgun in his hand in the backyard.

"It was dark, but I could make him out," Mrs Wallop said. "I knew something was very wrong so I called the police right away. I was devastated when I heard what happened to his family and poor Debbie Elliot."

"It's believed at this time that Anthony Bullock suffered a nervous or mental breakdown as a result of his recent divorce," Blue Creek Sheriff Earl Meyer said. *"It's unclear why he targeted the Watson home that evening and we may never know the exact reason for this tragedy."*

Other neighbours spoke of recent episodes of erratic behaviour from Bullock, including a heated argument with a town Works Department employee attempting to read Bullock's electrical meter.

Calvin Watson is currently recovering from the tragedy at Blue Creek Memorial Hospital. Information regarding funeral services for the Watsons and Ms Elliot will be forthcoming.

* * *

May 16, 1953
Orchard Bend

"Jason, don't go in there," Allie said on the verge of tears. "It's scary! We'll get in trouble!"

The Hansen children forgot all about the rabbit when they saw the shack (what Tom Reed later that day would refer to as a bunker). Jason thought it looked haunted, but stronger than the fear was a need to look inside.

"I'm going back!" Allie said.

"Stay there," Jason replied and he knew she'd do as he said. As he approached he promised himself that at the first sign of anything bad, he would run.

He stepped down through the door and the floor boards creaked. Dark shapes and shadows formed in the room as his eyes adjusted. When he saw the skeleton he went cold. He could just make it out. The skull lay on its lap as if looking back at him. He felt a powerful urge to run and came close to doing just that when something next to the skeleton's leg caught his eye.

There lay a small, dark rectangular box that looked broken in two pieces. Jason picked them up from the shadows and found they were held together by a thin, strong wire.

"Jason?!" Allie yelled, her voice shaky.

"I'm okay," Jason said, his voice also shaky, but not from fright. Fear had been replaced by excitement. He tried to fit the two pieces back together and it didn't work. He twisted the smaller piece around, thinking of the batteries in his dad's flashlight that had to be put in a certain way. With a click, the small piece fit into the larger piece and the little box lit up, startling him. Coloured lights flashed around on a little screen in the gloom of the shack. A bright red circle spun around, replaced by a solid green block. Grey smoke seemed to fill the room. In his hand there was a soft tone from the box and it went black. Jason shook the gadget and hit it gently with the palm of his hand, but nothing happened. The grey, smoky world had also vanished.

"Jason Hansen, I'm scared and I'm going home right now if you don't come out!" Allie cried.

Jason put the box in his pocket and climbed out of the shack.

"Allie, don't cry, everything's okay. We have to go get dad!" Jason said as he rushed towards his sister.

"Why?! What's in there?"

"I can't tell you," Jason said. "I have to tell dad!"

5

May 17, 1953
Orchard Bend

Books, boxes and antiques lined Peter Howard's office shelves. Despite the constant struggle for space, everything in the room was labelled and organized with precision. The office lay off to one side of the modest but ambitiously named Orchard Bend Historical Society Museum. This museum lay at the end of a corridor in the Town Hall where few ventured. In the museum, chairs, tables and other bits of antiquity made up most of the collection on display, surrounded by paintings and photos of Orchard Bend life captured over the years.

Tom Reed sat opposite Peter's desk, his notebook out, pencil in hand. Peter sat behind his desk

"I'm eager for you to hear this, Tom. I made this copy of the acetate a few years ago," Peter said, sounding like a child excited to share a new toy. "I wanted to keep the playing of the original 78 to a minimum. You can only play it so many times before it wears out."

Reed held up the 78 in his hands, nestled in its plain, yellowing sleeve. The label read:

Eloise Langford Memories 2 of 3
Recorded 06-06-35

"I have the other two 78s, but sadly Mrs Langford did not discuss Emery Dale on them," Peter said. He started up the reel-to-reel tape player. The sound of Eloise Langford's voice drifted from it, littered at first with the clicks and pops of an old record.

The night of the storm a stranger arrived, but none of us knew it right then. I listened to the wind all night. It gusted and slammed our tiny home, but my Da' said, "Sweetheart, nothing short of a twister is going topple over our home."

Reed sat and listened as the old woman in the recording told the story of what happened to Sam O'Toole and how he and the schoolteacher, Rose Adelaide, were saved from a gang of outlaws. Rose shot and wounded, but the hooded stranger who appeared took down the outlaws with only her knives and a sword. Reed had heard a variation of this story when he himself was a boy, but to hear Eloise Langford recount the events, Reed could almost feel he was there at the bridge in the ravine as it all played out.

After killing the outlaws, the stranger revealed herself as a woman, much to Sam's surprise. She dressed Miss Adelaide's gunshot wound and sent Sam O'Toole and the schoolteacher racing into town on the teacher's own buggy.

Reed smiled and Eloise Langford continued her story...

The stranger's name as you already know was Emery Dale and that was the day she arrived in Orchard Bend.

[At this point in the recording, Reed heard a rustling of paper.]

What's this? Oh, look at that! You did your homework, didn't you? This is from the early days of the Herald newspaper. You must have dug a might deep to find this clipping, dear. My oh my.

Well, it was written by the owner and editor of the Herald himself, Mr Thomas Buchanan. He invested all his inheritance in that newspaper and you can be right certain he was going to cover this story six ways to Sunday.

Oh, you want me to read it? Well, I'll do my best.

My word, Thomas Buchanan did write with such flare, didn't he? It was the style at the time, I suppose. You don't see this sort of colour in newspaper writing these days nearly as much.

Okay here goes...

The Orchard Herald, May 5, 1879
UNDERWOOD GANG TERROR COMES TO ORCHARD BEND
By Thomas Buchanan, Editor

The vicious brand of violence, larceny and death brought by the vagabonds known as the Underwood Gang was brought an end on the road west of town, at the stone bridge near the Staid farm.

Young master Samuel O'Toole and school teacher Miss Rose Adelaide encountered the gang at the bridge whereby they were set upon. There was gunplay and Miss Adelaide sustained a grievous wound to her shoulder.

The situation was most dire. For the benefit of readers unaware of the Underwood Gang's reputation as wanted men, what follows is an abbreviated account of their lawlessness.

In the summer of 1878, the Gang, consisting of Ernest Underwood (by all accounts the leader of this band of brigands), his brother Arthur Underwood and their associates, James Olsen and Andrew MacReady, assailed the Pine River Bank, making off with some $2,000. A Pine River deputy was gunned down as they fled on horseback. A posse pursued them, but lost their trail in the nearby Black Woods.

The Underwood Gang held up two more banks, one in Gravestone and another in Spring Pass. During the Spring Pass Bank hold-up, James Olsen was shot and killed by a local ranch hand who was at a neighbouring saloon and saw the gang flee the scene, again on horseback.

An extended manhunt failed to capture the gang. A reward was posted for their capture or death by means lawful or otherwise.

As winter gripped the region, the Underwood Gang for a time halted their nefarious predilections and were neither seen nor heard from until a Western Star stagecoach was ambushed. The driver met his end by the elder Underwood's bullet.

The reward money was doubled and following another bank heist in Yellow Brook, it was tripled.

The pastoral community of Orchard Bend was unaware that the Underwood Gang had cast its sights in that direction. When the Gang came upon Miss Adelaide and young master O'Toole, there is no doubt that these most evil of men had murderous intent in their heart.

Salvation came in a form most unexpected. Miss Emery Dale of parts unknown, or so the young lady identifies herself, was but a traveller and one with an uncommon skill, perhaps only seen this day and age gracing the boards of a big city theater or in a troupe of acrobatic performers. She had with her merely a sword and knives and with these did what armed men previously could not, she slew the Underwood Gang and brought to a close their foul deeds. May The Lord have mercy upon their souls.

Miss Adelaide was tended with heroic skill by Doctor Alfred Shaw and is expected to survive her injuries.

Peter stopped the tape.

"After that, Eloise Langford goes on at length about her family. That's all she says about Emery Dale. Personally, I'd have asked a lot more about her," Peter said. "I couldn't find that newspaper clipping she read, but I'll keep looking. The Herald archives are incomplete from that time period, which is a crying shame. There are a good number of more recent articles that mention Emery Dale's exploits, but a lot of it is rumour and legend, like Robin Hood. Where does the truth end and the myth begin?"

"The people described in the recording were real, I trust? Sammy O'Toole, Rose Adelaide, the Underwood Gang?" Reed asked.

"All of them, yes," Peter said. "I took the liberty of pulling this photo from the archives."

Peter handed the detective a framed school photo labelled *Orchard Bend School, 1880.* On the back were the names of the students and their teacher, Rose Adelaide. Reed also spotted Sammy O'Toole and an Eloise Picton. There was a David Langford in their class, as well.

"Eloise married David at some point?" Reed asked.

"In 1886," Peter replied.

Reed put the school photo down.

"And this is a photograph of her?" asked Reed, looking at the small, black and white image in one of the newspaper clippings.

"Yes, here's the source image the Herald used for that piece," Peter said, handing Reed an 8" x 10" photograph. Reed immediately saw the problem.

"This is a photo of a photo," Reed said.

"Yes, I'd like to find the original, obviously, but who knows where it is, if it even still exists," Peter said with obvious frustration.

Reed sat looking at the image, the only known picture of Emery Dale. She stood at three-quarter profile, looking to her right at something out of frame. Her blonde hair was in a ponytail with locks framing her face. The brim of her hat arced from shoulder to shoulder on her back and the hat's stampede string hung like an Old West string tie at her neck. Dale wore a dark jacket and a shirt only a little lighter in tone. Whoever took this photo of the original cropped off the lower portion. If Peter could ever find the original, there would be more to see.

"Any idea what happened to her?" Reed asked, putting Dale's photo down. "Anything in the legends and rumours about that?"

"Some say she left town, disappearing as mysteriously as she came," Peter said. "There's no grave, nothing marked, anyway, and the few official records of her seem to stop in 1895. It's all in the notes I made for you, including a rough timeline, starting with 1879 and her appearance at what's now the old West Creek Bridge."

"That was the bridge described in the recording, huh?" Reed asked.

"Yes, still standing after all these years," Peter said.

Reed started gathering up his notes.

31

"I have to ask, but I understand if you can't tell me," Peter said, "why the interest in her now?"

"Background information for a case," Reed said. "That's all I can tell you, Peter. And please don't mention to anyone that I've been asking about her."

"I'll give no words but mum," Peter said.

Reed gave him a quizzical look.

"Shakespeare," Peter said. "It means I won't say a thing to anyone. Cross my heart and hope to die. Just promise me that when you can tell me, you will."

"I will," Reed said. "Thanks, again, for all of this. If you find anything else, let me know."

"You know I will," Peter said.

6

May 3, 1879
Orchard Bend

Emery Dale stood at the edge of the road watching the buggy vanish over the hill. Blood belonging to the woman named Miss Adelaide still covered her hands. Dale had dressed the wound as best she could and figured Miss Adelaide's chances of survival were pretty good, so long as the doctor in town was halfway decent at his profession.

Dale looked at the bodies, figured they weren't going anywhere, so walked down the side of the bridge to the river. She put her hands in the cold water and started scrubbing, wishing she had soap or—

A pain shot through her head, bright and sharp. Dale clutched her temples and winced, teeth clenched. After a few moments it subsided and Dale sat hunkered down letting it pass before she finished washing the blood from her hands.

Walking back up to the road she thought about the migraine, the second one she'd had today. She also thought about her predicament.

She couldn't remember who she was.

She knew her name was Emery Ann Dale, but that was it. She had woken up at dawn in the wooded ravine, a few yards from the bridge, and didn't then even know her own name. In her confusion Dale had stayed put, watching the sunrise and taking a drink from the river while considering her situation. The first migraine came when she examined some wild berries, unsure if they were edible. It nearly caused her to pass out.

After the migraine passed, Dale took stock of her possessions, which amounted little more than what she had on her person, including a pair of cherrywood-grip knives. A sword in a scabbard lay on the ground next to where she awoke. Examining it, Dale surprised herself with a series of agile twirls and tricks. She wondered how she might fare against an opponent. The knives were much the same, as she could do things that seemed like they should be extraordinary to anyone else.

Maybe I can get a job at a circus, Dale had mused. *Knife Juggler Extraordinaire!*

Another discovery came as Dale looked at her wrist. There she found the thin black band she knew was a watch. The watch had a small display screen which lit up when touched. It showed her the current time and there were tiny glowing icons around it. The same sense of familiarity arose in her as when she handled the knives. She scrolled through the icons until she found one called *Settings*. She tapped it and after some searching came across an option for the device's identity. Dale tapped it and found herself looking at an image of her face, her expression serious and frowning.

Dale scrolled down and read her name:

Emery Ann Dale

"You should smile more, Emery," she told her portrait, but relief and excitement had welled up. She knew her own name now. She said the full name aloud in the hope that it would loose other memories, but it did not. She had a name, but nothing more.

Dale didn't have time to dwell on the discovery. Horsemen arrived at the bridge just then. Staying out of sight, she'd watched them argue about where they were and where they were going. Then the boy showed up and all hell broke loose. The rider shot the woman in the buggy and took aim at the boy. Dale had only time to scoop up a rock from the ground and pitch it at the horseman's gun hand. Beneath the adrenaline surge and thrill of combat reared a familiar sense of this being

34

something she knew and was good at. It wasn't an actual memory, but something like an instinct.

At the side of the road by the bridge now, Dale retrieved her knives. She left the one gun where it lay, still clutched by the outlaw's severed hand. She picked up the other of the shooter's guns from the dirt, a single action revolver she recognized but couldn't name right away. Frustration at the lack of memories floated under the surface and made her clench her jaw. She forcibly set the feeling aside and pondered the other sense she'd had since seeing the horsemen. Simply put, though she could not remember her own identity beyond her name, Emery Dale knew this was not her time. The horsemen, the woman and her buggy, the boy and his clothing, it felt like a movie...

I know what a movie is, that's good, Dale thought, though when she tried to recall a specific one, nothing came to mind.

Examining the bodies, she found a pocket watch on the man she'd impaled with her knife. Dale held it up and compared it to her watch. Years, generations even, separated the two pieces of technology.

Somehow this morning, Emery Dale awoke in the past.

* * *

May 17, 1953
Orchard Bend

Jason Hansen sat on his bed under the covers with a flashlight, the broken gadget in his hands. The two pieces sat separate before him, still connected by a thin cable. Jason wanted to get the gadget working again and had started by taking the two pieces apart the way he'd found them. Under the flashlight's beam he could now see markings and writing on the pieces. *Walker Electronics Co., Model: DN 876305*, proclaimed the stamp on the larger piece. On the smaller piece, printed very tiny on the side, was *BetaCell 120V*. He tried fitting the pieces together again and while they clicked into place, still nothing happened.

35

Jason sighed, clicked off the flashlight and came out from under the bed sheets. His room was cast in shadowy moonlight.

One of the shadows moved.

It moved towards the boy, the size of an adult, tall and thin. Jason still held the flashlight and turned it on, expecting the shadow to disappear in the light, having been only his imagination. Impossibly, though, the shadow remained, thin not just in shape, but in translucency. Jason could nearly see through it. He almost screamed before the noise of a voice filled his head.

I'm not going to hurt you, it said.

* * *

The odour of whiskey in Sheriff Thorn's office permeated the air. Reed smelled it even before he opened the door. The bottle itself sat half empty on Brian Thorn's desk next to a glass tumbler.

"Tom, where are you at with those bones from the Hansen place?" Thorn asked.

"I've been doing some digging, Sheriff," Reed said, "and I think I may have identified one of the remains. You're not going to like it."

"Is that so?" the Sheriff grunted.

"The female remains, the complete skeleton, appear to be Emery Dale," Reed said, bracing himself for Thorn's response. Sheriff Thorn only sat there, looking at the wedding photo on the edge of his desk.

"Is that so?" he said again.

"There was a badge with her name on it," Reed said, somewhat relieved. "And Dr Field's post mortem examination seems to support it."

Thorn reached for the bottle, poured a shot into the tumbler and downed it in a single gulp.

"Who else knows?" Thorn asked.

"All told? Me, you, Dr Field, Will Hansen and I think that's everyone," Reed said. "I trust Will Hansen not to say anything.

He's not too fond of publicity. Or people snooping around his property, for that matter."

"It'll be big news when it gets out," Thorn said. "Do you know what happened to her? And the other remains?"

"We have apparent causes of death for both, but as to what exactly happened in that bunker— or cabin, rather— I'm not sure," Reed explained. "It looks like there was a confrontation. She was stabbed in the neck and he was shot at least once, in the chest. I'm working on finding out his identity."

"Had a visit from Ty Brand this morning, looking for details," Thorn said. "Gave him the usual line, 'unidentified remains, investigation's ongoing,' but you know if he's sniffing around, the Barber is behind him somewhere in the shadows."

"The Barber," Reed snorted with contempt, looking out the window. Reed couldn't see the house on the hill, the McCabe home since the founding of the town, but Reed could picture it. And he could picture the old man inside. Reed shook his head.

"He won't want to hear the name Emery Dale, you can bet your ass," Thorn said, reaching for the whiskey bottle again. He picked it up and made to pour another drink, stopped and put it down, but not without noticeable effort.

"He may not have a choice, unless..." Reed considered his next words carefully. "...Unless this case ends up going nowhere, that is."

The Sheriff looked at the Detective and held his gaze a few seconds longer than Reed would've liked. When Thorn looked away, he stood up from behind his desk, capped the bottle and put it and the tumbler in a drawer. He adjusted his uniform and looked back at Reed.

"Find out what you can," Thorn said. "Steer clear of Tyler Brand as best you can and keep the circle closed, don't let anyone else in."

Reed thought of Peter Howard, not quite in the loop, but pretty close. He decided not to say anything about Peter just yet to the Sheriff.

"Keep Emery Dale's name off any documents for now and get out of the habit of saying her name," Thorn continued. "Those remains are *Jane Doe 13.*"

"Understood, Sheriff," Reed said.

Sheriff Thorn walked to the door of his office and took his coat from the stand.

"Have a good night, Tom," Thorn said.

"Give my best to Mrs Thorn," Reed said.

"Thank you, Tom," Thorn smiled.

* * *

May 3, 1879
Orchard Bend

Emery Dale sat in the cell not saying a word, simply watching the deputy sitting at the desk pretending to read the newspaper. She couldn't see his face. He held the paper between them, but she knew he wasn't actually reading anything. The deputy, named Wilson, would turn a page, glance at her, see her unwavering gaze and disappear behind the paper once more. Dale didn't move, she just sat with her arm on her raised knee and waited. It had been hours since the confrontation at the bridge, much of it spent behind bars.

Earlier at the ravine, when she heard the galloping of the horses approaching, Dale decided to meet the posse head on, standing calm in the middle of the road. When the riders appeared at the top of the hill, most of them looked more like farmers than lawmen. The posse saw her, stopped and levelled their rifles. Dale held up her hands.

"Don't you move, young lady," said an older man she guessed to be a sheriff.

"I don't plan to," Dale said.

"Turn around and get on your knees," the sheriff said. Dale did so. "Now drop the knives on the ground and don't go reaching for that sword, understand?"

"Yes."

Dale did as instructed. The posse approached and one voice said, "That boy wasn't kidding, was he?"

"Hush there, Wilson," the sheriff ordered. "Shackle her, then we'll take a look around."

"I saved the boy and the woman," Dale called out from her knees.

"We don't know you, lady," the sheriff replied. "We ain't taking any chances. I don't like finding three dead men in my jurisdiction first thing in the morning."

When Wilson had taken her wrist to shackle her, Dale knew she could fight back. It would've been easy to break his wrist, lock her arms around his neck, snap it and take his weapon. These were lawmen, though, and so far hadn't done anything to warrant retaliation. Dale allowed herself to be shackled and brought to her feet.

The sheriff climbed off his horse as one of the posse passed them and positioned himself on the other side of the bridge. Standing before the sheriff, Dale knew this man had seen a fair bit in his time.

"Okay, Miss," he said, "Tell me what happened."

"I was camping in the ravine there when these men arrived at the bridge," Dale explained. "The boy came along and then the woman. The woman got shot and they were about to shoot the boy, but I threw a stone that hit his gun hand. His shot went wild. That gave me time to take out the other two men before the first had a chance to draw his other gun. I killed his mount before he could kill me, then I killed him.

"After that, I tended to the woman's wounds and sent the boy to take her to town on the buggy," Dale concluded. "Is she going to make it?"

The sheriff scratched his stubbly face and said, "Doc Shaw was working on her. Mighty bad wound that was."

A wagon pulled up the hill just then and the sheriff waved them over.

"We're gonna load up these bodies and head back to town," the sheriff said. "You, Missy, are coming with us so we can sort this mess out."

"Sheriff!" came Wilson's voice.

"What is it?" the sheriff asked.

"Come here and take a look," Wilson said. "I reckon this is Arthur Underwood. And that there's his brother Ernest! This is the Underwood Gang, boss!"

* * *

The sheriff led Sam O'Toole into the jailhouse and Emery Dale sat up at once. The boy looked pale and fearful.

"Are you alright?" Dale asked, standing up.

"Hush now!" the sheriff said to her. He brought the boy forward. "Is this the woman, Sammy?"

Sammy stared at her and Dale sat on the edge of the cot, not letting go of his gaze.

"Well, boy, speak up," said the sheriff.

"Yes, sir," Sam said. "That's her."

"Okay, you can go," the sheriff told him and Sam bolted from the jailhouse.

Emery Dale rose from the edge of the cot and fixed her eyes on the sheriff. Unlike Deputy Wilson, the man didn't flinch.

"Did the boy confirm my story?" Dale asked.

"He did," said the sheriff, still holding her gaze.

"Then why am I still in this cell, sheriff?" she asked.

"Because I don't know who you are," he said. "You arrive at our doorstep and leave three dead men for us to clean up."

"And a dead horse," said Wilson behind him. The sheriff made as if he hadn't heard the deputy.

"Those three men arrived and would've left the woman and boy dead, and who knows how many others, had I not been there," Dale said. Despite the distinct lack of memories, she knew she did not like being in a confined space. It took a great deal of effort to keep her composure in the cell.

"We're grateful for your help," the sheriff said. "There's a reward for the Underwood Gang and some marshals are on their way to collect the bodies. I expect they'll have some questions for you. I suggest you answer them, take the money and press on to the next county. You're trouble this town doesn't need."

"Your gratitude and hospitality are both heart-warming, Sheriff...?" she said, fishing for his name.

"Anderson," he answered her.

"I'm not here to harm anyone, Sheriff Anderson," Dale said.

40

"You're not off to a very good start on that count, Miss...?"

"Dale. Emery Dale."

"'Emory' is a man's name," said Wilson.

"Not where I'm from," Dale said, her voice a touch cool, "At least, not exclusively."

"And where is that exactly, pray tell?" Anderson asked.

"Many different places," Dale lied, at least as far as she knew. "My family travelled a lot."

"Heed what I say and keep travelling then," Anderson said.

"I think that's good advice, sheriff," Dale nodded. Anderson gave her another once-over, then reached for the keys on the nail above the desk and unlocked the door. The hint of claustrophobia eased and Dale stepped out of the cell.

"Can I have my possessions back, sheriff?" Dale asked.

"Wilson, get her knives and her sword from the closet," Anderson said as he handed the keys to his deputy. Wilson went to the narrow door across the room and unlocked it, Dale following. The Sheriff stayed by the desk.

Dale slipped the knives into their sheaths, which hung under her arms in leather straps like a harness. The blades sat comfortably under her arms. Dale threw on the cloak before slinging the sword's scabbard over her shoulder.

"There's no need to be ready to draw, sheriff," Dale said without looking at him. "I'm not a threat."

Despite what she said, Dale knew the sheriff's hand never came off the grip of his gun until she left the jailhouse.

* * *

Ernest Underwood hit the ground as his horse threw him. The hooded figure first slashed the animal's neck, then drove the sword into its chest.

Who the hell carries a goddamn sword? Ernest wondered through his shock. He'd fallen from a horse before, so knew to relax as he hit the ground and rolled as best he could. His gun flew from his hand, but to his amazement, his mount crashed only a few feet from his other weapon. It was the gun he'd shot that bitch in the buggy with, that he'd tried to shoot that damn kid with before his hand had been broken by a thrown rock.

Earnest had read stories, dime novels and such, where highwayman and outlaws were sometimes known in a colourful, peculiar way as *hoods*. Their attacker now, cloaked in a hood, seemed to fit that description to the letter. The Underwood Gang was being set upon by a *hood*.

The *hood* pulled the sword out of his horse's body as Ernest scrambled for the gun. He planned to make this piece of shit pay for what had happened at the bridge. His hand gripped the weapon and he cocked it as he brought it around.

To his horror, he saw that he wasn't going to be fast enough. The *hood* and the sword were moving. Ernest saw the blood of the horse trailing behind the blade before it sliced through his wrist.

Jesus, Mary and Joseph, Ernest thought, *this asshole's just cut off my hand.*

Ernest didn't move, didn't have time to react to this loss, as the *hood* spun and drove the sword into his chest.

There came a moment of shock and horror as Ernest realized his end was upon him.

That's when he saw it.

That's when he saw the shadow at the side of the road, by the bridge, over the hood's shoulder. It was vaguely the shape of a man, though hard to make out. He could see through parts of it, but the head, the face (if that *was* a face, Ernest wasn't sure) looked around.

Ernest's eyes went from the shadow to the *hood*, looking under it, to see the face of a woman.

Well, how 'bout that? Ernest thought.

Past the *hood*, the shadow moved. It came towards him

Angel o' Death come to take me to Hell, Ernest thought.

Then a hissing, gasping, screaming noise of a voice filled his head.

No. I'm not Death, but you are dying, it said.

Time had seemed to slow down. The shadow was almost within reach behind the hooded woman currently impaling him

42

on her sword. Grey smoke seemed to be surrounding the bridge, the ravine and the trees.

What's happening? I see smoke... Ernest thought.

You're seeing *it. You're seeing* the Breach, the voice said. *However, death awaits you, not* that. *Farewell.*

As Ernest died on Emery Dale's sword, cold white consumed him.

*　*　*

Dr Alfred Shaw wrote at length about both the wound Rose Adelaide had suffered and his surgery to save her. He was seated at his desk in his office, which doubled as the foyer and waiting room. There was no hospital in Orchard Bend, for there were too few people. Shaw knew that would change in a generation or two. He'd brought up the matter with the town aldermen, but the their reply was that the town would need a proper government building, a Town Hall, long before it needed a hospital.

For the second time that day the door burst open.

"Doc Shaw!"

Henry McCabe was past the threshold and at the doctor's desk before Shaw's pen had stopped moving.

"It's time!" Henry barely contained his excitement. "The baby's comin'!"

Shaw glanced at the calendar on his wall as he rose from his desk and said, "I'd have given your mother a few more weeks."

"Mrs Wright says it's happening now and you should hurry!" Excitement and panic mixed in Henry's voice. Shaw looked to the back room, frowning under his thick moustache.

"Henry, go next door and find Mrs Reed. Tell her what's happening and that I need her to watch Miss Adelaide," Shaw instructed.

Henry bolted out the door as Dr Shaw gathered some supplies and instruments and put them in his large medical bag. Donning his coat, he walked to his exam room where Rose Adelaide slept. He took her pulse, which was strong, and checked her breathing. She seemed stable. He hoped that he

43

would not lose this patient's life as he was about to bring a new one into the world just down the road.

Outside his office sat one of the McCabe's wagons, ready to rush him to their estate. Dr Shaw closed his office door without locking it and a moment later Henry returned with Sarah Reed. Reed and her husband owned the Orchard Bend General Store & Feed beside Dr Shaw's office. They owned the property block and were his landlords. He'd known them a good many years and Sarah Reed was someone he could trust to watch Rose Adelaide in his absence.

"Dr Shaw," Mrs Reed said as she and Henry hurried to him, "Henry told me what's happening."

"Miss Adelaide is stable and resting. I don't expect her to, but if she wakes up, keep her calm and don't let her move too much," Dr Shaw explained, "I'll be back as soon as I'm able. Send one of the Statler brothers to fetch me if anything happens."

"I will, Doctor," Mrs Reed smiled at him through her anxiousness, but it vanished in an instant when Henry shouted from the wagon.

"Doc, we have to go!"

"You'll be fine, Mrs Reed," Dr Shaw said and he turned and climbed atop the wagon, taking the reigns from Henry. Across the street he saw the dark figure of Emery Dale on the boardwalk in front of the jailhouse. He did not yet know her name, but the cloak and sword identified her as the heroine from the bridge. She was watching the scene on the street and despite his fatigue and the long night he guessed lay before him, Shaw would've liked to speak with her. He settled for tipping his hat to her. She nodded and he pulled away with the wagon.

The McCabe house stood atop a gentle slope overlooking the collection of crossroads that formed the town of Orchard Bend. The McCabe apple orchards were blooming now, shining white in the late afternoon sky. The orchards curved around the path of one of three small rivers that met on the other side of town, giving Orchard Bend its name. Dr Shaw picked out the other two rivers in the distance, the lowering sun glistering off the water as it disappeared into the ravine. From this vantage point the angle was just right. He thought about Gertrude McCabe and her imminent delivery as he glimpsed the spot where Rose Adelaide had been shot that morning.

Maxwell McCabe was on the porch with Bill Wright, husband of the midwife, Ester Wright. Dr Shaw knew Ester was inside now, tending to Gertrude McCabe. Henry went to his father's side as the doctor hurried into the house. He paused only to take off his coat and hat. Halfway up the stairs there came a piercing cry from the McCabe's bedroom. Dr Shaw recalled delivering Henry McCabe ten years earlier in that very bedroom.

A little over an hour later, Owen Fredrick McCabe was born.

* * *

The Doctor tipped his hat to Dale and she nodded back, then watched him speed away. As he rode off, her gaze went to his office. The schoolteacher was in there, recovering. Sheriff Anderson had told her whom she had saved back at the bridge. Rose Adelaide, a well-respected lady of the town, both because she taught many of the townsfolk's children and because she was active in the community, so the Sheriff had said.

With nowhere to go until the US Marshals arrived, Dale stood in the shadow of the covered boardwalk in front of the jail, weighing her options. She had not a penny to her name, but that would change tomorrow. The marshals would deliver to her the reward money for taking care of the Underwood Gang and Dale planned to go back to the ravine as soon as that matter was dealt with. She hoped there might be some clue out there she'd missed about her identity, something to explain what was going on or where she'd come from.

And what then? Dale asked herself. *What if you find nothing out there? You're alone, a stranger in this town. One who's not exactly welcome here at the moment, despite saving those lives.*

The street was not busy, but a few passers-by gave her varying looks of curiosity, what felt like mistrust and perhaps a bit of fear. The doctor had tipped his hat to her, but no one else had. Mothers and children noticeably crossed the street to give her a wide berth and it was almost laughable to Dale if not for the sinking mixture of panic and fear in her stomach.

Who am *I?* Dale asked herself over and over. *Is this Hell? Purgatory? Is the afterlife just a one-horse town in the middle of nowhere, with no memory of your life before?*

Dale smiled in spite of herself, because if that was the case, that she was dead and couldn't remember anything of living, maybe that was for the best. No torment of regret or paying for your sins—

A blast of sharp pain filled Dale's head and she knelt forward, eyes clenched shut, somehow finding a post to lean on while she massaged her brow. This migraine felt different, if that was possible, the pain deeper than before. The post moved away from her. Her feet moved under her and through the pain she knew she was falling.

Then there was blackness.

7

May 18, 1953
Orchard Bend

In 1939, the US government's Work Projects Administration was helping the country climb out of the Great Depression. Orchard Bend, though not exactly in the Dust Bowl, was a farming community hit hard. There was some reluctance at first to accept aid from the federal government, but soon the promise of work and money tempered small town pride.

The 1939 WPA builds in Orchard Bend saw the roads and streets, improved, transformed from dirt and gravel to pavement. Sidewalks and parks sprung up around the town, as well.

Farmers and townsfolk at the west end of town were often the only people to use the old stone bridge at the ravine. The main road out of town ran at the southeast end, connecting Orchard Bend to Ashleyville, Blue Creek, Sutter Grove and, if you drove far enough, the big cities. The old bridge over the West River was built to last, but was not wide enough to accommodate the large vehicles which long since replaced the horses and wagons of the generations before. A new, wider bridge was built up river from the old stone one and the road was both widened and rerouted to it. Since the locals immediately favoured the newer bridge, the stone bridge and the older dirt road (now little more than a wide walking trail by comparison) were all but ignored at the ravine.

Tom Reed walked the last hundred yards up the hill which overlooked the ravine and stood at the crest of the hill. His car wouldn't negotiate the narrow, old path, so he'd left it parked on the grass next to the road. The morning was cool. The sun peeked over the trees and Reed stood at the top of the hill. He tried to imagine Eloise Langford's narrative from the day before, because it had played out here, at this very spot. He knew he stood about where Rose Adelaide took the bullet fired from Ernest Underwood's gun. Below him was the bridge and ravine where Emery Dale dispatched the three outlaws.

With long strides Reed walked down the hill, listening to the buzz of insects, smelling flowers in the fresh spring air. As he approached, the river babbled peacefully up ahead. Reed stopped a few yards from the bridge, guessing the showdown with the Underwood Gang took place at about that spot. The detective didn't know what he expected to see other than a virtually abandoned stone bridge. *It's not as though there would be any evidence of Emery Dale remaining seventy-plus years after the fact,* he told himself, but that hadn't dissuaded Reed this morning. He wanted to see the place, to stand in it.

"Emery Dale," Reed said to himself.

A breeze picked up and a soft crack came from behind him in the underbrush. As he spun around, for a moment, his imagination painted for him a cloaked woman in black emerging from the trees. But there was nothing. Reed remembered the storm from a few nights before and guessed it to be a loose branch somewhere.

Reed crossed the bridge to look around the other side before finally standing at its edge to watch the water ripple below him. As he turned back to the road and started towards the hill, he paused to pick up one of the many stones scattered in the dirt. He imagined trying to throw it at the hand of a man on a horse pointing a six-shooter.

Eloise Langford was not wrong, Reed thought, *you'd have to be a deadeye to hit that target. Or a major league pitcher, maybe like 'Vinegar Bend' Mizell out of St. Louis. Or you'd have to be extremely lucky.*

Reed turned the stone over in his hand in an absent fashion as he crested the hill. He turned to look back at the ravine as if to give it one more chance to tell him something, to offer some insight into Emery Dale, but the ravine sat serenely as it had all these years. Reed put the stone in his pocket and headed to his car.

* * *

Ed's Diner was located on Maplewood Lane, an inconspicuous side street off Wood St, near the town's primary intersection of Anderson and Wood. Tom Reed sat at the counter with his coffee, chewing the last bite of his scrambled eggs as he watched the town slowly coming to life that morning. The current newspapers from around the county sat a few feet from him. The paper on top was from the town of Blue Creek, down the road from Orchard Bend. A man there had killed his neighbours, it reported, before being shot by the neighbours' son. Reed had heard about the case over the weekend and wondered what the world was coming to.

Reed put thoughts of the Blue Creek murders and Emery Dale's case aside long enough to admire the scenery outside. The park across the street stretched from Maplewood to the Town Hall. A few blocks south was the middle school and almost as far north was the high school. Reed could see the students criss-crossing the park heading to their respective classes. A few cars went by. He downed the last of his coffee. With the steady traffic in and out of the diner, he didn't notice Ty Brand until the reporter sat beside him, notebook open.

"Good morning, Detective," Brand said.

"Ty," Reed said. He put down his empty coffee cup, placed some bills on the counter and stood up to leave.

"Detective, I was hoping to get a few words about the bodies found out at the Hansen place," Brand said.

"The investigation's ongoing, Ty, you know that," Reed said, picking up his hat and coat. Reed didn't bother asking Brand how he knew about the skeletons. Men like Tyler Brand (and his employers, both on and off the books) had their ways of getting that information. Even with Sheriff Thorn running some interference on the case, Reed knew it was only a matter of time before leaks to The Barber started forming.

49

Ed Howell put a cup of coffee on the counter next to Brand. Brand didn't look at it or even acknowledge Ed when he picked it up and sipped it black.

"Detective, you and I both know those remains were there for a long time," Brand said. "How long do you reckon they've been on the property? Herald readers will want to know."

"Long enough to make identifying them difficult," Reed said, hoping that Thorn would understand that throwing Brand a bone might make him ease off.

"Do you suspect foul play?" Brand asked.

"The investigation—"

"Yes, yes, it's still ongoing," Brand interrupted.

"You're catching on, Ty," Reed said.

"Looks like there's no story, then, huh?" Brand said, closing his notebook. "Shame, really, 'Mystery Skeletons Unearthed' would've made a splendid front page headline, something to frame on my wall, I think; like this one here from Blue Creek: *Local Man Murders Neighbours!*"

Brand held up the Blue Creek newspaper Reed had looked at earlier.

"But Orchard Bend doesn't spare a lot of time for the past, does it, Detective?" Brand continued. "The future is bright, isn't it? I can put my ego aside for the good of the community. Old news bores the kids today..."

Brand glanced out at the students walking past the diner laughing, schoolbooks under their arms.

"...And the same with their parents. Nothing doing when it comes to the dim and distant past," Brand smiled, putting down the Blue Creek paper and standing up. "We all have to accept that sometimes ancient history is just ancient history. Best to look to the future, don't you agree?"

"I think you need a haircut, Ty," Reed said, opening the diner door, "best see a barber about a taking a little off the top."

Just for a second, Tyler Brand's expression slipped before he replaced it with the usual self-assurance. It was around the eyes and Reed only spotted it because he looked for it. Yes, Tyler Brand and his employers could scratch up information, but Reed was a detective and information had a habit of sometimes coming his way. Brand was a loyal employee of the newspaper and its owner, but that position of confidence with The Barber would afford Brand *other* opportunities, with other members of The Barber's family, like one in particular.

"You have a good day, Detective," Brand said as Reed walked out of the diner. "Keep our streets safe."

* * *

May 3, 1879
Orchard Bend

Dr Shaw's office and exam room was a respectable size and he utilised it as economically as he could. There was just one exam table, but the year previously Shaw had been gifted by Reverend Thomas an unneeded church pew. Reverend Thomas had ordered twenty-four pews and twenty-five had arrived. Dr Shaw put it to use in his office as a place for family and friends to sit and wait when Shaw was examining patients. Dale Emery awoke on the pew after collapsing from her sudden migraine.

Dale opened her eyes, feeling the cool, damp cloth on her forehead. Sarah Reed sat over next to her.

"You passed out," Mrs Reed said. "How do you feel?"

Oh, where to even begin *answering that question?* Dale wondered, but instead said, "I feel fine now, thank you."

Dale sat up, pressed the bridge of her nose between her thumb and forefinger and let the fuzziness in her mind clear. Her memories were still absent and she groaned in frustration. When she opened her eyes, the shop matron handed her a glass of water.

"I'm Sarah Reed," Reed introduced herself. "Dr Shaw is at the McCabe's delivering their second child. You don't seem especially in need of his services."

"No, I'm fine," Dale said and sipped the water.

"Sheriff Anderson and the Statlers brought you here, but Dr Shaw had already left," Mrs Reed said.

"How long was I out?" Dale asked.

51

"Better part of half an hour," Mrs Reed replied.

"Have the US Marshals arrived?" Dale asked.

"I couldn't hazard a guess, I've been occupied with you and Miss Adelaide," Mrs Reed said.

"How is she?" Dale asked.

"Asleep," Mrs Reed said.

"Mrs Reed?" came a quiet voice from the examine room. Mrs Reed went to Miss Adelaide swiftly and Dale followed, pausing only long enough for a wave of dizziness to pass as she stood up. Standing discreetly at the threshold of the exam room, Dale listened.

"What happened?" Miss Adelaide asked, her voice a little stronger now.

"You're going to be alright," Mrs Reed answered.

"I remember... Sam O'Toole?" Miss Adelaide said with a noticeable mix of confusion and concern. "And three men..."

"Calm yourself," Mrs Reed said. There was a touch of gentle sternness in her words, her voice that of a woman accustomed to pressure and staying calm amidst it. Dale thought Dr Shaw chose her wisely to mind his patient in his absence. Mrs Reed continued, "Sam O'Toole is just fine. Those men are... well, they won't be troubling anyone anymore."

"My shoulder, it feels..." Miss Adelaide couldn't seem to form the words in her confusion and Mrs Reed tried again to calm her, but then the schoolteacher seemed to put it all together, saying, "I was... shot? Was I shot?"

Mrs Reed didn't respond, clearly not wanting to be the one to explain to her what had happened. But the shop owner also wasn't one to shirk the tough duty and said, "You were. Don't you fret none about that, you hear? Dr Shaw patched you up good and proper."

"Shot," Miss Adelaide said. It wasn't a question. She was processing the fact. "I was shot... by the big man on the horse."

"Okay, Miss Adelaide," Mrs Reed spoke now with more authority. "You have been through an ordeal today and you need to rest. I told you not to fret and I meant it."

Dale moved away from the door and under her boot a floorboard creaked.

"Who's that out there, Mrs Reed?" the teacher asked.

"That's...?" Mrs Reed started to reply, and then stopped. Dale could hear the uncertainty in her pause. Deciding it was the right thing to do and hoping it wouldn't startle the teacher, Dale stepped forward into the doorway.

"I'm Emery Dale," she said. "I saved you and Sam O'Toole from those men."

Rose Adelaide inched herself up on the elbow of her good arm and now looked at her rescuer. Dale expected fear or confusion, but instead the concern in the teacher's face seemed to vanish. What replaced it Dale could only guess was relief.

"Thank you," Rose said.

"You're welcome," Emery replied. She couldn't place exactly how or why, but in that moment some of Dale's own anxiety eased away.

"Okay," Mrs Reed said, now affecting her sternest, motherly tone, "I must insist you rest, Miss Adelaide. I'm sure Dr Shaw will be back soon and will not want to see you carrying on like this. Miss Dale, you're welcome to wait in the front office, but we don't want this patient getting in any more of a state, do we? No, we don't. Now let's go. Out. Out."

Sarah Reed shooed Dale out of the examine room. Rose gave Emery a small wave of her good hand and lay back on the exam table. Dale gathered her things and went outside.

* * *

Evening had set in on Orchard Bend when Dale stepped out of the doctor's office. The town looked almost abandoned, a fact betrayed by the sound of boisterous voices coming from down the street. Stepping off the boardwalk onto the dirt, Dale spotted what she reckoned was the saloon. A voice from came behind her.

"Not making to die on us, are you, Miss Dale?" Sheriff Anderson said. Dale turned as the lawman approached holding a paper. "Fitting an end to my day as that would've been, you can count me relieved we're not putting you next to the

Underwoods in the ice box right now, because I don't think there's room."

Behind Dale, the winged saloon doors clattered.

"Sully's place," Sheriff Anderson said, nodding towards the saloon. "He's got rooms you can rent. Just got word from the marshals, they're held up in Blue Creek and will be here first thing in the morning."

The sheriff held up what Dale could now see was a telegram.

"As inviting as Sully's establishment is, sheriff, there's the matter of my lack of funds," Dale said.

"Tell him you're on the sheriff's guest list and he'll set you up for the night," Anderson said. "You can settle that debt tomorrow after you're done with the marshals."

Anderson started away, back to the jailhouse.

"Thank you, sheriff."

Anderson turned, eyes narrowed.

"This isn't an invitation for you to put down roots, Miss Dale," he said. "I meant what I said about you and trouble. I see it just as soon as look at you. When this Underwood business is done, I expect you'll take your leave of Orchard Bend and we won't see you back here."

Emery Dale said nothing, only nodded. The sheriff tipped his hat. When he turned back to the jailhouse and started walking, Dale bit back her anger and frustration as tears fought to well up in her eyes. With some effort, she pushed the feelings back down and started toward Sully's.

* * *

Rose Adelaide knew the men at the bridge were trouble. Every thing about them was wrong, *dangerous*, and she had to get herself and the boy far away from that place.

"Sam O'Toole, come here!" Rose called to him, half rising from the seat of her buggy. Sam O'Toole was halfway to the bridge, a good distance away, but he started up the hill at her call. He was a bright student and it seemed to Rose that this situation might diffuse easily.

And then there was a crack in the air, followed by hot pain in her shoulder. Rose fell from her buggy and heard a second shot. Her mind raced. She felt warm wetness covering her shoulder. Rose's voice failed as she tried to call out to Sam. Maybe he could help her, the schoolteacher wondered. Maybe he could get her onto the buggy and they could drive off.

But that second shot...? Rose couldn't even fathom the idea that Sam O'Toole was dead. *What monster would shoot a boy?*

Through her dimming senses, Rose heard raised voices and the whinnying of horses. Fear came. A smoky darkness moved around her, seeping in through the trees and flowers. Somehow, the sky was still a bright blue above her and Rose focused on that, thinking that if she was going to die, she wanted to be looking toward Heaven.

"Miss Adelaide!" Sam O'Toole appeared at her side, but it was getting harder to keep her eyes open. Pain shot through her from the wound in her shoulder. She tried to focus on that. If she felt pain, she knew she wasn't dead yet.

"Sam," Rose said, "need...Doctor...Shaw."

Rose Adelaide tried to move, to get up so maybe they could get away on the buggy, but she had no energy left and fell back to the ground.

"NO! Miss Adelaide!" Sam cried, but to Rose the voice was far away. She forced her eyes open a crack and saw his silhouette kneeling over her. Behind him a dark shadow, like a person, came into view, looking at her with what seemed like curiosity. The powerful noise of a voice filled her mind.

I don't believe it to be your time, it said.

Who are you? Rose asked.

A prisoner, it said. *One who waits.*

I'm afraid of you, Rose thought.

A hooded person replaced the shadow figure. When the hood was pulled back, the female face beneath the cloth seemed to glow in the morning light. Rose tried to make out the features, but couldn't focus. She felt herself slipping away. The woman's voice spoke and Sam replied. Rose's eyes at last closed as she thought that if this angel of a woman was the last thing she saw, death might not be so terrible. Darkness swept over her.

8

May 4, 1879
Orchard Bend

Emery Dale awoke from a fractured sleep to the sound of knocking on her door. She was in her rented room above Sully's saloon.

"Yes? What is it?" Dale said as she stretched under the sheets.

"The marshals are here, ma'am," Deputy Wilson said from the other side of the door. "You're to come to the jailhouse, pronto."

"Alright," Dale said. "Thank you, Deputy."

She listened as his footfalls faded down the short hallway. She sat up and groaned. Dale had folded the single, thin pillow on the lumpy bed to achieve some measure of comfort, but the bed was not the source of her poor night's sleep. Nor was it the loudness of the ranch hands and cowboys drinking and gambling in the barroom below. Sleep was a long time coming, even after Dale had tried to relax by washing herself before lying in bed staring at a candle next to her bedside. Occasionally, she would look at the tattoo on her arm. The shape looked like a "P" with an "L" growing out of the left side, inked in red and black upon the inner forearm.

When sleep did take Dale, the dreams that came were a confused mixture of noises and images. In the light of morning, all she could recall was a handless Ernest Underwood impaled on her sword and Rose Adelaide covered in blood. Dread permeated the dreams, too, as if something stood behind her. Dale couldn't turn around to see what or who it was.

Dale dressed, made the bed and straightened the room before making her way downstairs. The proprietor, Sully, wasn't in the barroom, but a girl in her late teens swept the floor as Dale came down the stairs. The teenager saw her and stopped her chores.

"Did you sleep well, ma'am?" the girl asked.

"It was fine, thank you," Dale said.

As Dale passed her, the girl started to say something, and then stopped herself. Dale stopped and looked at her. The girl looked at the floor she had been sweeping.

"What is it?" Dale asked.

"No, ma'am, it's not my place," the girl said. "Only that there were men come to see you earlier."

"The marshals, I know," Dale said. "I'm going to meet them now."

"No, ma'am, not the marshals," the girl said, "Two men, who are in the employ of Mr McCabe."

"What did they want?" Dale asked.

"They asked around for you," the girl said, now visibly nervous. "I told them you hadn't come out of your room yet. They stayed and waited over at that table for a spell, but left when Arnie Wilson came in to call for you."

"Do I have reason to fear these men?" Dale asked.

"They work for Mr McCabe," the girl replied, as if that should answer the question.

"I don't know Mr McCabe," Dale said.

"Mr McCabe is an important man in Orchard Bend," the girl said. "If those men working for him want to talk to you, I thought it might be wise to, well begging your pardon, ma'am, that it might be wise to tell you, so you can see them coming, if you take my meaning."

Dale wasn't entirely sure she did, but she was smart enough to see that the girl's warning was not to be taken lightly. She adjusted the sword's scabbard over her shoulder and felt the reassuring presence of the knives beneath her cloak. It then occurred to Dale to perhaps step up her personal arms.

"Thank you, um...?" Dale said.

"Irene Sullivan, ma'am," the girl said, "My father owns this establishment. And thank *you* for what you did, rescuing Miss Adelaide and Sammy O'Toole. She was my teacher—"

Irene stopped herself before she started rambling, looking awkwardly at the floor again.

Dale smiled and said, "Have a good day, Irene Sullivan. I'll be back to settle my bill when I'm done with the marshals."

Outside, Dale looked around, taking in the light bustle of the town that Sunday morning. She kept a look out for two men who might have business with her, but saw no one as she made her way along the boardwalk.

Some heavily laden horses and a wagon stood in front of the jailhouse. Atop one of the horses, rifle in hand, sat a young man with a badge. A US Marshal, Dale figured. Approaching the jailhouse, Dale saw the wagon loaded with the wrapped up forms of three bodies. She knew they must be the earthly remains of the Underwood Gang.

Inside, the small jailhouse barely contained the lawmen gathered there. The strong smell of coffee filled the room. Dale's stomach growled. She honestly didn't know the last time she'd eaten anything.

The conversation stopped as she entered. The men all looked at her, eyes flicking from her face to her cloak to her sword. A few of the marshals let their gaze linger on her body and Dale could almost feel their looks crawling over her.

"Good morning, gentlemen," Dale said.

"Miss Emery Dale, marshal," Sheriff Anderson said to the man next to him. "She's the one that put an end to the Underwoods and saved the teacher and the boy. Expecting she'll be looking for that reward money."

"I've seen some peculiar things in my day, Sheriff Anderson," the marshal said, "but ain't nowhere near as you described went on out at yonder bridge."

The marshal stepped towards Dale and looked her in the eye, a tone of clear contempt in his voice as he spoke, "Go on, then, Miss, tell us what *really* happened."

Dale recounted the events at the bridge, starting with the arrival of the Underwood Gang, followed by the arrivals of Sam

O'Toole and Rose Adelaide. She told precisely how she'd saved the teacher and the boy and killed the outlaws. She concluded with her triage of Miss Adelaide and sending her with the boy into town.

The marshals listened and when Dale finished, they looked at each other, then to their boss.

"Bullshit," the marshal said.

Dale stood in disbelief. Her eyes went to the sheriff, who only shrugged.

"The boy's story matches hers," Anderson said.

"And there were no other witnesses? This school teacher...?" the marshal asked.

"Spoke to her this morning," Sheriff Anderson said, "She doesn't remember much after being shot."

"What is it you think happened out there, marshal?" Dale asked in a cold voice.

"The Underwoods were a quarrelsome bunch, prone to violence," the marshal said. "Like as not, they set upon themselves."

The other marshals nodded.

"And Ernest impaled *himself* on my sword?" the incredulity stinging in Dale's words now. "After he cut off his own hand?"

"*No one* is that fast with a blade, be it knife or—"

The marshal didn't have time to finish as Dale had, in two swift motions, drawn both her knives. She let one fly with uncanny accuracy into the face of a *Wanted* poster on the wall behind her. The knife sunk deep into the wood. In almost the same motion, the other knife, still in her hand, was at the throat of the marshal nearest to her. The other men reached for their sidearms, but not nearly fast enough. Dale noted that Sheriff Anderson, though having the clearest shot, had not gone for his weapon. Instead, he watched her very closely. As the men went for their guns, Dale stepped back and sheathed her knife.

The marshal in charge, one hand on his six-shooter, raised the other quickly, saying, "Whoa there, boys."

The other marshals relaxed. Dale looked from the marshal to the sheriff and back again.

"I think you should give her that reward money, Saunders," Sheriff Anderson said to the marshal. "The warrant says 'Dead or Alive,' doesn't it?"

Marshal Saunders kept his eyes on Dale, but nodded, "Yes, sir, it does."

The man then let forth a hearty laugh. Dale took a few steps back and retrieved her knife from the wall. The other marshals filed out of the jailhouse, a few tipping their hats to her sheepishly.

"Anderson," Saunders said, "you'd well be the smartest man in the county if you deputized this lady. She's a firecracker, ain't she?"

Anderson sat down behind his desk, eyes still narrowed on Dale. She felt his gaze and it unnerved her just a little, even as the adrenalin rush ebbed.

"How much is the reward?" Dale asked.

Saunders looked at Anderson.

"You didn't tell her?"

Indifferent, Anderson put his hands up as if to say *not my job*. Saunders looked back at Dale and said, "Five hundred dollars."

Dale wanted to ask if that was a lot, but compared to the prices she saw around town— the menu at Sully's and the cost of a room for the night —she began to understand that her frame of reference for the value of a dollar was very far off. It further intensified the notion that she was not from this time.

And five hundred dollars here and now was a lot of money.

"How much for his guns?" Dale asked.

Saunders blinked.

"I beg your pardon, ma'am...?" he said.

"Ernest Underwood's guns and belts," Dale said, walking forward. "I'd like to buy them."

* * *

May 18, 1953
Orchard Bend

Owen McCabe sat on the porch of the house where he was born seventy-four years prior. It had been his home all that time, apart from brief periods away at school or travelling. He'd watched the landscape of the town slowly change year by year. Orchard Bend stretched out before him in the clear spring evening. It was an impressive view, but Owen didn't notice. His attention was on the car coming through the gates and up the short curved driveway towards the house. He tapped the old black leather-bound ledger on his lap like a metronome.

The car parked and Ty Brand climbed out. The reporter adjusted his tie, using the driver's side window as a mirror. McCabe could clearly remember cutting Brand's hair at his family's shop all those years ago when Ty was a boy. Owen McCabe cut just about everyone's hair in town during his long barbering career. His great-grandfather, Liam McCabe, had helped found the town with his orchard and mill. Liam's son, Sean, had become a barber, but both men's real passions were real estate, community involvement and local politics. Sean's wife, Mary, had died of pneumonia, and Sean left the mortal coil by way of a heart attack, leaving Maxwell, an only child, the entire McCabe fortune and estate. Owen came along later and wasn't an only child. He'd had a brother at one time, lost before the turn of the century. Owen didn't like to think about that even now, all these years on. He tapped the ledger harder, pushing away thoughts of his brother Henry.

Ty crossed the lawn to the porch steps. Owen looked back out at the sunset. The reporter reached Owen and stood in respectful silence. Owen tapped the ledger as if marking time, knowing Ty Brand would wait as long as needed.

"Is it her?" Owen asked.

"Yes, it is," Brand replied. "Reed was evasive, but it was in his eyes."

Owen cast a stern look at the reporter. Brand pointed to his own eyes, saying, "These lie detectors don't fail. Reed knows those bones are Emery Dale and he knows why I was asking. What are you going to do?"

"*My* business is *my* business," Owen said, looking back out at the town. Brand was skilled and had his uses, but the reporter in him sometimes didn't know when not to ask a question.

Brand again waited as Owen tapped the ledger a few more times. Owen thought of a dog he once owned, Buster, who would sit at his master's heel waiting to be fed, waiting to fetch, waiting to be acknowledged. When at last Owen would turn his attention to Buster, Buster would be so grateful, so excited, as if even the smallest morsel of affection validated the dog's very existence.

Without looking at Brand, Owen said, "The headline will read: *Unidentified Remains Found.* No mention of *her*, details of the skeletons will be vague. This will be second page reading, no photo. She should have stayed in that shithole to rot, but at least we can keep the memory of her from coming back."

Brand nodded and said nothing. Owen suspected there were questions in the reporter's silence but the younger man kept his peace, which was wise. Owen rewarded Brand's restraint by not keeping him waiting a moment longer.

"Thank you for your efforts in this matter, Mr Brand," Owen said, looking at Ty, and whether the reporter knew it or not, the old man's acknowledgment was sincere.

"You're welcome, Mr McCabe," Brand said. As he turned away, the front door opened. Gabrielle McCabe, Owen's granddaughter, stood silhouetted in the doorframe, her form tall and slender, her dark hair shining. Ty hesitated before her, straightened up and tipped his hat to her.

"Good evening, Gabby," Brand said.

"Tyler," she said politely before turning her attention to Owen. "Grandpa, would you like me to bring you your brandy out here or are you coming in soon?"

"I'll be in when I damn well please, thank you very much," Owen replied.

"Alright, but don't be long. It's getting chilly now," Gabrielle said. She looked back at Brand, who hadn't moved from his spot since she appeared. "Well, good evening then, Tyler."

"'Night, Gabby," Ty said. She closed the door and Brand walked down the steps and headed to his car. Owen watched him go, once more tapping the ledger.

* * *

May 4, 1879
Orchard Bend

Emery Dale sat at a table in Sully's, having just finished her meal. Other patrons were also at Sully's, playing cards, drinking and eating. There were two men at the bar, talking to the bartender, Irene Sullivan's mother. They were there when Dale had returned from the jailhouse. Dale supposed they were the men Irene had warned her about. Their clothes were sharp and each had a gun on his hip. Dale wore a pair of her own now, formerly belonging to Ernest Underwood. Marshal Saunders had been a bit surprised by Dale's request to buy the guns, but saw no reason not to sell them. The Underwoods had no apparent next of kin and were destined for a state-paid burial. For an even twenty dollars Dale bought the two guns, what ammunition the Underwoods had, a nice leather satchel and other such items Saunders said were bound to be auctioned off.

The men at the bar had tried to be inconspicuous watching her at the table as she ate, but Dale caught every glance cast her way, so was not at all surprised when they stood up and approached her table. Irene came and cleared Dale's plate, giving her a look that told Dale these were indeed the men. Dale gave a slight nod and said, "Thank you, it was a pleasant meal."

Irene scurried off and the men stood before her.

"Might we join you, ma'am?" said the tall one.

Dale looked them over more closely, making as if she only now saw them.

"To what do I owe the pleasure of your company?" Dale said in return.

The men exchanged a look and the short one said, "Let us make your acquaintance, ma'am. I'm Burke and this is my associate Miller. We're in the employ of a Mr McCabe. Perhaps you're familiar with his name?"

"I cannot say I am," Dale replied.

"As a recent arrival to Orchard Bend, that's to be expected," Burke went on. "Mr McCabe is a man of means and an active member of this community, Miss...?"

"Dale. Emery Dale," she said, figuring they very well already knew.

"Miss Dale, word of the goings on yesterday at the bridge has reached our employer," Miller said. "Your heroic actions will surely make the front page of the Herald tomorrow. Such deeds do not go unnoticed by Mr McCabe and he wishes an audience with you."

"Well, gentlemen," Dale said, "I'm flattered, truly. I was hoping to catch a stagecoach out of town shortly, so if I decline, I hope Mr McCabe does not take it as a sleight against his person."

The two men exchanged a curious look and then Burke said, "Miss Dale, it being the Lord's Day, there's no stage arriving or leaving today."

"It would seem, then, that you have time after all to accept Mr McCabe's gracious invitation," Miller said.

"Dinner this evening would be most agreeable for him," Burke added. "He will send for you here at 6 o'clock."

"Very well," Dale said. "I look forward to meeting your employer."

"Good afternoon, then," Miller said as the two men left Sully's.

Dale watched them go and took a long sip of her beer.

* * *

Leaving her reward money unattended in her room at Sully's was out of the question, so Emery Dale began to feel a little like a pack horse as she carried her knives, sword, guns and satchel to Dr Shaw's office.

64

There she found the Doctor looking haggard and tired at his desk.

"Miss... Dale, is it?" he said, getting to his feet.

"Dr Shaw," Dale said pleasantly.

"No headaches or dizzy spells today?" Dr Shaw asked.

"Mrs Reed told you?" she asked.

"That she did," he answered.

The doctor came over to her as she unburdened herself of the satchel and her sword, placing them on the pew.

"If you'll permit an examination, I might be able to help," Dr Shaw said.

"Can I count on complete confidentiality, Doctor?" Dale asked.

"Of course you can," Dr Shaw.

"I'll consider your offer, but the purpose of my visit is to see Miss Adelaide," Dale said.

"I'll see if she's awake," Dr Shaw said.

He disappeared behind a curtain covering the doorway to the exam room. Dale heard him speak to his patient in hushed tones.

Dale looked at the degrees on the office wall. Military certificates, including discharge papers, hung next to them, as well as a photo of a young Dr Shaw in a uniform.

Shaw came out and said, "You can have a few minutes."

Dale nodded and Shaw let her into the exam room.

Rose smiled as Emery entered. Her face no longer looked ashen. Colour had crept back into her cheeks and the schoolteacher had an encouraging alertness in her eyes.

"Good afternoon, Miss Adelaide," Emery said.

"Call me Rose, please," the teacher said.

"You may call me Emery," Dale said. "How are you?"

"I can squeeze my hand. Dr Shaw says that's a good sign," Rose said.

"It is, it means you'll still have the use of your arm," Emery said.

Rose smiled, but tears were welling up in her eyes.

"Are you in a lot of pain? I can get Dr Shaw in here," Emery said, but Rose shook her head.

"No, no. The pain is dull," Rose said. "It's the idea of... of, well... all of it, really."

Rose's voice wavered and Emery scrambled to change the topic, but could think of nothing. She cursed her absence of memory and not for the first time.

Then Emery did remember something. "Irene, Sully's daughter, she spoke of you today. I'll ask her to visit, if you wish?"

"Irene Sullivan," Rose said, her voicing relaxing. "One of my first students. A bright girl. Her beau was Alan O'Dell. He was a hard worker but book learning wasn't his strength. Irene helped him and they fell in love. They talked of marriage, but poor Alan needed money and went to work for Mr McCabe. There was an accident and Alan was... But that was some time ago and I shouldn't chatter on so. Tell Irene to come see me when she can and we can catch up."

Dr Shaw entered and Emery knew her visit was at an end even before he said, "That's enough visiting now, ladies."

Emery squeezed Rose's good hand and said goodbye. She gathered up her satchel and sword and left, wondering about the fate of Alan O'Dell.

* * *

May 18, 1953
Orchard Bend

Owen McCabe sat in his study and sipped his brandy. His damn fool doctor ordered that he keep his drinking down to a single glass of brandy, but Owen was celebrating and knew he could handle a little extra tonight.

The town's memory of Emery Dale would remain dim and distant, a curious footnote in whatever archives there were and half-truths told by parents to their children. Owen knew that even those stories would fade and today he'd struck another nail in the coffin of that bitch's legend. That was cause for celebration and screw his doctor, celebrate he would.

Before taking his first sip, Owen had written in his ledger:

May 18, 1953
Spoke to Brand, then telephoned Simmons and killed Orchard Herald front page story about Dale. He wasn't happy. Screw him. She's staying dead. Time for a drink.

Under the entry, Owen had left space for the newspaper clipping, the small piece he'd told Brand to write. The editor at the Herald, Simmons, had wanted to run a full front page piece on the discovery of the remains, not even knowing who they were. Well, Owen owned the damn paper and vetoed it. An annoyed Simmons knew enough not to argue. In a way, that made Owen happier. Emery Dale's remains could be big local news, sparking interest in her history and what she did in Orchard Bend. The town might even declare some half-ass *Emery Dale Day* and the townspeople would have a parade and all that crap. With a phone call, Owen had put his aging foot down and stamped it out the way a smoker stamps out a cigarette butt with his heel. He would have preferred her bones stay lost out there, but that wasn't in the cards, as they say.

So now Owen sipped his second brandy. He wouldn't go past that, he wasn't stupid, no matter how delighted he felt.

A shadow moved out of the corner of the room and dread cut through Owen's pleasure. Owen knew immediately who it was even before the harsh voice entered his mind.

It has happened, said the Prisoner, *the other one has come through the Breach as expected.*

Owen sat unmoving. He didn't need to go back through the ledger's many pages to understand what the Prisoner was telling him, having long ago memorized the passages he himself had chronicled over the years. Page after page of notes, newspaper clippings and diary-like entries all formed Owen McCabe's unique, meticulous record, a history of sorts of Orchard Bend no one else living or ever having lived in the town knew. Some of the record came from events in McCabe's own lifetime and some of it came from the Prisoner. Each piece connected in one fashion or other to the person he hated: Emery Dale.

The visit now by the Prisoner brought Owen's thoughts to the Breach, a crack of some sort in time and space, one that existed just under the surface of reality in and around Orchard Bend. And it was growing in stops and starts as days and years passed, not widening but with its threads spreading. The Prisoner wasn't always clear on details. He communicated ideas to Owen through a combination of thoughts, words and images, all of which formed the noise that filled the mind when he 'spoke.' Owen tried to draw the Breach in his ledger. The crude sketch looked as an automobile windshield did having suffered a spider web crack that crept along in different directions.

The Prisoner always evaded Owen's questions about how he became trapped in the Breach and Owen came to realize the Prisoner might not remember everything that happened to put him there. Owen had pieced a few details together with the help of his notes and long hours of study. The best he could figure was that the Breach allowed for a method of time travel, a way of moving from one point to the other, such as from one's present to the past. Slip through that crack and come out the other side in another time. However, because the Breach lay under the surface of reality, so to speak, some damn fool couldn't just walk along and fall through it the way you might stumble down an abandoned mineshaft by accident. Stripping away that layer of reality was the key to reaching the Breach.

And by Owen's further best guess after years of pondering the clues, the Prisoner had found a way in, but could not get out for some reason, despite others having entered and exited, others like Emery Dale, who had arrived in 1879 from some future point in time. The Prisoner was convinced another traveller would arrive in Orchard Bend through the Breach one day. With the passage of years and the advancement of age, Owen had begun to doubt this other time traveller existed.

After all this time? Owen asked.

The Prisoner bombarded Owen's mind with images in an angry barrage, what seemed like a hundred years of seasons, lives lived and lost. Owen couldn't make sense of it all, what looked like lights, faces and machines.

Time?! The Prisoner said. *You haven't experienced* time *as I have.*

So what now? Owen asked.

This traveller has something I need, the Prisoner said. More images weaved in and out of the voice, now running so fast that Owen could make sense of none of it. *You will find the traveller and all debts will be paid.*

How do I find this person? Owen asked.

A single image came from the Prisoner into Owen's mind and the old man gasped in horror.

9

May 4, 1879
Orchard Bend

True to Miller and Burke's invitation, a coach belonging to McCabe arrived at Sully's to pick up Emery Dale. Miller accompanied the coach driver. As before, Dale carried what amounted to all her worldly possessions on her person, not trusting the feeble lock on the door of her rented room at the saloon.

At the McCabe house, Miller escorted her inside and to the dining room. Candles glowed and a fire crackled in the small fireplace.

"Mr McCabe will join you presently," Miller said, standing by the door in a manner that told Dale two things: she was expected to stay in the room and that it was his job to see she did. A knot formed in her stomach and though the room wasn't small by any means, she felt the tell-tale edginess of her claustrophobia beginning to rise. Somewhere in the house a baby started crying. There were footsteps above her and a moment later the crying stopped.

Dale set her satchel on the floor against the wall next to her, followed by her sword and cloak. If necessary, she wanted a full range of motion. The weight of the guns on her hips reassured her, as did her knives under her arms.

Maxwell McCabe entered the room only minutes after Dale's arrival.

"Please excuse my tardiness, Miss Dale," he said, "My wife and I only just welcomed our second child into the world and he requires a good deal of our attention."

"Of course, think nothing of it," Dale said.

He extended a hand and Dale reached out to shake it, only to be surprised when McCabe kissed it and said, "It is a pleasure to meet you, Miss Dale. I'm Maxwell McCabe."

Unsure how to respond, Dale simply said, "Nice to meet you, too."

"My wife is still recovering from the delivery, you understand, so will not be joining us. Please, do sit down. Can I interest you in a glass of wine?" McCabe asked, sitting down at the head of the table.

"Thank you, yes," Dale replied. She sat, careful to keep her back to the wall.

The door opened and a matronly woman entered. Dinner was served. The cooking was much better than at Sully's, but Dale could not shake the feeling of being enclosed in the room. Several times she cast a look at Miller, who stood impassive at his post, watching them eat.

"Would it be presumptuous of me to ask after your history, Miss Dale?" McCabe asked.

"It's not a subject I'm fond of discussing, Mr McCabe," Dale replied.

"We all have a past, I suppose. I ask only to better appreciate your skills with a blade," McCabe said. "The events of yesterday morn were described to me and are becoming the talk of Orchard Bend. It's been my experience that few come by such abilities naturally and even then, a good many years of practice are a necessity to hone them."

"You would not be wrong in that assumption," Dale said.

"And those Colt 45s? Until recently the property of one of the Underwoods whom you felled. Are your talents in sufficient measure with them, also?" McCabe asked.

"In sufficient measure for *what*, if I may answer your query with one of my own?" Dale responded. She poured herself another glass of wine, relieved as the trapped feeling abated.

"I am to be travelling on business in the coming days and will be gone for a week," McCabe said. "Normally, this would be an opportunity for my family to partake in the many wonders of the city with me, but with a newborn and my wife not fit for travel, they're to stay in Orchard Bend."

Dale sipped her wine as McCabe spoke, but now asked, "And what would you have my role be, Mr McCabe?"

"I pride myself on being a good judge of people and your actions yesterday demonstrated not just proficiency with your weapons, but more importantly you are a person of sound character. And because of that, I feel I can trust you with this assignment. You protected innocents and I would ask of you to do the same for my family in my absence," McCabe explained. "You will be compensated and provided lodgings here for the duration. Miller will also be on site for this duty."

"Are you expecting any specific trouble?" Dale asked, downing her wine and reaching for the bottle again.

"I can't say I am," McCabe said. "And perhaps this is paranoia brought on by husbandry and fatherhood, but I'd feel much relieved knowing they are under competent protection."

Dale looked from McCabe to Miller, then around the room, her gaze falling upon the window. It was dark outside, so much so as to be black. She didn't know what she expected to see, some light from Orchard Bend perhaps, but she saw nothing.

"Very well, Mr McCabe," said Dale. "I accept your offer of employment."

* * *

May 19, 1953
Orchard Bend

Gabrielle McCabe arrived at her house a little after midnight. The winds had picked up and clouds now blotted out the moon and stars. Her long coat fluttered about her dress as she walked from her car to her front door. Without turning on the lights, she set her keys and purse down in the narrow front hall and slipped her heels off. In the living room, she turned on a lamp.

"You're late," a voice said behind her. Startled, Gabby turned around to see Ty Brand sitting on the sofa.

72

"Dammit, Ty! You almost gave me a heart attack!" Gabby said.

"Sorry, sweetie," Brand said, getting up. "I was starting to wonder if you were even coming home tonight. I was about to leave."

"That cantankerous prick insisted on staying out on the front porch for hours after you left," Gabby said, taking off her coat. "If only he'd frozen to death out there, it would've saved us a lot of trouble."

"I've said it before, sweetie," Brand told her, "it's time to get out. You and I can be so far away from here when he wakes up..."

"Don't tempt me, darling," Gabby sighed, lighting a cigarette.

"Why not? The money is there, let's use it. I've got it all figured out, listen," Brand said, putting his arms around her from behind, "We drive to the city, get a room, and in the morning when the banks open, we take out everything you stashed, get on a plane and disappear. Leave your asshole of a grandfather to die alone just from the shock of it."

Gabby took a drag of her cigarette, looking out the window to where the trees swayed in the wind. The branches and leaves made shadow shapes against the streetlights.

"No, it's not time yet," Gabby said, relaxing a little in Ty's embrace. "Leaving isn't enough. He'd miss his money, but certainly not me, except maybe as a doormat. And he wouldn't suffer enough and *that's* the important thing. I want him to understand that I took everything from him. Only then will we leave the son of a bitch to die alone and broken."

Gabby snuffed out the cigarette and turned to Ty, kissing him with such intensity that he staggered back a step.

* * *

September 29, 1945
Orchard Bend

Gabby McCabe was ready to kill herself.

The sun shone in the blue autumn sky, birds were chirping and Gabby had never felt so much pain in her life. The world around her still revelled in the end of the war. The soldiers would be coming home soon. Gabby's girl friends swooned at how good a man looked in uniform and not long ago she had agreed with them.

Then her parents were killed in a car accident and everything became a surreal nightmare. The McCabe's car had swerved off the road near the bridge over the west river. Gabby, sixteen, had been home alone waiting for her parents to return from a party when Sheriff Thorn arrived to deliver the news. Not wanting the girl to be alone, Thorn had driven her to her grandfather Owen's house, on whose porch she now sat.

Three months after her parents died, Gabby noticed the change in people around her. Their expressions of sympathy began to wear thin as they repeated the same condolences again and again, the words becoming more and more perfunctory. But Owen McCabe somehow made the entire loss worse by barely mentioning his son and daughter-in-law, even when discussing matters of their estate and her inheritance. Owen planned the funeral without input from Gabby and it seemed all she had to do was show up and cry. And cry she did, the recipient of everyone's thoughts and prayers, everyone but Owen's. He met with the undertaker to plan the funeral, shook hands at the wake and thanked everyone politely, but in the quiet of his house seemed unmoved. At first, Gabby thought he was simply grieving in his own way, but it became clear he was not grieving at all and had little time for her anguish. Unable to comprehend what she was going through, Gabby's friends became distant, with the excuse of giving her time to mourn. She saw it for what it was, though, their inability to cope with the darkness consuming her. And Gabby just did not care. The one good thing about her grandfather's apathy was that he did not insist she go back to school right away. Gabby knew she couldn't handle classes, homework or teachers. Allowed to simply stay at home, sometimes she didn't get out of bed all day.

All the while the blackness of her grief filled her soul. The decision to end the pain by ending her life came two days ago. That afternoon, she'd watched a robin feed its young in the nest in the tree outside her room.

If the mother bird left the nest to get food and was killed by a hawk, Gabby thought, *what could the chicks do but die?*

In that moment it hit her.

Die and be done with it. Anything would be better than this emptiness and pain.

The question now was how to do it.

Gabby was on the porch thinking about this when she saw Ty Brand on his bicycle coming down the hill heading toward town. He sped by at a pretty good clip, saw her and waved. She didn't wave back, so he waved again. He didn't see the small pothole in the street and tumbled off the bike, hitting the pavement hard. Horrified, Gabby dashed from the porch to her classmate.

Ty sat up clutching his knee as she reached him. His pants were torn and his skinned knee bled.

"I should have watched where I was going!" Ty said through his gritted teeth.

"Can you move?" Gabby asked. "Come inside and I'll patch it up."

She helped him to his feet. Ty limped through the gates with his bicycle and the two walked up the driveway to the house.

Owen McCabe was at work at the barber shop, so only Gabby was home. In the bathroom, she began dressing the wound.

"Don't overdo it, okay," Ty said. "My mom can clean it up when I get home."

"Are you in a hurry?" Gabby asked.

"No, not exactly. I just don't want to put you out is all," Ty said.

"How is your mom?" Gabby asked.

"She's good!" Ty said.

"She and my mom were in the Drama Society together," Gabby said. "She sent a nice card. Tell her thank you."

"Yeah, I will," Ty replied.

"How's school?" Gabby asked.

"Well, you know," Ty said, "Same teachers, same people. Well, you're not there, though."

Gabby looked up from her work on his knee. Ty looked like a rabbit about to get run over.

"I mean, we all know why you're not there! I didn't mean to say... well, I what I meant was..." Ty babbled.

"I know what you meant," Gabby said, going back to her work.

There was an awkward silence, then Ty asked, "What's it like?"

"Losing my parents? It's hell," Gabby said.

"I'm sorry," Ty said.

"I get that a lot," Gabby said.

"Well, I don't know what else to say, Gabby," Ty muttered.

"There's nothing else *to* say," Gabby sighed. "No one can help. No one can bring them back."

Another heavy silence fell between them. Gabby finished and stood up. Ty could walk and could bear more weight on it now.

"Hey, what do you know? That's some great work, Gabby," Ty said.

Gabby took him by the collar and kissed him so hard he nearly lost the footing on his wounded knee. When she let go, he was looking at her, speechless. She was unable to articulate what came over her, the sudden, intense desire to be with him. She took Ty's hand and put it on her breast, leaning into his touch, breathing a little heavier. Ty took the hint and caressed her with both hands. She closed her eyes and let her arousal wash over her. She started undoing the buttons of her blouse and Ty stopped.

"What about your grandfather?" he asked.

"He won't be home till eight o'clock," Gabby said.

She took his hands put them inside her open blouse. He cupped her breasts through her bra. She began undoing her jeans and Ty moved forward to kiss her again. She dropped her pants and started taking off his. She could feel how hard he was and knew she wanted him inside her. Ty's hands left her body as he balanced on his good leg to kick out of his pants and drop his drawers. Lust filled her eyes and she pulled down her panties. Ty turned Gabby around and bent her over the sink. She spread her legs and he wasted no time entering her.

As he eased in and out, Gabby welcomed the rush of a feeling. For the first time in months, she felt something stronger than her grief. The pain was still there, only dulled as the fresh thrill of her first time surged through her. Gabby knew she needed this; she did not want to die a virgin.

* * *

Not long after Ty left, Gabby stood below the window of her grandfather's study. She had tried to pick the lock, but had no idea how, so gave up. The previous winter, on Christmas Day, Gabby and her parents had come to see Owen, as they did every Christmas. There wasn't an abundance of cheer at the house and the visits rarely lasted more than a few hours. The last such visit had ended in an argument between Owen and his son. Gabby didn't get all the details, but the argument seemed to be around Owen's health and mental well-being. Her father spoke on the drive home of getting a lawyer and filing for power of attorney over the elder McCabe's estate. Gabby thought it would all blow over in a few days, but it did not. Her father spoke to both an attorney and a doctor. Gabby feigned obliviousness to the situation, but would overhear parts of telephone conversations and discussions between her parents. Gabby never got a chance to see how far this family squabble would go, because on a rainy May evening, her father lost control of their car and plunged both himself and her mother off the road near the new west river bridge. That was that.

That Christmas Day, however, before her family left amid angry voices, Gabby and her mother played outside in the snow. They'd built a snowman and caught snowflakes, then somehow got into a snowball fight. Gabby's mother made a wild throw and hit the window of the study, knocking one of the small panes of glass loose from its moulding in the wood frame. The glass didn't break when it fell into the snow. Standing on a snowdrift, Gabby and her mom fit the glass back in place, wedging little bits of broken moulding in around it to help keep it in place. The infamous argument broke out while the ladies were still outside and Gabby forgot about the window until a few days after her parents' deaths. She had walked numb around the outside of the house, trying and failing to think of nothing as the pain of loss tore through her. At one point she found herself staring at the window, seeing the pane her mother had knocked loose.

Now here Gabby stood, knowing it would help her end her life. In a way it was her mother helping her and tears rolled down her cheeks. She set an apple crate below the window, stood on it to reach the loose pane and pulled it out. Reaching inside, she undid the latch and slide the window open. She hopped up, crawled through the open window on her belly and slid it closed behind her.

Gabby had been in this room once before with her father, helping him look for a dictionary so he could finish a crossword in the newspaper. Before he shooed her away from Owen's desk, Gabby had gone through some of his desk drawers and found a pretty-looking wooden box. She'd opened it and found inside it a revolver. The handle was pearl and a box of bullets sat next to it. The gun had scared and fascinated her. Gabby wanted to touch it, but resisted the urge, closing the box and the drawer just as her father called her away from the desk, telling her to look on the shelves.

Standing at the desk now, she opened the drawer and saw the pretty wood box still there. Her heart raced and she thought of the sex she'd just had with Ty Brand in the bathroom. There had been pain at first, then relief. Gabby expected putting a bullet in her head might feel the same. Pain as it killed her, then sweet relief from the grief tormenting her. She opened the box and there was the gun, just as it had been years before. The bullets were sitting next to it.

The revolver was heavier than Gabby thought it would be, so she used two hands. Looking down the cylinder, she saw the empty chambers and knew the weapon wasn't loaded. She had a panicked moment as she wondered how to get the gun open to load it, but fidgeted with the little switches on the side and the gun opened. Not wanting to take a chance, Gabby loaded six bullets into the chambers and closed up the gun. It locked with a satisfying click.

Gabby wondered if she should sit down for this, park herself behind her grandfather's desk and eat the bullet right there. It would be more dignified than standing, pulling the trigger and falling to the floor, so she sat on the thick, cracked leather seat and it creaked under her weight. She put the gun down to get comfortable and saw her grandfather's black ledger sitting on a stack of dusty books. Gabby looked at it, just sitting there on the desk. The clock on the wall told her Owen wouldn't be home for a few hours, so she pulled the ledger to her and opened it.

It was like a scrapbook, full of notes, newspaper clippings and dated entries. Gabby thumbed through it, noticing names like *Emery Dale*, *Henry* and *the Prisoner*. Gabby flipped back to page one and saw beautiful, delicate drawings of landscapes and people, most without description, but those which did bear notation gave the names of individuals and places. A few dates were scribbled throughout the sketches, placing them more than sixty years previous. There was even a little map next to a drawing of a carving on a tree. Gabby recognized the river and the bridge illustrated on it.

The sketches seemed to stop partway into the early pages of the book and new entries in a different hand, her grandfather's hand, took over. Gabby started reading.

A strange mix of local history, family history, spite, anger and *madness* filled the ledger. There was no other explanation for some of the things her grandfather had written, some of the confessions and revelations which otherwise made no sense. However, some of the things, too awful to fathom, were true, supported by some of the older newspaper clippings. Gabby wondered if her parents knew half of what was in this ledger.

Maybe they did, she wondered. *After all, they were trying to get Owen committed before they died. Maybe Dad saw this or Grandpa spoke of it.*

After a while, the newspaper articles began to repeat the same old information, particularly about this Dale woman and the larger town history, so Gabby skipped ahead to the most recent entries, wondering if any entry mentioned her.

There were newer clippings, pieces about the McCabe car accident. Gabby's eyes watered and her lip quivered as she saw the paper's photos of her parents. She flipped back a few pages to the date of their death and found a handwritten entry there.

May 21, 1945
Idiot lawyer called yesterday about competency hearing so I gave the word to Officer Gillespie to _off_ James and Maria. Shit's gone far enough. James ain't no goddamn son of mine no more. Fuck'em! Him, his bitch wife. Hope they burn in hell tonight.

Gabby's encounter with Ty in the bathroom had dulled the pain of grief, but reading this entry replaced it fully with something else: raging hate, focused at her grandfather.
He killed them, Gabby thought. *He had them* murdered*!*
She could picture it, this Officer Gillespie running her parents' car off the road in the rain. It was late, there were no witnesses. Gabby re-read the article and wasn't surprised to see Gillespie was on the scene first, the officer who reportedly found the McCabes after the "accident."
Gabby looked at the revolver and considered sitting here until Owen came home and just putting six bullets in the old man. In her monstrous rage, she knew she could do it.
The rage ebbed a little after a few moments, but the anger still burned hot and that's when Gabrielle McCabe started formulating her real revenge plan.

* * *

May 19, 1953
Orchard Bend

Gabby lay naked atop the dishevelled bed in the dark of her bedroom, listening to Ty's footsteps as he descended the stairs. She heard him open the door of her house, then close and lock the door behind him. Gabby lit a cigarette and basked in the afterglow, thinking about what Ty had said. They could leave

80

right now, they certainly had enough of her grandfather's money.

No, Gabby thought, *it's not time.*

Her plan was a good one and so far it was playing out the way she'd envisioned all those years before, sitting at Owen's desk with the revolver.

Just a little further to go, Gabby told herself. *I can't walk away now.*

Outside, the wind still moaned and the shadows from the trees danced on the walls and ceiling. Gabby watched them, picking out shapes.

One of the shadows appeared as a dark figure and Gabby sat up. The shadow figure moved toward her and she screamed. Something like an arm reached out from the dark shape and covered her face. The cigarette fell from her fingers and she tried to grab her assailant, whose body felt like a swirling column of wind. The air around her face became a vacuum. The wind seemed to fill the room, pressing her down on the bed. As thick and black as the shadow smothering her was, she could just about see through it. The shadows of the trees still danced on the walls, but otherwise everything was normal. Gabby struggled, trying to scream, but there was no sound.

And then she saw the smoke seeping around her and noise filled her mind. The shadow was talking to her.

You are going to die, it said in a matter-of-fact voice. *I need Owen. And in a way, I owe him for what he is going to do when the traveller arrives.*

Gabby's struggles eased as she lost the energy to fight and her consciousness faded.

I was there, you know, the shadow said. *I watched you take out the gun and read Owen's ledger. I was in the room, though you didn't see me. But you read about me. I'm the Prisoner your grandfather wrote about. I've always been in Orchard Bend. Watching...*

Gabby lost consciousness hoping that if she truly was going to die now that she'd find her parents waiting for her on the other side. She did not wake up as smoke filled the room, the smouldering fire sparked by her cigarette igniting the bed sheets.

When she died, white replaced the darkness.

10

May 10, 1879
Orchard Bend

Emery came downstairs on the afternoon of her third day guarding the McCabe family. She gave serious thought to a cup of coffee. It was Saturday afternoon. Miller and Henry were outside playing catch.

"Miss Dale, please join me," Gertrude said. Dale said nothing, but crossed into the parlour. Owen was in his bassinette asleep and Mrs McCabe looked tired, yet pleasant. Until now, Gertrude and her son, Henry, kept mostly to themselves. Henry went to school during the day, escorted by Miller, who stayed in town and then returned home with the boy before dinner.

"Perhaps a nap as your son sleeps would be more wise than talking with me, Mrs McCabe," Dale suggested.

"Please, call me Gertrude," she said. "It's not a courtesy I'd afford to Mr Miller, but you and I are ladies and I hope we can speak as friends."

"Then do call me Emery," Dale said.

"Emery, such a curious, yet not unpleasant name for a woman," Gertrude smiled, pouring two cups of tea. "And you're right, I should enjoy a chance to rest when I'm able, but since you are charged with keeping my family and me safe, I'd be very much interested in knowing more about you."

Dale tensed, but sipped her tea.

"Now, now, it's not my intention to pry into your past," Gertrude said, "It's abundantly clear that you prefer to keep that to yourself. Such is the way of many who come West in search of new opportunities. No, I won't ask where you come from or ask after your childhood. Instead, I would like to know about *you*, perhaps your plans for the future."

"I don't much know what I plan to do after this," Dale said, nodding at the room. "It would be an understatement to say this probably isn't where I planned to be, arriving in town as I did. I can't go back to where I came from, that path seems lost to me, and staying here after your husband returns, well... It's been suggested I move on."

Gertrude sipped her tea, nodding, her expression difficult to read. While only in her mid-twenties, Mrs McCabe appeared older, carrying a weathered countenance common to many Dale saw around town.

"Well, I should not keep you from your duty any longer, Emery," Gertrude said after a moment's quiet, "but come find me before you take leave of us at the conclusion of this assignment. Please, do me that courtesy, will you?"

"Of course," Dale replied. She finished her tea, thanked Gertrude and headed outside to sit on the porch.

* * *

May 13, 1879
Orchard Bend

The grandfather clock in the upstairs hall chimed midnight. Downstairs, Emery Dale took care not to open the door to the study too fast. Like the rest of the house, blue and black shadows bathed the room, broken up by dancing moonlight from the trees swaying in the wind outside. On previous nights, she'd moved through the halls of the McCabe house by the light of a small lantern, but as she became more familiar with the layout, she found its dim glow more of a hindrance. It was simply too weak to properly illuminate the dark rooms and halls, but was bright enough to throw off her night vision. She had a *Lamp* application on the wristwatch she no longer wore, but now kept in a pocket of her cloak. Wearing it would be to invite questions about her origin, questions she couldn't answer. She and the watch were from another time and place and it was best to keep that information to herself.

The study was clear. Dale checked the latches on the windows again and paused to look outside. The waning half moon was still enough to brighten the gentle hills of the countryside beyond the McCabe estate. She took a moment to reflect how peaceful and quiet everything looked, then closed the curtains and turned away from the window to continue her rounds.

Someone's shadow stood in front of her and Dale drew one of her guns in surprise. There was a shadow, but no person. She blinked in the darkness to try to focus on it. It vanished for a moment, only to reappear again as the thin shafts of light cut through the curtains. Dale trained her gun on the shadow, now certain this anomaly was real. A shadow cast by no one, yet there in the room with her, appearing to look around. An odd feeling of familiarity gripped her and Dale's mind raced to find a connection somewhere. The memories were almost there, but another stabbing migraine cut through her skull and she couldn't help but fall to one knee, still clutching the gun still aimed at the dark shape before her. When at last she could hold out no more, Dale closed her eyes against the pain, but did not lose consciousness. She waited for the migraine to subside and through sheer force of will opened her eyes again.

The shadow was gone.

Dale holstered her weapon and wondered if she'd really seen what she'd seen. There was no doubt in her mind something or someone had been there. Dale rose to her feet and collected her wits, breathing deeply. There was water in the kitchen, so she decided to continue her rounds in that direction and left the study.

Dale's head was mostly clear again when she reached the kitchen, but she poured a cup of water anyway and sat on the stool in the corner to drink it, trying to make sense of what she had just witnessed. She couldn't shake the feeling that the shadow, whatever it was, was familiar to her. After a few long, intense minutes turning the experience over in her mind, Dale was no closer to understanding it.

85

Setting the empty cup down on the counter, Dale left the kitchen, walking down the hall back toward the front of the house.

A noise made her stop, a clicking sound coming from behind her, from the kitchen. Dale listened, unmoving in the dark. The clicking came again, louder and more urgent. Dale again drew a gun and from the shadows of the hall peered back into the kitchen she'd just left. Everything was as she'd left it.

When the sound came again, Dale locked in on its source. It wasn't just clicking now, but the gentle rattle of the handle of the door leading outside. Dale had inspected the door on two separate visits to the kitchen during her rounds and it had been locked. Now someone was outside trying to get in.

* * *

May 7, 1879
Blue Creek

United States Marshal Ed Saunders and his men made camp for the night outside the mining town of Blue Creek. It was their latest stop as they made their way to the city, transporting the bodies of the Underwood Gang. The Orchard Bend undertaker had embalmed the bodies for the journey, but Saunders knew they'd start rotting regardless, so planned to get there by this time tomorrow.

Dusk had fallen and the sky was a deep blue. Saunders checked that the coffins were secure in the wagon and walked back to the fire where his men were cooking dinner.

"They ain't goin' nowhere, boss!" Marshal Hoss called to Saunders. The other men laughed and Saunders smiled.

"They've given the law the slip more than once. I ain't puttin' nothing past'em, Hoss, even two days dead," Saunders joked back.

"Tell you what," said Marshal Clarke, "This has got to have been the strangest few days I ever witnessed on this job. The Underwoods taken down by a single woman."

The men grumbled their agreement and Saunders poured himself some stew.

"No gun. Three armed men on horseback," Clarke continued. "If she hadn't drawn those knives on us in the jail, I never would've believed it possible. Where'd she learn to do that, you reckon?"

"Saw one of them Wild West shows a few years back," said Marshal Raines, through a mouth full of tobacco. "There was a knife thrower there, bull's-eyin' apples off the tops of pretty girls' heads. I thought of that fella when I saw that lassie with her blade to your throat, Hoss."

"*Tarnation*, Hoss, I thought your days were done," said Clarke. "The lady darn near got her pretty head blown off with that stunt. And boss, what were you doing making like she was lying about what she did? You knew she was telling the truth, we all heard the sheriff say it."

Saunders shrugged.

"I wanted to get a sense of the woman," Saunders said. "Get a girl riled up and you'll learn the truth of her, just as you will giving a man a bottle, so my father says." Saunders pointed to the young man, "Remember that lesson, boy, but also remember when *not* to get her in a state; that is to say, not when she's within reach of a blade!"

The men laughed.

"I do apologize, Hoss. I expected her to go off, but I didn't expect you'd have a knife at your throat when she did," Saunders said.

"You buy the first round when we get home and I'll consider the debt paid, boss," Hoss said, but before he reached the end of the sentence, the whiney of a horse on the road drew their attention.

The dark shape of a man on his mount crested the low hill, paused there and then proceeded toward the marshal's camp. The lawmen drew their guns and stood ready.

When the rider reached them, Saunders called out, "United States Marshall Service! State your business."

"Hold your fire, Ed!" said the rider, dismounting.

Saunders knew the voice.

"Robert? Robert Quinn, is that you?" Saunders asked.

Quinn approached the campfire, looking harried.

"Ed, I've been riding since before sun-up! It's your father!" Quinn said.

Saunders holstered his weapon and went to the man.

"What about my father?! What's happened?" Saunders demanded. "Speak, boy!"

"He... He took his own life," Quinn said.

"He did *what?*" Saunders asked, unable to comprehend.

"With a hangman's noose," Quinn said. "I'm sorry to tell you this way, but—"

Saunders grabbed him by the collar and yanked the younger man so close their faces were inches apart. The other marshals hurried forward.

"What are you telling me, Quinn? WHAT ARE YOU SAYING?!" Saunders erupted in Quinn's face, ignoring his men who tried to pull him off.

"He took his life," Quinn pleaded. "Hanged himself last night."

Saunders lost all his energy, let go of Quinn and dropped to the ground.

"What happened, boy?" Hoss said to Quinn. "Tell us everything."

"I don't know the whole story, but there was a land deal Mr. Saunders had and it fell through," Quinn said. "He lost everything, all his investments, I reckon. There was a mortgage on the property..."

Quinn trailed off when it became clear the details of the business venture didn't much matter now. Ed Saunders got to his feet, pushed past his men and stumbled into the darkness. He dropped to both knees and let out a pained howl.

* * *

May 10, 1879
Sutter Grove

Ed Saunders had not waited for the others to awaken. He rose before dawn and told Hoss, the man on shift keeping watch over the camp, to proceed to the city with the Underwood's bodies. He'd meet them back there in a few days. He and Quinn rode hard and arrived in Sutter Grove in late afternoon. His father's remains were with the undertaker and Saunders went straight there, demanding to see him. The son wept angrily over his father's body until Quinn convinced him it was best to bring him home.

The following day, people came, paid their respects and Saunders greeted them. No one commented on the smell of alcohol coming off the US Marshal, his frequent sips from the flasks in his coat or his quiet mutterings when standing alone next to the body of his father. Quinn was concerned for his friend, though, and as the day grew long, Quinn tried to speak to Saunders, only to be met with an angry shove. Quinn took his leave of the man and so too did the other mourners.

After the last one left, Saunders made dinner and ate it on the small front porch of the house. A toxic combination of anger and regret seeped through him. His thoughts were shattered and incomplete from a lack of sleep. In the pale blue dusk a rider approached.

Saunders took a swig of whiskey from the bottle next to him, ready to send this last well-wisher away just as soon as the stranger said his piece. The man dismounted, tied his horse to the hitching post and approached with his hand outstretched.

"You'd be Royce Saunders' son?" the stranger asked.

"I am, mister," Saunders said, at the edge of his politeness. "The hour grows late. I thank you for your thoughts and regret to direct you back to the road at this hour, but I expect you understand the circumstances."

"The name's Henderson," the stranger said. "I suspect I understand the circumstances better than you do."

"You best start making sense, stranger," Saunders said. "My patience has reached its end."

"The loss suffered by your father was not his alone," Henderson said. "*My* family's meagre holdings are gone and there are others who share this fate."

"You and the others have my sympathies," Saunders said, "All I can offer you is a drink from this bottle."

"Thank you, but you may be more interested in what *I* bring *you*," Henderson said, "The identity of the man who brought ruin upon so many. And the opportunity for vengeance."

The spiralling thoughts in Saunders' head snapped into sharp focus. If he could avenge his father's death, he could find peace.

"You have my attention," Saunders said.

* * *

May 13, 1879
Orchard Bend

A click came from the kitchen's outside door. In the shadows, Emery Dale knew the lock had been picked. When the door opened, she slipped further back into the darkness and watched as three men entered. They wore bandanas around their faces and their guns were drawn. They moved with purpose through the kitchen. They slowed when they reached the narrow hall, which twisted at right angles, flanked by a sitting room and a water closet, all interconnected. Dale had the advantage here, knowing both the layout of the house and being able to navigate it in the dark.

The intruders entered the sitting room and one of them pointed to the fireplace.

"There," he said in a harsh whisper to the man next to him, "Light it and we'll take care of everyone upstairs. Then we burn the place to the ground."

They left the man to start the fire. As he stood pondering the fireplace, Dale emerged from the shadows behind him and drove a knife into his back, covering his mouth with her hand. The intruder sucked in a gasp of air and seemed to hold it, unable to exhale as he died.

Dale left the body in the sitting room and slipped into the water closet, drawing her guns. From there she reached the door to the front hall and emerged into the shafts of moonlight pouring in from the windows.

90

"Henderson!" called out one of the intruders as Dale appeared in front of them.

Emery Dale opened fire, both guns levelled at the men intent on killing everyone in the house. The intruders' own bullets ripped past her. A vase exploded on the side table inches to her right and chips of wood from the table next to her sprayed her back and cheek. Thick smoke and the smell of gunpowder filled the hallway in seconds. Dale's ears were ringing with thunderous echoes from the half dozen shots fired between them. She instinctively dropped back into the water closet, holstering her smoking guns, which were hot against her legs even in their leather holsters. Drawing a knife, she heard the shuffle of feet and moved to intercept them near the kitchen.

She made it to the sitting room. The body of the first dead intruder still lay prone on the floor. A second intruder stumbled in clutching his stomach with one hand and his gun in the other. He drew down on Dale and fired. As she moved, the bullet tore through her shirt and grazed her arm, but she already sidled, driving her knife into the man gut. The blade impaled his hand even as it sunk deep into his stomach. Both the intruder and Dale's feet entangled with the body on the floor and they went down hard. The man writhed and kicked and punched at Dale. From upstairs she heard two more gunshots and a crunch as something heavy hit the floor.

"Run, Henry!" Gertrude cried. Another gunshot thundered upstairs.

The intruder's blows were not so much strong as they were desperate, those of a wounded animal in its death throes, and at last the man stopped moving. Dale got to her feet, stepped over the bodies and went to the hallway. She drew a gun and held it tight in a hand thick with the intruder's blood. Taking the stairs two at a time she reached the second floor and Gertrude's bedroom in seconds.

Miller lay dead on the floor, his gun next to him. Gertrude was unmoving on the floor against the wall, clutching the baby Owen. Dale's heart filled with sadness and anger at the thought of her death. When she moved to the pair, Gertrude blinked and looked at her. That's when Dale saw the bullet hole in the wall mere inches from her head. The mother clutched the baby to her breast and whispered, "Henry."

"Gertrude! Where is Henry?" Dale asked.

"He ran," Gertrude said. "The man ran after him."

Gertrude's gaze hadn't shifted from the door connecting Henry's room to this one. Dale followed the route of the boy and the last intruder. She re-emerged into the upstairs hall. At the far end, toward the rear of the house, she saw the small door swaying open. It led to the narrow servant's stairs. Small drops of a dark liquid on the floor confirmed that someone bleeding had come this way. Dale followed. Downstairs, she found the rear kitchen door open and wind blowing in from outside. At the door, Dale could just make out tracks in the grass leading from the house to the barn forty yards away. She took off at a run and reached the open door to find the last intruder bearing down on Henry with an axe. Henry pled and cried and the man muttered, so low Dale could not make out his words. The man was too close to the boy for her to try shooting him in the dark. The risk of hitting Henry was too great. And as confident as she was in her skill with a knife, all it would take was the man or Henry to move at the wrong time and Henry could be killed by her weapon.

Emery Dale drew her sword and charged.

"Intruder!" she shouted, hoping to pull the man's attention from the boy. He turned, his bandana now hanging around his neck. As he swung the axe at her, she blocked the blow easily. Dale hesitated when she saw the face of her opponent.

"Saunders?" Dale said.

"Lady Firecracker," he replied.

There was no sanity in his eyes and Dale had no time to wonder why. Saunders drew his gun, but not at her. Henry still cowered next to him and the barrel of Saunders' gun was about to find its mark. Cold fear and focus steeled Dale as she prayed she'd be fast enough.

Dale would remember the click of Saunders cocking the gun's hammer for the rest of her life, the barrel glowing silvery in the moonlight.

*　*　*

Emery Dale *was* fast enough.

*　*　*

The blade of Dale's sword flashed through the shaft of moonlight, taking Saunders' head from his shoulders. The marshal's finger squeezed the trigger and Henry cried out as the bullet grazed his cheek.

Dale stood shaking as the adrenalin rush ebbed, then went to the boy.

"Don't look at him, Henry," Dale said. "It's over. You're safe now. Let's go see your mother, okay?"

Henry nodded, wiping the tears from his face, looking from the dead marshal to Dale. He was slow to his feet, but once up and walking hurried with Dale out of the barn.

11

May 13, 1879
Orchard Bend

Sheriff Anderson's jaw noticeably clenched as Emery Dale walked him through the McCabe house. He asked very few questions as Dale detailed what happened, leaving out the strange encounter with the shadow in the study. The bodies were covered, but left where they'd fallen the night before.

Upstairs, Dr Shaw attended to Gertrude and the boys in a guest bedroom. The body of Miller still lay on the floor of the master bedroom. Gertrude, holding Owen in her arms, came to the bedroom door to watch Dale and the sheriff as the two went to where Miller lay. When she made eye contact with Dale from across the hall, Emery saw a wealth of emotion behind her eyes. Behind Gertrude, Dr Shaw tended to Henry.

Inside the master bedroom, Anderson pulled the sheet from Miller's body.

"Shot in the heart," Anderson muttered. He looked to the blood on the wall opposite the body. "But before that he got off a round himself and hit his target."

"I was downstairs with the other one when I heard two shots," Dale said. "I guess the first was Miller's and the second was Saunders', then Gertrude yelled for Henry to run and Saunders fired at her before running after the boy. He must have thought he killed her. Or wounded her and would come back to finish the job. I don't know. I followed his blood trail to the barn."

Dale led Anderson down the hall to the servants' stairs, out the kitchen and to the barn. Anderson had seen the decapitated body of the US Marshal earlier. Then as now he made no overt display of his feelings and Dale tried to read his expression as the sheriff stood in the shaft of sunlight over Saunders' remains.

"When I arrived, Saunders was approaching Henry with the axe. I drew his attention," Dale said. "He swung at me, I blocked it, then drew his gun to shoot Henry. That's when I killed him," Dale said. "I saw his eyes, though, and they weren't those of a sane man. Do you know why he came here?"

Anderson grunted a negative, picked up Saunders' pearl-handled revolver and emptied the cylinder into his hand. All the shells were spent. The Sheriff looked to the bullet hole in the barn board wall, the one that grazed Henry's cheek. He looked at Dale and Dale understood. The Marshal had fired at Henry with his last round, knowing that no matter what, Saunders would be dead by Dale's hand an instant later.

Pearl-handled revolver in one hand and spent shells in the other, Sheriff Anderson walked out of the barn, head down, with Dale following.

* * *

Activity filled the house that evening. Word of the assault on the McCabe home spread quickly. Gertrude's friends arrived to check on her. A few insisted she stay in town, at Sully's or with them, but Gertrude would have none of it.

"This is *my* home," she'd said more than once, "and I will not be driven out by vagabonds."

A wire was sent to the city to notify Maxwell and a few hours later, another arrived back saying he would catch the earliest train to Orchard Bend, but wasn't likely to be home until the following day.

Tired as she was, sleep wouldn't come for Dale. She gave up and went to sit on the porch in the late afternoon light. Two of Gertrude's friends were visiting and she left them to join Emery on the porch.

"I have yet to thank you for your heroism, Emery," Gertrude said.

95

"It almost wasn't enough," Dale replied. "It didn't save Miller."

"Mr Miller's death saddens us, Henry especially," Gertrude said. "Dr Shaw said to expect nightmares for a long while."

Dale nodded and asked, "Miller was not married?"

"No," Gertrude said. "And he had no children, no family left to provide for. I've left instructions with the undertaker that Maxwell and I will cover any expense for laying him to rest. It is the least we can do for him."

"How are *you* feeling?" Dale asked.

Gertrude didn't answer right away, but looked out at the road leading to town and sighed, letting the weight of the night's events show through.

"I am strong enough to remain composed until my husband returns," Gertrude said. "We still have you to protect us and for that and your deeds last night I am eternally grateful. It is a debt I will never be able to pay back, but there *is* something I'd like to share with you, further to our conversation the other day, the one where you expressed doubt about being here and what to do in the days to come."

Gertrude held up the black leather ledger and sat down next to Emery. She opened the book and Dale saw that Gertrude had been using the pages not for business record keeping, but as a sketchbook.

"My husband has many of these unused in his study and in the absence of anything else to use, I continue my artistic pastime in them," Gertrude said. "I have a full one in the bedroom. It's a bit of self-indulgence, I know, and with the children occupying much of my time, I have fewer opportunities to partake."

Mrs McCabe flipped through the pages, revealing images of trees, the sky, scenery and people.

"These are amazing," Emery said. "You're incredibly talented!"

Turning the page, Dale saw Gertrude had clipped the front page article of the Orchard Herald, the one about her stopping the Underwood Gang and saving Sam O'Toole and Rose Adelaide.

Gertrude paused and looked at Dale.

"I hope you don't mind these next few," she said. "I was working by candlelight from my bed. Not the most ideal of conditions, I dare say."

Gertrude turned to the next page and there were two sketches of Emery, one looking at three-quarter profile and one looking away.

A sense of familiarity arose in Dale and she feared another migraine would overtake her. None came. Instead, she was left with a sense that she was looking not just at herself, but at someone else, someone she might have once known. The feeling was so strong, but without context or memory, all Dale could do was again lash out in her mind at the vast chasm where her identity had once been.

There were tears welling up in her eyes and Gertrude produced a handkerchief.

"These are exquisite," Emery said. "Thank you for sharing them, Gertrude."

"You're kind to say," Gertrude replied, "but what I wished to show you is something altogether different."

Gertrude turned the page again and revealed a sketch of a shape carved into a tree. Emery knew this shape and rolled up her sleeve. The tattoo on her inner forearm, the one which looked like an "L" growing out of a "P," was more stylized in the sketch, but essentially the same.

Emery looked her question to Gertrude, who answered, "That carving is on a tree in a grove of aspens to the west, not far from the bridge where you first came into town. I saw the marking on your arm the other day and at once came to remember this tree. I had not given it much thought in a very long time. I drew a map here to help myself remember where it was and if you wish to copy it, to perhaps see the carving for yourself, you are welcome to do so."

Dale believed someone with knowledge of this symbol had placed it on the tree at some point in the past and now here she was, bearing the mark. She knew this could not be coincidence.

"I hope you're right," Emery said, looking from the map to Gertrude. "I hope this answers some of my questions."

12

October 24, 1945
Orchard Bend

It wasn't the first time Gabby McCabe returned to the house where she grew up, but it was the first time she did so by herself. Previously, Gabby had been escorted by Owen, who sat impatient in the kitchen as Gabby gathered clothing and personal items from her room. Lost in her sorrow, Gabby had only wanted out of there, taking the bare essentials and leaving the remains of her old, happy life behind.

This trip was different. When she unlocked the front door, she dreaded what awaited her, clutching her schoolbag tight. She closed her eyes and walked inside.

She stood in the foyer and said, "I'm here."

There was only silence, but already the familiar smells of the home triggered flashes of memory. A hint of pine reminded her of Christmas morning, opening presents with her parents. A musty scent brought the powerful image of her father in his cardigan by the fireplace. It might have been her imagination, but Gabby was certain she caught a whiff of her mother's perfume, the same one she wore the night she died.

"I'm going to open my eyes now," she said to the house. Her voice cracked as she added, "Please don't hurt me."

Her damp eyes opened and she waited to see if this once joy-filled place would embrace her or reject her. Soft morning light poured in through the windows and Gabby felt at home. She sat on the stairs and cried until her throat ached. When the sobs slowed to hoarse gasps, Gabby got up, adjusted her dress and climbed the stairs. She went to her parents' room first. It was almost untouched from the night they died and Gabby picked up items in no discernable pattern. She held her mother's compact, then her father's reading glasses. On the nightstand, she found a book, one her mother had been reading, about someone named Charlotte Darkey Parkhurst. She opened it to the bookmark, read a few lines and wondered if her mother had gotten to that part. She closed the book and put it back. She opened her father's dresser drawer and found his pocket knife. She opened it and smiled at the satisfying click it made when locked open. She closed it and slipped it into her school bag.

Gabby left her parents' room and went to her own bedroom. She lay on her bed, curled up so her knees touched her chin and closed her eyes. She slept a few hours and her dreams were calm and peaceful.

When she awoke, the sun was lower in the sky. Gabby didn't notice until she sat up that she felt different now. The dread of being home was gone. She belonged here. She was welcome here. This was *her* house was again.

"Thank you," she told the house.

Gabby left with a few more of her possessions and returned to her grandfather's house. He was sitting on the porch, something he did a lot, and she joined him there. She left a chair between them, but he shifted in his seat as she sat down.

"I'm ready to go back to school," Gabby said.

Owen nodded.

"Good. You've been out too long, I reckon, but you'll catch up quick," Owen said, not looking at her.

Gabby looked past him, seeing Orchard Bend sprawl across the countryside. Autumn was here and the town was coloured gold and rose red. The first summer without her parents had come and gone and soon the first winter without them would come cold and harsh.

"You got something else to say?" Owen asked.

Her gaze returned to him.

"Don't sell my house," she said.

Now Owen looked at Gabby. His gaze casually pressed on her, but she didn't flinch and didn't look away. She also didn't breath in those few seconds.

"We don't need to sell it, though it had crossed my mind," Owen said. He looked back out at the town and Gabby let out a long, silent breath. "You can have it when you finish school. Not high school, but *college*. Your parents left you enough to see to your higher education. If you want the house, you finish school and it's yours. Agreed?"

"Yes," Gabby said. It galled her, but she added, "Thank you, Grandpa."

Owen waved a dismissive hand and said no more on the subject. Gabby rose, collected her schoolbag and went inside.

***

July 14, 1946
Orchard Bend

At every opportunity, Gabby McCabe would sneak into her grandfather's study and read from his ledger. Sometimes she would pour over the pictures her great grandmother drew, idyllic scenes of an Orchard Bend she never knew. Other times, she would read the diary-like entries and try to understand the insanity of her grandfather's mind, all the stuff about the Prisoner visiting him, telling him things about the town, its history and this other place called the Breach.

Her revenge would take time and at first Gabby had only a vague idea what she should do. She would bring about the ruin of her aging grandfather by becoming the most important person in his affairs. Somehow. Her determination to destroy him was enough to pull her from the brink of suicide and give her purpose, if not much peace. With this new reason to live, Gabby returned to school and concentrated on her education like she never had before. With her girl friends, talk of things like dating and music was little more than an act, a disguise behind which she hid the vengeful hate. Gabby's real interest was gaining an advantage over her grandfather.

So it was that Gabby made her way to the abandoned bridge one summer day. She had her own hand-drawn copy of her great grandmother, Gertrude's, map. The one which led to the tree with the odd symbol carved into it. She walked her bicycle through the underbrush along the river bank, careful to keep the rushing water in sight. She was looking for the landmarks on the map, like the S-shaped twist in the river and the old abandoned cabin. When she came to the spot where the cabin should have been, there was only a stone foundation covered in a quilt of moss. Beyond the foundation was a grove of aspen trees and Gabby knew she was close. She leaned her bike against the stone foundation and entered the grove.

The tree Gabby sought was somewhere in there, according to the map. Hot, thick air and the drone of insects filled the ravine and the grove. The aspens were like columns around her, as if she were in some natural cathedral of white and green. The unkempt grass was the only undergrowth and it tickled her bare legs as she moved through the trees, trying to examine every one, a near impossible task.

After a while, Gabby stopped and rested against one of the aspens, rubbing her eyes and thinking perhaps it wasn't worth the bother to just find a stupid carving on a tree. What would it matter if she saw it? How could it help her plan for revenge? Yet, she had come this far and if the tree still stood, it was connected to Owen's ledger and that was reason enough.

Gabby opened her eyes, but before she could press on, she found herself staring at the strange "L" and "P" shape. It was on a tree about five yards away and Gabby almost thought her eyes were playing tricks on her. She walked to it and touched it, tracing it with her fingers. Gabby started to laugh and said, "I don't know what you mean, but you're real and that's all I need right now. Mom? Dad? Grandpa Owen is going to suffer for what he did to you."

Gabby turned from the carving and a pale shape of a person was there before her. There was no time even for fear as the smoke-like figure reached out to her. She heard the whisper of a voice in her mind.

I'm not going to hurt you.

Gabby was on her back in the grass surrounded by the aspens. Panicked, she sat up and looked around. The tree with the symbol was next to her and she tried to remember what happened. Her head throbbed like a migraine and her mouth was dry. Her right hand felt cramped and her arm was sore, as if she'd spent hours writing. She stood up and brushed the grass from her body, confused and a little frightened. The heavy summer air seemed to press in on her. Gabby remembered finding the carving on the tree, then... nothing, just waking up on the ground.

Gabby licked her lips, but there was little saliva in her mouth.

Heat stroke, maybe, she thought, *I'm dehydrated and I probably passed out.*

The insects were still buzzing and the sun still sat high, so Gabby figured she had not been out for very long. Thirst gripped her and she decided to head back to town. She collected her bike from the where it leaned on the stone foundation near the river and stared up the path to the bridge. She paused long enough to scoop a handful of water and sip it, splashing another handful on her face.

Walking her bicycle back the way she came, Gabby left the grove behind her.

* * *

May 15, 1879
Orchard Bend

Apart from the bullet hole in the tree by the road, left by Ernest Underwood's failed attempt to shoot Sam O'Toole, Emery Dale found no evidence of what had happened at the bridge in the ravine. The overcast sky softened the colours around her and there was a chill in the air. She suspected an approaching spring rain. The clouds had rolled in as she walked west from the town.

The wind picked up now as Dale moved along the bank of the river. An old wood-framed cabin sat unused on a stone foundation up ahead, just as Gertrude said there would be. When Gertrude was a child, she'd played with Isla Cormack, the daughter of the family who once lived there. That's when Gertrude first saw the carved symbol in the tree, which Isla's father said was probably put there by Indians.

Dale peered into the small, abandoned cabin as she passed and then continued toward the grove, the white trees bright even in the gloom of the grey sky. Entering the grove, Dale systematically examined the trees around her, moving slow, deliberate in her gaze, not studying each individual aspen, but letting her eyes try to find a break in the pattern of the bark.

Several yards in, a soft beep from the pocket inside her cloak broke Dale's concentration. Startled, she stopped, then remembered she kept her wristwatch in that pocket. As she reached inside, it beeped again and she scrambled to take it out. Text appeared on the screen:

Signal Acquired
Connecting...

Dale stood in the grove, bewildered and excited.

A signal? she wondered. *Out here?! And in* this *time?*

Dale knew the watch could not connect to any Global Positioning System or any such communication signal simply because there was nothing at this point in history to connect to. There probably wouldn't be for a hundred more years. Yet, now her watch had found a signal it could read and all she could do was stare at the screen in disbelief.

A new message appeared:

No Signal
Searching...

"What?!" Dale said, looking around as if the source of the problem might be somewhere in the grove. She tapped the screen with her fingernail, uttering in frustration, "No! *No!* Not when I'm this close!"

Dale held up the watch and walked forward, turning this way and that.

"Come on! *Come on!*" she said. "Where are you?"

Dale moved past the trees, to which she paid almost no attention now. So fixated was she on her watch and reacquiring the signal, nothing else mattered. Muttering to the little piece of technology in her hand as she went, Dale felt her heart sinking.

She caught her breath as a new message appeared:

Signal Acquired
Connecting...

Dale stopped moving, standing motionless in the grove, afraid to even lower the watch to eye level. The pounding of her heart flooded her ears and her mouth went dry. Another beep came and a new message appeared:

Signal Connected
Syncing...

"Yes, yes, yes," Dale whispered.
Then the display read:

Sync Complete
1 New Message
Device Clearance Recognized
Maj. E. A. Dale
Enter GvSci Passcode

– – – –

Drawing a complete blank on what the passcode could be, Dale looked around, hoping for a clue and fighting off bitter disappointment. She didn't know if it was wishful thinking, but

104

she felt so close to unlocking some of the mystery of her predicament. She wasn't ready to give up. The message, whatever it contained, was stored in the watch's memory, so she would have time to work out the passcode code even after she left the grove. The bigger question was what had her watch just synced up with? It had to be another such device, something broadcasting the signal. Guessing it could be related to the carving, Dale ventured further into the grove, aware that the sky grew darker but otherwise disregarding it.

Emery found the tree with the "L-P" symbol not far from where she acquired the signal. She stood staring at both it and her tattoo for a long time, touching her inked skin and then the carving, hoping for some insight.

"What do you mean?" she asked the symbol on the tree. "Who put you here and why? *Was* it for me? Are you a message?"

No answer came to Dale and the first drops of rain made her look up. With the sky now dark grey, she decided to head back to town.

Dale tucked the watch back into her cloak pocket as she walked out of the grove, past the abandoned house and to the river. At the bridge, she raised her face to the rain and let it wash over her skin, licking her lips. Dale looked back the way she came, remembering something else and smiling, saying, "I was a Major then, huh? At least I learned that much."

She then covered her head with the hood of her cloak and started back on the road to Orchard Bend.

13

June 11, 1953
Orchard Bend

Cal Watson sat in the sun on the park bench in front of the Town Hall trying not to think. Thinking inevitably lead to remembering and that felt more and more like one of the worst things he could do to himself. It wasn't so much remembering his parents and Debbie, but the little things about his life in Blue Creek. The other day he'd sat in Ed's Diner and the Lloyd Price song "Lawdy Miss Clawdy" came on. Cal's thoughts turned to the time he and Debbie sat holding hands in the bleachers of the Blue Creek High gym, watching the school dance below. Anger sprung from deep inside and Cal had to get out of there. He had not been back to Ed's Diner since.

After the murders of his parents and girlfriend, Cal had no choice in moving to Orchard Bend and living with his aunt, uncle and cousin. His house in Blue Creek would be sold just as soon as Cal's Uncle Ray got it ready to go on the market. Many times Cal found himself worrying about it sitting vacant. He'd asked his Uncle Ray if he could go with him on one of his uncle's drives to Blue Creek to check on it, but Ray's answer was always the same, "No, Cal, it wouldn't be good for you. Later, maybe." Even the day of his parents' funeral, the request to go by the house was denied ("Too much to do. Maybe later, huh?"). The one small bright spot that day was the few minutes he had sitting outside the church hall with his friends and classmates during the reception. Todd King, Cal's best friend since the first grade, handed him a duffle bag of things from the house, some clothes and mementos from his bedroom.

"Me and The Fish snuck in there a few days ago," Todd said, pointing to their friend Freddie 'The Fish' Beauchamp. "We thought you'd need some of this."

Cal clasped Todd's shoulder, his eyes wet. Todd's girlfriend Katy gave Cal a hug and said, "Anything you need, any time, you call us, Cal Watson. Understand?"

Cal agreed and soon after he was called back inside. He hadn't seen Todd, Katy, The Fish or any of his friends since. He wondered what they were up to in Blue Creek. Probably in class or writing exams, he figured.

After the funeral, Principal Stein came to see Cal and his aunt and uncle, to tell him that being so close to the end of the school year, he'd been allowed to finish the year with the good grades he'd earned. His uncle and Principal Stein had arranged for him to start at Orchard Bend High this coming September for his last year.

In the meantime, everyone in Orchard Bend had to either go to work or school. Cal's choices were to either sit at home while his aunt Helen scrubbed the kitchen floor or walk around town and try to get to know his new home.

So, Cal walked and eventually came to this park bench, where he tried not to think about the last month, when a shadow loomed over him.

"Shouldn't you be in school, son?" Sheriff Thorn asked.

Cal looked at Thorn.

"No, sir," Cal said, "I just moved here."

Thorn looked around and shook his head.

"I don't like kids running amok on my streets when they have somewhere to be," Thorn said.

Cal caught the odour of alcohol from Thorn, cutting through the otherwise pleasant smell of the trees and flowers around them.

"It's the last day of school and my cousin, Melissa, is going to meet me here, sir," Cal said, looking in the direction of Orchard Bend High School.

Thorn leaned in close and the smell of alcohol was undeniable.

"You giving me lip, boy?" Thorn asked.

"If you'd let me explain, sheriff—" Cal started to say, but Thorn cut him off when he grabbed Cal's collar and hauled the teenager to his feet.

"Loitering's against the law and I don't like your attitude, boy," Thorn said. "You're coming in with me."

"What?! I didn't do anything!" Cal protested, pulling away and slipping from Thorn's grasp.

Thorn stood fuming and reached for his nightstick, but a hand grabbed the sheriff's shoulder and Detective Reed stepped between the two.

"Sheriff, this young man was just getting on his way," Reed said, turning from his boss to the boy. "Isn't that right, kid?"

"Yes, sir," Cal said, backing away. "Thank you, sir."

Cal ran from the scene, not waiting to see if the sheriff would overrule his detective. He crossed the street and continued down one of the tree-lined avenues. He thought it uncanny how some of them resembled the streets in Blue Creek.

This one almost looks like Freddie The Fish's street, Steel Drive., Cal thought. *There's even a Studebaker in the driveway over there, like Old Man Redding drove, who lived across the street from The Fish.*

He rounded a corner and halfway down the block passed the burned out husk of a house. Old police tape still circled the scene of the recent fire. Cal stood on sidewalk looking at it, hoping no one had been inside when it caught fire. The police tape reminded him of something Todd King had told him at the funeral, that there was still police tape around his house. Normally, thinking of home brought too much pain, but the anger of his near arrest just now trumped it and that was just fine with him.

Cal took a few deep breaths as he looked at the burned out house, then continued on to the school to meet Melissa.

* * *

"Sheriff, this young man was just getting on his way," Tom Reed said. He turned to the boy and added, "Isn't that right, kid?"

108

"Yes, sir," the boy agreed, backing away. "Thank you, sir."

The teenager took off and Reed turned to his boss, who was gnashing his teeth in barely contained rage.

"Kids like that need to be scared straight, detective," Thorn said, dropping his nightstick back onto his belt. "I won't stand for delinquency in my town."

"Sheriff, I have an important matter to discuss, about...," Reed looked around before saying it, "Jane Doe 13."

Thorn, who had been watching the boy cross the street and disappear down Maplewood Lane, turned to the detective, his eyes suddenly sharp and focused.

"What about her, Reed?" Thorn asked.

"Her possessions are gone from the evidence room," Reed said. "No one signed them out after I signed them back in two days ago, but I just went there now and they're gone."

Thorn's expression went solemn.

"Well, that's it then, I suppose," Thorn said.

"The Barber," Reed said. "Owen Fucking McCabe."

This time Thorn grabbed Reed's jacket and pulled him close. Reed smelled the booze just as Cal Watson had moments before.

"Watch it, Reed," Thorn said. "You got close and by the grace of God Almighty and whatever's going on in The Barber's head, you didn't get run over with this. The man just lost his only granddaughter, so don't think for a second he'll take too kindly to you knocking on his door asking if you can please have Emery Dale's shit back. The case is closed, time to move on."

"There are still questions that need answering," Reed said. "Like who was the other person. What were they doing out there?"

Thorn shook his head.

"None of it matters, Tom. It's ancient history and Emery Dale stays a half-forgotten legend," Thorn said.

The sheriff patted him on the shoulder and walked back toward the Town Hall, leaving Tom Reed to stand alone in the park.

* * *

"So, what did you do with yourself today?" Melissa asked as she and Cal walked the tree-lined streets. A school bus rumbled along past them, followed by a convertible full of teenagers waving to a group of girls on the other side of the street. Music poured out of the car's radio, a tinny blues song Cal could almost identify, but then the car raced off and he shrugged.

"Not much," Cal said. "I walked out toward the train tracks. There wasn't much to see there, so I looped back. Was waiting at the Town Hall where we said we'd meet, but the sheriff thought I was loitering so I left. Passed a house that burned down not far from the school."

"Oh! I know which one you mean," Melissa said. "That was awful. A woman died in that fire. It was all over the newspaper. She was the granddaughter of someone really important in town. I'm terrible with names... McCurty?... McMaster...? Something like that."

They walked in silence for a while. Cal noticed his cousin glancing at him out of the corner of his eye and knew she wanted to know more about how he was doing. He could try to tell her, but even if he could put some of it into words (which he couldn't do), Melissa wouldn't really understand. He suspected she knew that, too.

The street ended and they were in front of the Town Hall, with the park on the far side. Cal tensed a little, his eyes darting about for the sheriff, but he was nowhere to be seen. He remembered the heavy odour of alcohol on the man's breath and shuddered a little. A twinge of anger turned in his gut, but Cal ignored it.

He and Melissa crossed the street, rounded the Town Hall and walked through the park, passing the gazebo. On the other side, Cal stole a glance at the park bench where he'd had the run in with the sheriff and noticed someone sitting there now. He would not have given the woman a second thought (except maybe *I hope the sheriff doesn't try to arrest you, too, lady)*, but she turned and he recognized her.

Earlier in the day, on one of his explorations of the town, Cal reached the train tracks, stopping there to wonder if this rail line was the same as the one which ran through Blue Creek. He suspected it was as he parked himself on the bank of the tracks, looking in the direction of his home. How nice it would be to simply start walking on the tracks and not stop. He sat there a long time. Later, he climbed back up the bank to the road which ran parallel to the tracks and walked along it for a while, until the road ended at the Orchard Bend freight yard.

Cal was about to turn down another road back to town when he saw someone sitting on the opposite bank in an olive drab army field jacket. The woman took a drink from a canteen and looked back and forth along the tracks as if waiting for a train. It didn't seem that she saw him and Cal didn't think much of it except that it was curious she was wearing an army jacket like that. He turned down the road back to town and kept walking.

Now here she sat, on the bench he'd recently occupied. The jacket lay next to her, draped over the back of the bench, and he could pick out the canteen under it. A duffle bag sat at her feet.

Cal's head started to ache and he pressed the bridge of his nose between his thumb and forefinger until it passed.

"What's the matter?" Melissa asked.

"Just a headache," Cal said, opening his eyes. He led them away from the woman and onto the grass. He glanced at her and saw her gaze cast in the opposite direction now. The headache came back stronger. If Cal didn't know any better he'd think she was the cause.

"I think I need a drink," he said.

"Want to stop at Ed's? It's right across the street," Melissa asked.

"Nah, I'll be fine."

"Are you sure?" Melissa gave him a look he'd seen from her a few times, one which seemed to say she suspected he wasn't being entirely forthcoming.

"Too much sun, probably," Cal said. The headache eased, but didn't quite go away. Cal guessed that he was just tired and as much as he dreaded going to sleep these days, he figured he'd have a nap when they got back to his aunt and uncle's house.

* * *

Jason Hansen stepped off the school bus with his sister, Allie, behind him. They started walking toward the driveway to their house.

"I can't wait to start summer vacation," Allie squealed as she skipped along the road, kicking up dust.

"Yeah, me too," Jason said, but his thoughts were elsewhere and Allie had noticed.

"Why are you acting weird?" she asked.

"I'm not acting weird," Jason said.

"Yes, you are," Allie kicked a dusty rock from the side of the road. "Ever since you went into that haunted house you've been acting weird. You don't play outside anymore unless mom or dad tell you to."

Allie was fond of calling the old hunter's cabin where they'd found the skeletons the haunted house. Jason had stopped trying to correct her.

"I just like being in my room, that's all," Jason said.

"What do you do in there?" Allie asked.

"Nothing," Jason said as they turned up the driveway. "I read. I play with my stuff. I just like to be alone, so what? Mind your own business, Allie."

"Mom says it's not healthy to be inside so much," Allie said.

"Are you going to be a nag all summer?" Jason asked, just wanting his sister to leave him alone.

"I'm not a nag!" Allie said.

"Tell you what, I'll race you to the house and give you a head start," Jason said.

"Okay," and Allie started running up the driveway to the house.

After a few seconds, Jason jogged after her, letting her win.

"Beat you!" Allie said.

"Yeah, you did," Jason replied, walking up the steps to the porch as she stood panting on the grass.

"Soon I won't need a head start," Allie said.

"I believe it," Jason said and went inside.

* * *

Cal Watson's headache wasn't getting any better when he and Melissa arrived at the house. The smell of ammonia from the kitchen didn't help. The throbbing was so intense as he climbed stairs, he didn't hear his aunt Helen ask how his walk went. In his room, Cal wended his way through the boxes of clothes and collapsed on the bed. He missed his bed in Blue Creek. At some point Cal's bed would be brought from Blue Creek to Orchard Bend, but until then, he was left with the spare bed in what used to be the spare bedroom.

As his head hit the pillow, the pain in Cal's head reached levels he'd never experienced before. He let out a moan and rubbed his temples. He'd heard somewhere that it would help, but it seemed to do little. From Melissa's room he could make out the static-filled sound of the radio and the crooning of a singer. She was getting ready for an end-of-the-school-year party and sang along.

The pain reached migraine proportions and tears rolled down Cal's cheeks. Cal curled his knees to his chest, lying on his side, and just as he thought he'd pass out, the pain broke and sweet relief washed over him. Cal opened his eyes, intending to get up and change his clothes, which were now damp with sweat. What he saw instead scared the hell out of him.

* * *

Ty Brand sat in his car fighting the urge to drink. He'd parked across the street from what used to be Gabby McCabe's house. The roof of the house was gone and the bedroom where she died was recognizable only by the burned out frame of the walls and windows. It was the room where they'd made love and the room where he'd left her. Earlier today, some punk walked up the street, stopped at the house and stood there looking at it. Ty had watched him, expecting him to get his look in and move on, but the boy had stood there a good long time. Ty tapped his finger on the steering wheel and was ready to climb out of the car and tell the boy to get lost, but hadn't needed to. The kid kept walking and Ty went back to his own vigil.

This wasn't the first time Ty had done this, sat in his car across from Gabby's destroyed house, but he hoped it would be his last. The previous visits had found him drunk, sometimes beyond remembering he'd even gone there, but this time he was two days sober.

Two days. Just to be sure he was thinking straight and just to be sure his plan went off without a hitch.

Another plan, huh? spat his doubt, *just like Gabby's plan to rip off Owen's money and ruin him?*

"Shut up," Ty said, fully aware he was talking to himself and not caring.

Two days ago Ty woke up late for work. He called in sick, thought he actually *would* be sick and while on his knees waiting to vomit, the idea came to him. It was perfect and simple and dangerous. Ty got through the wave of nausea without puking, but forced himself to cook up a hearty breakfast of greasy bacon and eggs to fight the hangover. He also forced himself not to drink anymore until he executed and completed his plan. There could be no room for error and he had to be sober to pull it off. Just to be certain, Ty resolved to stay sober for the next two days, to completely clear his system. His binges had been intense and frequent, but not constant. He went to work dry as a bone (unlike a certain sheriff he knew) and never missed a deadline at the newspaper. This last binge had been one of the worst, though, so Ty needed to be extra careful.

Two days to sober up.

Then Ty would steal Owen McCabe's black leather-bound ledger.

* * *

114

Cal stared in horror at the world around him. He recognized the bedroom and its contents, but everything seemed to be shades of black and grey. Jerking his head left and right, he opened and closed his eyes in a frantic attempt to regain normal vision, but each time he saw only the monochrome version. Even his own hands held to his face were devoid of colour, made up of a thin film under which was a smoky fluid.

"Oh god, maybe I'm dead!" Cal said. He looked to his bed, expecting to see his own dead body there, having succumbed to the migraine somehow, but the bed was empty. He touched the bed and felt the soft fabric of the checked blanket he had just been lying on. In the weave, he could just make out some hints of colour, some shades of the red and green in the pattern, and leaned closer.

Yes, definitely colour there, Cal thought. Yet, there was more. There was a flowery patterned sheet under the checked blanket and somehow Cal could see a bit of that as well and the fitted sheet below that and even further to the mattress.

Holy cow, Cal thought, *I'm seeing* through *the fabric.*

Cal held up his hands again, closer to his face and felt his stomach turn over at the vague shapes of the bones beneath his skin.

I have to be dreaming, Cal thought, *there's no way any of this is real.*

Cal lay on the bed as he had during the migraine and closed his eyes. Instead of the usual black, there was only dark, blurred grey and he realized his eyes were trying to see through his own eyelids. His eyes sprang open wide at the horror of it. Even lying down he felt dizzy with fear and panic.

Unable to grasp what he was seeing or why this was happening, Cal stayed curled up on his bed for a long time.

Maybe I've gone insane, he thought. *Maybe after everything that's happened I've finally lost all my marbles.*

Cal had heard about hysterical blindness and shell shock, conditions that affected soldiers in the war. It was a little relief to think that maybe this was all in his mind, that his sight had simply decided to go haywire on him. Still, Cal had no desire to remain like this, to see the world through this crazy grey vision. He sat up, his fear turning to anger. He pressed his hands to his temples and closed his eyes, trying to will back his normal sight.

There was no change.

Drawing the deep breaths of a man frustrated, Cal tried again, but still there was no change. He got up and paced the room, his anger giving him focus. There was a way out of this, he knew it, and he just had to find it.

There was a knock on his door and before he could stop her, Melissa had walked in. Cal stood frozen, waiting for her to react, to see something terrible and different about him.

"Cal, I was wondering if we could talk," Melissa said. When he didn't answer, she asked, "Is everything okay? I mean, is it a good time to talk now?"

Cal found his voice, but the surreal sight of his cousin appearing as so many smoky layers was difficult to process. He could see her face, but just under the surface he could make out her teeth behind her lips and the sockets of her eyes containing her eyeballs. It was faint, but it was there. He could also make out her undergarments beneath her clothes and looked away.

"Yeah, um..." Cal stammered. "I just feel really strange right now."

"Oh, I'll bet. I can't even imagine what you're going through," Melissa said.

Kid, you have no clue! Cal thought, his panic ebbing somewhat. Whatever he was experiencing, she was oblivious to it. He half expected that maybe his eyes were glowing or had turned a hideous black, but Melissa appeared to see nothing wrong with him, at least not related to whatever was going on with his sight.

"I wanted to show you something," Melissa said. She held up her hand and even before she opened it, Cal saw she had something in it. Opening her fingers, she revealed a small broach.

"Your mom gave this to my parents for me when I was born and I kept it safe in my jewellery box," Melissa explained. "I wore it at your parents' funeral, too, but I don't think you noticed. You had a lot on your mind, of course. It's meant a lot to me, I've always loved it and I plan to wear it at my wedding someday, but I never thought I'd wear it to their funeral. After I stopped crying when my mom and dad told me what happened, it was the first thing I thought of for the funeral, like the first thing I thought of to wear... Sorry, I'm babbling. You know what I mean, though... Anyway, I wanted to show it to you."

There were tears in Melissa's eyes and she took in a small sniffle as she handed him the broach. Cal took it and held it up, admiring the design. A wave of sorrow cut through the confusion of what was happening to his sight.

"Mom always had a great eye for jewellery," Cal said, fighting the lump growing in his throat. Without warning, Melissa hugged him. Pain stabbed the inside of his hand. The sudden act of her hug made him clutch the broach. The pin drove into the fleshy part of his hand below his little finger. He let out a shout of pain and Melissa pulled away.

"What?! I'm sorry, I thought..." and then she saw what had happened. "Oh no, I'm sorry! Here, don't move, I'll take it out."

With a quick pull, Melissa freed the broach's pin from Cal's hand, but this time he didn't notice the pain as it came out and only barely felt the dull throb from the wound.

His sight had returned to normal.

The smoke-like monochrome world pulled back, seeping into the natural shadows as the pain from the broach pin surged through Cal's hand.

"It's bleeding a little, hold on," Melissa said. She grabbed a tissue from the box next to his bed, left there by his aunt Helen should he ever need it. And he had needed it most nights. Melissa pressed the tissue to the wound and a new stab of pain came with it, but Cal was too relieved to care. She told him, "Just keep that pressed there. Make a fist. I'll get a Band-Aid."

Melissa hurried from the room and Cal sat down on the edge of the bed, looking at his good hand, wriggling his fingers, content to not see through his own flesh.

Melissa had put the broach down on his little bedside table and a dab of his blood spotted around the pin. Cal blinked out a tear and thought, *Thanks, Mom.*

Again he admired the design of the broach and wondered where his mother had bought it. The little "P" and "L" squiggly shape was interesting.

* * *

The end-of-school party was ostensibly at the Baker house, but in reality it took place at the far end of the Baker's vast farm property. Melissa's best friend, Angie Freeling, found a spot and parked the car. A dozen or more other vehicles littered the field of tall grass. Cal was in the back seat, next to the cooler full of soda and potato chips, watching the glow of the bonfire a dozen yards away. Music played and voices were laughing, yelling and singing.

"Everyone remember where we parked!" Angie said and she hurried out of the car. Melissa grinned and looked at Cal.

"I'm glad you decided to come," she said. "How is your hand?"

"It hurts, but it's okay," Cal said.

Angie knocked on the driver's side window and said, "Are you two coming? Get moving, huh?!"

The two climbed out. Cal carried the cooler and they walked the length of the path to the bonfire. A car sat with its doors open nearby, its radio pumping out the music. Teenagers sat on logs and rocks and a few lawn chairs around the fire.

A girl spotted them and rushed over.

"Melissa! Angie! You made it! And are you two just looking the Dollies tonight?" the girl squealed. She saw Cal standing behind them. "And who's this fella you brought?"

"Brenda, this is my cousin, Cal," Melissa said, pulling him forward. "Cal, this is Brenda Baker, it's her party."

"Nice to meet you," Cal said.

"Angie girl, Mike Garrett is here somewhere and I think he's gotten off that thing for Patsy Delmont," Brenda said, taking Angie by the arm and leading her away. "He was asking about you. According to Louise Finch..."

Angie threw a wink and grin back at Melissa as Brenda led her off, filling her in on the situation. Melissa giggled and spotted someone else she knew on the other side of the bonfire.

"Back in a jiff," Melissa said and skipped off.

Cal watched her go. He found a decent spot just away from the throng of revellers, opened a soda and sat on the cooler. From the radio, the DJ announced the latest Fats Domino record, "Please Don't Leave Me," and a group of kids who were clustered around the car jumped up in excitement. Cal tapped his foot to the piano-driven number and took another gulp of soda. Looking back at the car, he saw a girl leaning against it, lighting a cigarette. Her short hair made Cal think of Audrey Hepburn. He stole a glance at her legs below the hem of her skirt and then watched the bonfire some more. When he looked back at her, her gaze was in his direction. Cal jerked his head back to the fire. He took another pull from the bottle of soda. Trying his best not to be obvious, he directed his view back to the car. He was both relieved and disappointed that the girl was gone. Cal shrugged and went back to watching the flames. He took another sip and held the bottle up against the light, watching the odd way the flames danced through the curved glass. The memory of seeing through his own hands sent a chill through him. He lowered the bottle quickly.

"See something you didn't like in there?" asked the voice of a girl. Cal turned with a start. The girl from the car stood almost behind him, the hand holding the cigarette resting on her hip.

Cal stood up at once and the girl sat down on the cooler, leaving a bit of room next to her.

"Well? Cat got your tongue?" she asked, then took a drag from the cigarette.

Cal held the bottle up to the flame again and said, "I was looking for a genie in the bottle so I could be granted a wish."

"You might want to look in an oil lamp," the girl said, flicking ashes from the cigarette. "Genies are not known for hanging out in soda bottles."

"Mind if I sit down?" Cal asked.

"It's your cooler, Daddio," she said.

Cal sat down, hyperaware that there was only so much room on the cooler and that his thigh was now against hers. The girl gave a wave to someone across the field.

119

"My name is Cal Watson," he said, putting his hand out, "Nice to meet you."

"Grace Pine," she said, shaking his with her free hand and taking another pull from her smoke with the other.

"Friend of Brenda's?" Cal asked.

"Not really," Grace said, letting the smoke drift from her mouth. "We're classmates, but not exactly thick a thieves, if you get my drift?"

"Sure, I guess," Cal shrugged, "It's a place to hang out. Something do to."

Grace looked at him and said in a matter-of-fact tone, "Yes. Exactly. It's something to do. You nailed it on the head, Cal Watson."

"What can I say? I have a way with words," Cal smiled.

"A regular Shakespeare," Grace nodded.

"Uh oh, you just broke Rule Number One," Cal said.

"And which rule is that?" Grace asked.

"Where I come from, Rule Number One is 'No talking about school at the end of the year party,'" Cal informed her.

"Is that so?" Grace said with mock indignation. "And where are you from, Cal Watson?"

"Blue Creek," he said.

"You don't say," Grace said, feigning horror, "Your Trojans beat us to the semi-finals last year. Here I am fraternizing with the enemy!"

"If it makes you feel any better, I'm moving to Orchard Bend to live with my aunt, uncle and cousin," Cal said.

"Melissa or Angie?" Grace asked. "I saw you arrive with them."

"Melissa is my cousin," Cal said. "My mom was her father's sister."

"'Was'?" Grace asked.

Cal nodded, expecting her to ask more, but she only took another drag from the cigarette.

"What the hell is this bullshit?!" came a male voice behind them full of quiet anger.

Grace closed her eyes and let out a sigh, "Rats."

Cal turned to see the owner of the voice was broad-shouldered and well-muscled. His hair was cropped short, almost as if he had been in the army, but Cal could see this guy was about his age. The bonfire glinted off his horn-rimmed glasses, which sort of made him look like a well-read farmer.

The music from the car played on, "Your Cheatin' Heart" by Hank Williams, which Cal now wished someone would turn off. Grace flicked her cigarette away and faced the newcomer.

"Gracie, you better explain in a real hurry what you're doing here," the big guy said.

"For Pete's sake, it's a party!" Grace said without a hint of apology.

"Don't take that tone with me," the guy said, stepping towards her. "You know you got a mouth on you and you know I hate it."

"We broke up, remember that?" Grace said. "Stop acting like my boyfriend and stop acting like my father!"

Cal was aware now that others in the immediate vicinity were watching them. Grace's ex-boyfriend stood fuming and his gaze went to Cal and then back to her.

"Who's this?" the ex asked.

"Someone I'm talking to," Grace said, planting her hands on her hips. "You're making a scene, you know that? Just split, would you? You always do this. You always show up and embarrass me!"

"Oh, I do, do I?" he asked, talking over her.

"Yes, as a matter of fact."

"You're embarrassed?" he asked.

"Just go," Grace said, turning away from him.

Her ex turned to Cal.

"How 'bout you? You embarrassed?" he asked.

Cal put his hands up, saying, "Maybe you should give her some time, big guy."

"What's with the hands there, fella," he mocked Cal, "you surrendering?"

"Terry, stop it!" Grace said, pivoting around. "What are you going to do, huh? Are you going to hit him? Sheriff Thorn would love to throw you in jail just like your dad. Grow up! We're finished and all this... this *horseshit* of yours isn't winning me back!"

Terry stood stunned. Around them, Cal could hear the shocked mutterings of the other teenagers.

"Gracie, I just..." Terry stammered and Cal actually thought the big guy would to breakdown in tears.

"Terry, don't. Just go," Grace said, her arms crossed.

Terry cast a dark look at Cal and slumped away. Cal looked around and found many faces looking at him. He looked to Grace, but she was walking away in the other direction.

The music hadn't stopped, and now playing was Bill Haley with Haley's Comets' "Crazy Man, Crazy," and Cal saw Brenda Baker reach into the car to turn the volume up. One by one, the kids' attention drifted from Cal back to the party, all except Brenda, who had marched over to him.

"I have a good mind to send you packing," she said to Cal.

"Why? What did *I* do?" Cal asked, indignant.

"Just stay away from Grace Pine," Brenda told him. "She and Terry are having a spat and you getting all lovey dovey with her just confuses things."

"I wasn't getting—"

"My party, my rules, understand?" Brenda said with a stern look.

"Yeah. Whatever you say," Cal just couldn't be bothered arguing anymore.

Brenda's expression went right back to cheerfulness as if someone flicked a switch.

"Excellent!" she said and went off to mingle with her guests. Cal watched her go, shaking his head.

Crazy, man. Crazy.

14

June 12, 1953
Orchard Bend

Time to get up, said the noisy voice of the Prisoner.

Jason Hansen muttered in his half sleep and rolled over.

Get up now, *Jason, it's time to take a walk,* the Prisoner ordered.

"What time is it?" Jason asked.

It doesn't matter what time it is. I need you to do this for me. We're friends, right? I've done a lot for you, haven't I? asked the Prisoner.

"Yeah, you have," Jason said out loud, keeping his voice low, the way he always did when they talked. And they talked often since the day Jason found the skeletons in the cabin in the woods. At first, Jason dreaded and feared the shadowed presence, despite the Prisoner's assertion that Jason wasn't going to be harmed. That first night, the Prisoner offered Jason a deal.

Help me fix that device, the Prisoner had bargained, *and I will help you.*

Knowledge and images poured into Jason's mind about how to fix the box, how to make the flashing lights return.

What you saw in the cabin was the Breach, the Prisoner had told him, *I'm trapped there and need the box you're holding to help get me out.*

Jason had the know-how, but repairing the device took time. Everyday after school and every weekend, Jason had carefully followed the Prisoner's instructions. In return, the Prisoner told him things. Things about the town Jason never knew. The stories the Prisoner told Jason were a combination of words and images, sometimes like having a movie play in his head. Jason saw his teacher, Miss Gibson, stealing a pair of shoes from Kenner's Clothing and a few days later noticed she wore those very shoes at school. The following day, Miss Gibson gave the class a surprise geography test and Jason, not having done the homework (he'd been working most of the evening on gluing bits of wire and metal together inside the device), sat in stark panic at his desk. He was both going to fail the test and face the wrath of his parents at home. But the Prisoner helped him, giving him some of the answers. The ordeal unnerved Jason, despite getting a respectable 19/25 on the test (enough to pass well, the Prisoner told him, but not enough to draw suspicion). That night, he didn't work on the device. The Prisoner was not happy, but Jason was too angry to care.

The next night, Will Hansen took his children to the Old Western Movie House. Greta Patterson was there. She was in Jason's class and sat a few rows ahead of him. She wore a pretty blue dress that Jason could have admired all night.

"We're going to get our seats, champ," his father said. "You coming?"

"Yeah, I just want to say hi to someone," Jason replied.

His dad and sister went inside and Jason walked to where Greta was standing by the concession stand.

You can buy her a Coke and some popcorn, said the Prisoner. The appearance of the voice was so abrupt Jason stopped and looked around, but didn't see the shadow anywhere. The Prisoner spoke again, saying, *Go to the garbage can. Trust me.*

Jason did so, walking to the garbage can with the dusty ashtray built into the top. It stank of old cigarettes.

Look behind it, the Prisoner said.

Jason looked and saw a crumpled dollar bill there.

"How...?" the boy asked.

Dropped by the tall bald man heading into the theatre. He didn't notice it when he took out his pack of smokes, the Prisoner explained. *Now go buy Greta Patterson something from the concession stand.*

Jason pocketed the dollar and went to Greta, who was now joined by her younger sister, Janey.

"Hi, Greta," Jason said.

"Hi, Jason," she replied.

"I like your dress," Jason said. "You look nice."

"You're so sweet, Jason Hansen!" Greta said, grinning.

"Greta, come on, we're going to be late!" said Janey, pulling at her sister's arm. "I don't want to miss anything!"

"We have time, Janey, don't worry," Greta said. She looked at the concession stand menu. "I can't decide between a candy bar or popcorn. I only have enough for one."

"I was just coming over to get something myself," Jason said, hardly believing the sudden bout of confidence brought on by money in his pocket. "If you get the popcorn, I'll get you the candy bar. I can afford it."

Jason took out the dollar and held it up.

"Are you sure? I mean, that sounds great, if you can afford it!" Greta said, beaming.

"Greta, hurry up!" Janey whined. "We're gonna miss it."

"I think I'll have enough for Janey to have some extra liquorice, too," Jason said. "How does that sound, kiddo?"

"I'm not a kiddo!" Janey said.

Jason laughed.

"She reminds me of my sister," Jason said to Greta.

"She's right, though," Greta said. "Let's hurry."

They ordered their food and rushed to the door. Jason saw his dad with Allie on his lap, both eating their popcorn. Gesturing to Greta, Jason indicated he was going to sit with her. His dad gave him a wink and a thumbs up.

It went on like that for the last four weeks, the Prisoner imparting more secret knowledge to Jason Hansen and Jason feeling a sense of power and control that comes from such knowledge.

* * *

Jason climbed out of bed, seeing it was just a few minutes after midnight.

"Where am I going?" Jason whispered.

I'll show you, you'll be taking the device there, said the Prisoner and he showed the boy exactly where to go and how to get there. It was going to be a long walk.

Jason got dressed, being extra careful not to make any noise. He went to the back of his closet and pulled out a short piece of floorboard, under which he had placed an old shoebox. Inside the shoebox, wrapped in newspaper, was the device. Jason had at last repaired it to the point where it worked again for just a moment. That had been on the Sunday before. The Prisoner had showed/told him that the smaller piece had been a power cell, a battery and it had lost what little charge remained when Jason had turned it on upon finding it. That hadn't concerned the Prisoner much and the goal remained to get it working again. Jason had covertly scavenged the materials he needed, following the Prisoner's instructions. Replacing the dead power cell was a length of power cord Jason took from the family's discarded toaster, found in the barn where his father kept a lot of old junk and his tools. The fathers of some of Jason's friends were meticulous about their tools, organizing them with almost military precision in their workshops. Everything in its place and a place for everything a handy man would need. Not Will Hansen, though, who did succeed in keeping most of his smaller tools in a beat up old tool box, but everything else, like his saw and his large wrench (the one he used to fix the kitchen sink when it leaked every six months), was scattered about the tables and shelves on the back of the barn, surrounded by spilt jars of screws and nails, washers, off-cuts of wood and other detritus. Jason's mom kept a tidy house, but the barn was his father's domain. Though it could have used a little of Ann Hansen's touch, its casual sense of order made it easy for Jason commandeer what he needed to work on the device. After finishing the work Sunday and testing it, Jason had put everything back, including the old toaster power cord, now burnt out and never to carry an electrical charge again. On the Prisoner's instruction, Jason had wired it to the device where the power cell had been, had plugged it into the wall outlet in his room that night and turned the box on. The red circle spun again on the screen and the green box appeared. Jason had barely been able to contain his excitement. He pressed the green box and a soft hum came. The smoky film returned around him and the colour drained from the room. Looking at the device, Jason saw he could almost see through it. The layers of wires and what the Prisoner called circuit boards, all the things Jason had seen inside the box while working on it were just visible through the outer shell. He almost dropped the device when he realized he could see through his own hands.

"Successful test," the Prisoner said, but this time the voice wasn't noise in Jason's head, it was behind him and Jason turned. Standing there was the dark form, much more tangible than the shadow which Jason had gotten used to seeing. What he saw was very much a person, but still hard to make out. Parts of the Prisoner were nearly transparent, other parts more opaque, but somehow blurred and less defined, the way an old photograph just doesn't have the detail one could see in newer pictures. The Prisoner's face was cloudy and dark, with deep black pools where the eyes and mouth should have been.

There came a whiff of burning plastic and Jason turned to see the old cord spark and light up at the wall outlet.

"Unplug it!" the Prisoner ordered, but Jason had already yanked at the device in his hand on instinct to pull the plug from the wall. It worked and the device winked out, its power source gone. The smoky film over the world slipped away. As the world went back to normal around him, Jason looked to the corner where the Prisoner had stood and saw the familiar shadow there.

"What was that?" Jason asked.

The Breach. My prison, came the noise of the Prisoner's voice.

"But...what *is* it?" Jason asked.

A flood of images and sounds came as the Prisoner forced the knowledge into Jason mind. It was dizzying, but after a few seconds of it, Jason thought he understood. He saw a dark city of light and electricity. Places like New York and Chicago looked like this in the movies, but there were differences. Smaller cars dotted the streets and bright electric signs towered over the citizens. It reminded Jason of science fiction movies, including one his father had taken him to, a silent movie called *Metropolis*. Will Hansen had gotten bored about thirty minutes in, but Jason had enjoyed it. The world the Prisoner was showing him resembled that Fritz Lang movie in some ways. Jason understood that this was where the Prisoner came from, some city of the future.

Jason had pieced together other parts of the story, interpreting the images and information as best he could. There had been scientists and they had found the Breach. They studied it, having found a way in, a doorway or a portal. Entering a portal allowed one to pass through the Breach and arrive at a different point in time. Jason couldn't quite make out what happened next. There was a fight. Soldiers were firing and the portal was open. People died, but some went through the portal, including the Prisoner (or rather the one who would become the Prisoner). After that, there were only scraps of knowledge, images unconnected. There was a place of white trees. A flag with a dragon on it. A scared man being told "We're going home. Right. Fucking. Now."

What you experienced was a view of the Breach, the Prisoner explained, *but it was not a portal. Those are... more complicated.*

* * *

Jason crept outside, his beat-up leather backpack tight on his shoulders. In it was the device, still wrapped in newspaper. Getting downstairs was the hardest part, each step he took creaked so loud he expected his parents to come flying out of their room looking for an intruder. Jason would take a step, pause, shift his weight little by little and take the next step, one by one. After he was downstairs, it was easy slipping into the kitchen and out the back door.

He left the house at 12:34, according to the grandfather clock in the living room. There was no moon and dark blue light painted the landscape. Jason stopped, letting his eyes adjust. He wasn't normally too scared of the dark, but his journey was

128

going to be long. In the pitch blackness of the new moon night he whispered, "I should get a flashlight."

You won't need one, the Prisoner told him.

"But—"

Trust me, Jason.

A cold sweat gripped the boy, but he stepped down the back stairs, rounded the side of the house and paused once more at the front yard. He took a deep breath, trusting the Prisoner, and walked away from the house. His feet crunched the driveway gravel and the early summer air made a lonesome sound in the trees. The stars were bright without a moon and Jason picked out the few constellations he knew, such as Leo and Hydra, but the rest were just a dazzling array of pinpoint lights. The Milky Way itself stretched across the sky and Jason noticed a shooting star. He began to think this might not be so hard.

He reached the end of the driveway and looked down the road. It was mostly black under the low trees. Butterflies began to flutter in his stomach

"Are you still there?" Jason asked, not bothering now to whisper.

Yes, I am, the Prisoner said. *We're doing this together. There is nothing in the dark that will hurt you, Jason.*

"Okay," Jason said and started on down the road toward town.

The steady rhythm of his footfalls soothed the fluttering in Jason's stomach, easing it into a tense calm. His eyes darted back and back forth, picking out shapes in the dark trees. In places where the trees opened up, Jason could see across the fields and felt a little like he was on another planet.

The Prisoner's directions led him to another road and as he crested a hill, Jason saw the glow of the town ahead on him. He walked on in the middle of the road. He walked for over an hour, but did not feel at all tired. He passed under the train bridge and thought of trolls, which made him jog ahead until he was clear.

Jason reached the first street light at what felt like half an hour later, though without a watch on, it was hard to judge the passage of time. He kept moving, but with a greater sense of vigilance. It was more likely now that a car would drive by. A ten year old boy out for a walk at this time of night (whatever time it was) was certain to draw suspicion.

As if on cue, a car approached behind him. The Prisoner instructed him to duck behind the bushes and Jason did so. He heard the car approaching, then it rocketed by and away from him. He waited a few seconds before venturing on.

Though he moved right through the center of Orchard Bend, the Prisoner's route kept Jason to the lesser-used side streets, zigging and zagging past the diversity of the town's homes. Properties alternated between lush gardens with white picket fences and unkempt lawns with disassembled cars and broken toys scattered about. He passed Orchard Bend High School and considered how eerie and unnatural a school building looked at night. As with the bridge earlier, Jason stepped up his pace to leave the school behind.

Another car approached as he reached the corner. Jason didn't need the Prisoner to tell him to move into the shadows. He ducked behind the overgrown shrubbery of the nearest house's front lawn. He lay on his stomach, almost willing himself to disappear into the grass. The car went on its way and just as Jason rose, another car shot past. Jason almost didn't get out of view in time. Three more cars went by, going in different directions, and Jason wondered if he'd end up trapped on this strange lawn until the sun came up. When the last car came and went, Jason waited a moment, then got up and brushed the grass off.

The feeling of losing precious time welled up in Jason and he broke into a jog to try to make up for the delay. The sound of voices came from up ahead and Jason saw the lit porch light of a house and several men moving about. There was a smashing of a bottle and cheers of encouragement, followed by one angry voice giving the offender a piece of his mind.

To your right, came the voice of the Prisoner, accompanied by images of a route through some backyards. *A short cut.*

Jason jogged up the dark driveway of the house and into the backyard. He moved to the side of the garage and pushed between the tall bushes. He was in the yard of the house behind it now. He crossed diagonally and through a broken section of fence into the next neighbour's backyard. There, Jason paused to look at the burned out shell of the house. A dim memory of a newspaper article surfaced, of a recent house fire where a woman died. His father had said she was probably smoking in bed or it was the electrical wiring, one of the two. The idea that faulty wiring could burn down a house stuck with him as he himself did the delicate wiring work on the device. Jason wondered if this was that house and felt bad for the woman, whoever she was. What a terrible way to go.

A dozen blocks after the burned out house, Jason turned onto the road leading up the hill to his destination. He broke into a jog again, despite the upward slope, knowing that once this leg of the journey was finished he could head home.

There were no streetlights out here. Jason was back in the starlit darkness of the countryside, but there was no fear this time. He was close and adrenalin had kicked in.

Then he saw the car parked on the shoulder a few yards ahead of him. In the starlit darkness, it had not been visible until he was almost upon it.

It was too late to worry if anyone inside had seen him, so Jason simply stood and waited to see if there was any reaction from the occupant. There was none, so Jason approached with caution. As he got closer, inching around it, but giving himself a wide berth, he could see the car was empty. Jason looked around, up and down the road, and saw no sign of the owner.

"Guess they had car trouble or something," he said. There was no reply from the Prisoner and Jason at once sensed the absence. He almost called out, but the destination was not far now and Jason resumed jogging. He turned off the road and walked through the open gate to the large house atop the hill. The windows were dark. He wondered who lived there and if anyone was inside. A curious sensation came of being watched. Part of him wanted to run away, to run home and not look back, but another part, the same part that led him into the old tumble-down cabin in the woods, where the skeletons were, *that* part urged him forward.

Jason crossed the lawn, climbed the steps to the porch and took the newspaper-wrapped device out of his pack. He placed the package on the chair nearest the door and felt a sense of relief and accomplishment. The Prisoner was still away and Jason wondered why he'd been left to reach the house on his own. When the Prisoner returned, Jason was going to ask.

Letting out a long breath, Jason looked out over the town and marvelled at the view from the porch. He'd never been out this way before, living well in the farm country on the other side of town. He longed to just sit and rest and watch the eventual sunrise, but the desire to get home before his parents woke broke the spell and a different kind of panicked urgency took him over. Jason tried not to think about the long trip back through town as he bolted down the stairs and jogged across the lawn, leaving the McCabe house behind him. In his haste to get home, Jason didn't notice one important thing when he jogged back down the road in the opposite direction. He didn't notice that the abandoned car on the side of the road was gone

15

June 12, 1953
Orchard Bend

It would have surprised Jason Hansen to know this, but one of the cars that went past his hiding spot on the lawn was the very car he passed on the road to the McCabe house.

When unbeknownst to Ty Brand he passed Jason Hansen, Brand had been so focused on the task ahead that even if he'd seen the boy, he would not have given him much notice.

When Brand was close to Owen McCabe's house, he swung around and parked on the side of the road. He hoped he wouldn't be out here long enough for the car to be seen.

Brand walked up the sloping road, aware of every footfall and crunch under the soles of his father's worn leather shoes. They were a size too large, but were worked in so much that they didn't click or creak on the pavement as he walked. With the dark pants and dark brown cardigan, Brand knew he looked ridiculous as a cat burglar, at least from what he'd seen in the movies and read in comic books.

When he approached the McCabe house, another childhood memory came to him, the day he crashed his bike in front of Gabby, who had been on her porch. She'd rushed to help him, patched him up and to his utter surprise she'd taken his virginity, and he hers'. He stopped and stood about where he remembered taking that tumble and looked at the large house, practically a mansion. The porch was dark, but in his mind's eye, Tyler could see Gabby rushing towards him, looking as pretty as the day is long.

That perfect memory cross-faded into hot anger. Owen McCabe had killed Gabby's parents and then had killed Gabby herself. The timing of her death was too perfect. Just as she was about to spring her plan to steal her grandfather's money and leave his murderous insanity exposed, Gabby dies in a house fire? Brand wasn't one for conspiracy theories, but this was too neat. Owen must have found out, at least about the money. Gabby had assured Ty over and over that she was covering her tracks in legitimate paperwork. She had positioned herself as his sole heir to take everything, his entire estate. She wanted to destroy the man for what he'd done to her parents, but didn't want to kill him. Even the best staged death would cast suspicion on her. She would inherit his wealth, so even if a police investigation cleared her, the stink of rumors in a small town would never go away. Exposing Owen was the key. Let the men in white coats drag him away as he raved about a Prisoner and a portal and Emery Dale and his brother. The ledger was damning and Gabby even more so, playing the reluctant granddaughter. She would reveal to the world that living with the elderly man was a nightmare in the worst moments of Owen's delusions. Gabby's claims would be supported by what the man had written in his ledger over the years. Then the police would investigate the murder of Gabby's parents, looking squarely at Owen. Even if there was no charge or conviction, Gabby would have Owen committed because of his insanity alone and the estate would be hers.

Without Gabby, though, the plan fell apart.

Except for the ledger.

It could still do damage. Written in Owen's hand, it was still pretty damning evidence. Brand could think of a few people who would love to read it.

Under the blue-blackness of the moonless sky, Brand darted up the driveway. He stayed under the trees where the shadows were thicker and rounded the side of the house. As he passed the windows, more thoughts of Gabby arose, of her telling him about breaking into the study to use the gun to end it all. That was the same day as she and Ty had had sex in the bathroom. Gabby had been in the darkest possible place, ready to kill herself. She told him reading the ledger stopped her suicidal thoughts, but Ty believed he had a part in her decision, too. After all, what prompted her to stop and read the ledger in the first place? Ty had never told her he felt that their lovemaking had given her something beautiful in the midst of her pain. She paused long enough because of him to read the ledger when she was on the verge of using the gun on herself. Ty believed that. It fuelled his desire to mete out this small bit of justice against Owen.

Brand reached the back of the house and the rear door which led to the kitchen. He fished in his pocket for the small ring of keys and pulled them out. Gabby's spare set, left at his house over a year before. They had sat undisturbed all that time, resting on the little table inside his front door. They'd been there so long, Ty had forgotten about them. When his aching brain began formulating this plan, their existence and importance came barrelling through his thoughts. There had been a terrifying moment when he doubted they were still there. Somehow it seemed too perfect to be true. Still nauseous from the previous night's drinking binge, Ty had forced himself up and lurched as fast as he could to the front hall. The keys had been there, right where Gabby had left them.

At Owen's house now, Brand tried one key, then another and at last the third key slid into the lock and turned inside it. There was the tell-tale resistance and then the satisfying click as the door unlocked. Brand turned the handle and it creaked. Careful not to let the hinges make any noise, he eased the door open.

The kitchen was near black. His eyes had adjusted to the moonless outdoors, but here there was not even the small amount of starlight to help. In the dark the floorboards groaned under his weight. Wishing it wasn't necessary, Brand pulled a flashlight out of the pocket of his pants. He had covered the end with two old socks. A hole cut in each of them reduced the beam to a small sliver, but it was enough. The thin line of light moved around the room and gave him his bearings. He turned the light off and inch by inch, Brand crossed the kitchen to the door leading to the hall.

Another quick flash of the light revealed his surroundings and he moved through the twists of the hall, until he stood at the study door. He tucked the flashlight under his arm with the tiny beam still alight. He took out the keys, doing his best to not let them rattle. To Brand's relief, the first key unlocked the study door and he went inside. Gabby said that when she would read it as a girl she always found the ledger in the same spot on the desk, even after Owen had made new entries. Brand went to the desk, but didn't see it. He shone the light over every inch of the desktop and amid the papers and other books, found nothing of the ledger. There were official documents with Gabby's name on them and Brand read them. Health insurance, home-owner's insurance, bank account information. Ty felt a chill inside. All the money Gabby had siphoned from her grandfather was laid bare in these papers. There was no doubt in Brand's mind now that Owen knew Gabby stole from him and there was no doubt Owen would kill her to put an end to it. Ty wondered if the old man suspected he, Tyler Brand, was involved. Would Owen come after him next, not just for being involved with Gabby, but for betraying Owen's trust as one of Owen's lackeys?

All the more reason to find the ledger, Brand thought.

He looked in the desk drawers and found the case containing the pearl-handled revolver. He fought the urge to take it upstairs and just use it on Owen right now, just to be done with the old bastard. Brand walked the length of the room, examining the bookshelves and still did not find the ledger. The thought of having to search the entire house was disheartening. Not only would it be impossible to do in one night, it would be virtually impossible to do over multiple visits without eventually waking Owen up.

Brand stood in the study, clicked off the flashlight and considered his options, the least palatable being to just give up and go home. He pictured the ledger in his mind, Owen clutching it, tapping it at their meeting on the porch a month prior. Owen had held it like a bible as Gabby's coffin lowered into her grave. Brand had wondered that day, watching the geezer's expressionless face, if he slept with the damn thing, too.

And Owen might indeed sleep with it. It made perfect sense, Brand thought. When Gabby grew older and Owen grew more dependant on her as a caregiver and executor, Owen had entrusted her with keys to the house and rooms (including a spare set). Owen would not, of course, entrust her with access to the ledger filled with his incriminating insanity. So he kept it with him at all times. Over the years, Brand guessed, that practice would become a habit. Owen probably did sleep with the ledger, meaning it was upstairs and that was where Brand had to go.

Ty didn't wait a moment longer. He exited the study and in the dark moved slowly up the stairs, hoping Owen didn't lock his bedroom door at night.

Turns out, the old man did. Brand could hear steady snoring from inside the room. He reached into his pocket and his fingers clutched the key ring, but Brand knew it would be too much to rattle the keys in the lock mere feet from the man and not expect him to wake up. Brand also knew he had come too far to turn back. The ledger was on the other side of this door, it had to be. It was all or nothing now.

An idea popped into his mind. He let go of the keys and took out the flashlight, moving away from the door to the stairs. There, he slipped off one of the socks covering the lens of the flashlight. He reached into the other pocket and wrapped the sock around the keys to muffle any clinking or jangling they might do. Brand put the flashlight in the crook of his armpit again and turned it on. It was brighter now with one less sock on it. With a meticulousness borne out of the instinct to not get caught, Brand looked at the keys. Two he now knew were for the backdoor and the study. That left three more. He selected one of the three and folded the others together in the sock, the key sticking out from the cloth. He turned off the light, put it in his pocket and took his time sneaking back to the bedroom door. He slipped the key in, but it would not turn. He gave it a few tries just in case the old mechanisms inside were being stubborn, but it was clear this was not the key. All the time he listened to the steady snoring of Owen McCabe.

Brand moved away from the door again and repeated the selection process for the next key. It also did not work, not even fitting the keyhole.

Third time's the charm, Brand thought. If this one didn't work, Brand didn't know what else he could try, short of kicking the door in.

The key slid in and when Brand turned it, there was resistance, but it moved. Brand let out a quiet sigh of relief. He turned it as far as he could and there came a *CLINK* from within the lock.

Brand froze in place.

The snoring stopped. There was a cough, then another, followed by the creak of bedsprings. From under the door, Brand saw a light turn on in the bedroom.

Brand remained perfectly still, his hand clutching the key in the lock. The steady tick-tock from the grandfather clock in the upstairs hall counted off the seconds behind him.

There were more creaks from the bed and Brand knew the old man was getting up. The creaks stopped, replaced by the groaning of wooden floorboards.

He's going to open the door and find me standing here! Brand thought. He couldn't let go of the keys without their rattling giving him away, nor could he remain standing here when Owen opened the door.

Brand decided that if his goose was cooked, he was taking the old son of a bitch with him. Owen would open the door and in his moment of surprise, Brand would club him with the flashlight. Brand figured putting down a 74 year old geezer shouldn't be that hard for a healthy adult male in his prime. There might even be enough time to drive to the city and catch a flight down to Mexico, maybe. Brand had a little of his own money saved up and with luck would be long gone before anyone found Owen McCabe murdered in his bedroom.

The footsteps were moving around the bed now toward the door. Brand braced himself. Owen's shadow came into view under the door, shuffling along. There was a bout of coughing and swearing as McCabe cursed his tired, wretched body.

Owen reached the door and Brand was ready, his free hand now gripping the flashlight and pulling it from his pocket.

Any second now, Brand thought, but to his surprise, the shuffling continued past the door. A moment later there was a creak of a door and a soft click. Brand saw the light pour out under the next door down in the hall. He heard the distinctive latching sound as a door closed and Brand realized Owen was going to the bathroom.

The reporter's relief was broken when the grandfather clock behind him ran through its hourly chime. Brand acted almost without thought, twisting the key back and pulling it out under the cover of the clock chiming. He turned the handle and opened the door. The door to the bathroom was indeed closed and he could hear the disgusting sounds of the old man doing his business.

As the clock rang out for each hour, Brand's eyes darted around the room, but didn't see the ledger. He moved to the only place he could think it would be, the bedside table, and slide open the drawer.

There it lay, black and thick and well-worn.

The last hour rang out from the clock as Brand scooped up the ledger and closed the drawer. There came the sound of a toilet flushing in the bathroom and Brand creaked back across the floor, knowing full well his caution was lessening under the urgency of the moment. He fought the desire to run and backed out of the room. The sound of a faucet came from the bathroom, with more coughing and swearing from Owen. Brand was closing the door and heard the bathroom door creak open. There was another fit of coughing. Brand shut the bedroom door. He waited. The light from the bathroom went out.

Owen shuffled back across the room, grumbling and throwing a few more choice curses out. The springs creaked as he climbed into the bed. The light clicked off and still Brand waited. The grandfather clock tick-tocked along, but Brand was too focused and wired up to notice it. He was listening for Owen's snoring and after long, excruciating minutes, it came, low and steady. Brand waited a little longer before slipping the key back into the slot and locking the door behind him. Owen would find the ledger gone in the morning, but the locked door would hopefully put him off the scent of who could've taken it. Gabby would be the only one with a key to the room and with her gone, Owen might look in his direction, guessing Brand had used hers. Owen might figure it out after some long consideration, but not before Brand could deliver the ledger to the right person. Or so he hoped.

Brand's heart was racing and he wanted to just run down the stairs and out the door in victory. Instead, he made his way out of the house, back the way he came in, and locked the rear door behind him. Once outside, he moved along the side of the house, across the lawn under the trees and down the driveway.

Brand passed through the gate, turned down the road and stopped.

Someone was standing at his car further down the hill. The person was a dark shape standing in the middle of the road looking at the car. They slowly rounded the vehicle. Brand realized he or she was focused on the car and had not seen him. He backed up and dropped into the ditch, thankful the night was moonless. Peeking his head up, Brand saw the figure jogging toward him. He ducked back down and listened as the footfalls first stopped at the gate and then continued up the driveway.

Ledger in hand, Brand climbed out of the ditch. He couldn't see the other person, but hoped they were far enough away to not hear his footfalls as he ran to his car. He'd picked the spot well, knowing that the view was such that this short stretch of road couldn't be seen from the house.

Still, the car had been seen. Climbing in, putting the ledger down on the passenger seat, Brand knew there was nothing he could do about whoever had just gone to McCabe's house. If they'd thought to take down his license plate and were now telling McCabe, Ty Brand would not be long for this world. He may not have murdered McCabe, but Brand knew he had to get the hell out of Orchard Bend as soon as possible.

16

June 12, 1953
Orchard Bend

Cal Watson sat on the front steps of his aunt and uncle's house in the dark as the boy rushed down the sidewalk. Every few moments, the boy looked over his shoulder as if being followed. Cal thought it odd, but then he himself had slipped out for the odd late night constitutional from time to time so who was he to judge? Still, Cal was a number of years older. He was about to say something to the boy to the effect of "You should get on home, kid, it's late," when the mind-shattering headache hit. There was barely any time to react and no sooner had the pain come than it was over and Cal saw into the strange, grey, smoky glass-like version of the world. It didn't seem to matter that it was night time because everything was visible around him. He looked at his hands again and saw the same slight transparency.

The boy was moving up the street. Even as he passed stationary objects like trees, Cal could make out the boy's form through them. Unlike the last time, Cal didn't panic. The first time this happened, pain had brought his sight back to normal and he expected he could hurt himself again and restore his vision. The boy hadn't seen Cal and crossed the street. Cal stood up and looked around.

That's when he saw the shadow person moving a dozen or so paces behind the boy, trailing him, but without a doubt following. Cal walked the stone footpath to the white picket fence at the edge of the property, keeping both the boy and the dark shape of the shadow in view. Watching the shadow, Cal could nearly make out arms and legs and a head. The two continued up the block and Cal moved to pursue them.

The boy slowed down at the end of the block and Cal stepped behind a tree, watching as best he could through the tree's layers. Up close, the trees were a fascinating combination of textures. The boy crossed the street and turned down another. Cal kept pace, half a block back. It looked like the two were heading to the edge of town.

Cal followed the boy and the shadow as they turned onto a road where the town's streetlights ended. Rounding the corner, Cal saw the shadow stop and look back. Cal could just make out a face. Where the eyes should have been were large black pools, like the eye-sockets of a skeleton. What stood before Cal, though, was no skeleton, but the full form of a man. Cal could almost make out the shape of clothing. There was a dark hole of a mouth, which Cal just glimpsed as he hid behind a tree. Through the tree he saw the dark shape moving toward him. Cal bolted across the grass and down a short slope. A low brick warehouse sat abandoned at the bottom of the hill. He moved along the wall, running at a crouch, hoping the shadow person wouldn't see him. He dodged to his left around the side of the warehouse. He came to a hill, a long, high mound of earth which once had been a mere pile of excavated dirt. It was now almost overgrown with thick, coarse grass. Cal went up the mound and over the other side, taking cover behind it. The grass was tall and camouflaged him well. Looking back, he saw the warehouse, and a moment later the shadow person came around the corner. The other features were harder to make out from a distance, but the terrible black eye sockets and round mouth hole were easy to distinguish. The head moved back and forth, looking around. Cal had not been this scared since Blue Creek. It was an unhinging kind of terror, the kind he felt could result in madness. Cal could not take his eyes off the shadow, especially when the head stopped scanning and fixed in his direction.

It sees me! Cal thought in a panic. He froze, terror preventing him from moving. All he could do was watch the shadow staring at him.

Because of this, Cal failed to notice what was moving right next to him until it was almost upon him.

His head whipped to the side. He saw another face there, looking at him. Or almost a face. All the features were there in the pale smokiness of her form. Her beauty was so much different from the shadow's nightmarish face. Looking at her, Cal at once thought he was seeing the face of Debbie. He felt his sanity loosen, but it reasserted itself as he saw it was not the face of his dead girlfriend. Debbie had been a strawberry blonde and had a sweet, round face. This ghost's hair was a much darker shade. Brown, perhaps, or black, it was difficult to quite make out, so spectral was her form. The shape of the face, the sharp features, even in their misty-like opacity, Cal knew it wasn't her.

Oh God, that means there's another one! Cal's mind cried out as he watched this second ethereal being gazing at him.

The ghost (the only thing Cal could think to call her) regarded him with a quizzical expression. She looked to the shadow being and Cal's gaze darted in that direction in time to see it moving slowly toward him. He looked back at the ghost and she mouthed words he couldn't hear, gesturing with the wispy hand. She pointed to herself and then in the direction of the shadow. Then she pointed to Cal and to the other direction, away from there. Not waiting to see if Cal understood, the ghost ascended the hill. Cal watched as she strode across the shadow's path. The shadow stopped. The ghost flitted across the grass, the ashen form of her legs skipping. She danced and moved in an arc away from Cal, pulling the shadow's attention from his hiding place. She kept moving and the shadow pursued. Cal took off at a run in the opposite direction. After a block he glanced back over his shoulder, hardly slowing. In the smoky grey vision he could see neither the shadow nor the ghost.

Cal's shoe caught the lip of the manhole cover jutting up from the asphalt and he was in a rolling heap before he could brace his fall. When he came to rest, Cal's palms and elbows screamed and his back muscles felt pulled in four different directions. He laid there, chest heaving. Around him, the world had gone back to normal, his sight restored with the sudden blast of pain. When he sat up he looked back the way he came and still saw nothing of the shadow or the ghost.

They're out there, Cal knew, *even if I can't see them now, they're there. Somewhere.*

Cal got up from the pavement and started back down the street, looking at the scratches on his hands and the small dots of blood appearing there. The wound from the broach throbbed, too, and though his jacket wasn't torn, he expected his elbows would be bruised.

Making his way back to his aunt and uncle's house, Cal wondered why the ghost had saved him? And who was the boy and where was he going with the shadow trailing behind him? His thoughts turned to the smoky shadow world as he wondered what it all meant and why he could suddenly see it. Was it this town? Was it him? The headaches came each time, like migraines, and then he could see that world. The first headache had come when he walked home with Melissa. The second time was when the boy passed by.

But that wasn't entirely accurate. The first time had been when he saw that woman in the park by the Town Hall, the one with the army jacket and canteen. Cal had also seen her at the train tracks. The first headache, the really bad one, had started when she looked at him.

So who was she?

* * *

Sully's Saloon was empty except for Tom Reed. He sat at the bar on a stool that only seemed to get more comfortable after each beer he polished off. By his count, he had just downed his third.

No, make that four *beers*, Reed remembered.

Next to the bottles behind the bar was a collection of sepia-toned photographs taken of the original Sully's tavern. The watering hole of that by-gone age looked much different from the one Reed found himself in now. The property was the same, but renovations and changes of ownership had updated the

144

layout and décor such that you'd never know it had been the same place. For starters, where Sully's had been two stories, offering guests room and board. Nowadays, the upper story was a cluster of low rent apartments.

In the photos of the exterior, Reed could make out a few buildings which still stood today. The jailhouse was gone, but the post office building was there, now the Nook & Cranny Bookshop. Just out of frame, he knew the Reed General Store & Feed would be almost across the street. His great-grandparents, Edmond and Sarah, had been pretty successful in their business. After Edmond passed away, Sarah had continued running the store with her sons.

Jack Preston, the bartender and current owner of Sully's Saloon, came to clear Reed's empty pint glass. Preston was lean and lanky, bald on the top of his head, but sporting a distinguished half-crown of dark brown hair from ear to ear around the back of his head. He had a thick moustache he kept immaculately waxed.

"Jack, you're probably too young to remember," Tom said, tapping his finger on the dark oak bar, "but there was a time when the Reed family was a big deal in Orchard Bend,"

"You have a street named after you, I know that," Jack said. "Reed Street. My aunt lives there."

"Named after my ancestor, old Doc Reed," Tom explained. "He helped found this town, side by side with a handful of families, including the McCabes. The Reeds had influence in Orchard Bend before the Depression. Now the Barber owns damn near half the town."

"It's late, Tom," Jack said. "You should get on home. You don't want to go to work hungover. You might catch a big case."

"Already caught a big case," Reed said with a heavy sigh. "Biggest case of my career. Biggest case this town has seen in at least sixty years."

Reed put his fists together and mimicked an explosion, adding, "Poof! All gone."

Preston rinsed the pint glass and started drying it, saying nothing.

145

"And you know what, Jack?" Reed asked. "It wasn't the glory I was after. It wasn't a promotion or anything like that. It was *justice*! Justice for the victims, justice for..."

Reed trailed off. Jack Preston finished drying the pint glass and put it away under the bar. He threw the towel over his shoulder and leaned forward.

"I'm closing up, Tom," Jack said. "Go home, get some sleep and things will look better in the morning, I'm sure."

Reed stood up and pointed to the photos behind the bar.

"Does Peter Howard know you have those?" Reed asked. "The Orchard Bend Museum should have copies."

"Where do you think I got them," Jack smiled. "When I re-opened Sully's, I went there and Peter let me photograph the pictures in his archive. He's got a hell of a collection."

"Don't I know it," Reed said, putting on his jacket and straightening his tie. He took out his wallet, counted out some bills and put them on the bar. He put on his hat and waved to Jack as he walked out.

"'Night, Jack!"

"Stay out of trouble, Tom!" Jack said as he counted the money.

Outside, Reed looked up at the moonless sky. Anderson Street was quiet and his shoes clicked as he walked to his car. He opened the door to get in, then stopped and closed the door. He wasn't ready to go home. In fact, he wanted another drink. His head was spinning in that pleasant, drunk way. Even though the streets were dead this time of night, he thought it might be better to walk home.

The beer had slowed the spiralling thoughts about the stolen evidence in the Dale case, but they still crept in on him. Everything but the *Jane Doe #13* case file was gone. It had survived because he had kept it with him. Now he kept it hidden. There was a safe in his modest house, in the closet of his bedroom. If McCabe decided to send someone to hunt for the file, just to complete the job of sinking the case, they'd have to haul the entire safe out. Of course, they wouldn't get the case file because Reed hadn't put it in the safe.

Reed snickered to himself as he passed the Nook & Cranny Bookshop. Wasn't he so clever?

Why, yes. Yes, I am!

He kept his gold detective's shield in that safe, along with vital records and some other valuables, so anyone would naturally assume that's where he would hide Emery Dale's case file. But no, the file was safe behind the disused grating in the floorboards below the old wood stove. You couldn't even see the grate unless you got down on all fours and looked for it. Reed had hidden the file there earlier this evening.

Reed turned the corner onto Wood St. As the Town Hall and the surrounding park came into view, he slowed to a stop. He stood on the sidewalk with his hands in his jacket pockets, listening to the leaves rustle in the trees. The dark windows seemed to look back at him.

As his mind buzzed from the alcohol, several truths spoke to him.

McCabe has someone on the inside, very likely a police officer. There's no other way he could have stolen the evidence found at the hunter's cabin.

McCabe wants Emery Dale erased from Orchard Bend history. If he could go back in time himself and kill her, he probably would.

McCabe appears willing to do anything, to move heaven and earth to get what he wants.

And that meant...

McCabe will probably try to destroy the few existing records of her that Peter Howard has in the Museum archives.

An idea popped into Reed's head and he started chuckling on the sidewalk. It was so crazy it might just work.

McCabe couldn't steal what was already stolen.

The plan came almost fully formed in his mind's eye and Reed knew he had to try it. After all, how hard could it be for a cop to break into Town Hall?

* * *

"Brian?"

Brian Thorn was deep in a dream where he was telling some back-talking, snot-nosed teenager what goes and what stays in his town. Tom Reed was there, urging him to lay off the boy, but the sheriff pushed him aside and gave the mouthy teen a jab to the gut with his nightstick. Nothing too serious, just a love tap. It would shut the kid up before the sheriff would drag him from the park and tossed him in a cell. Thorn would let him stew for a while behind bars. That should be enough to cure the boy of his bad attitude. Kids today needed a firm hand, rules, and sometimes you had to put them in their place, whether it was with a gentle poke with a nightstick or a night in a jail cell to scare them straight. Or both.

Sheriff Thorn took the boy by the ear. He had doubled over coughing after his meet-and-greet with the nightstick. The sheriff dragged the boy inside the Town Hall, heading toward the holding cells in the Sheriff's Office.

"You're thinking this is a bad day, boy?" Thorn said, "Just wait till I call your folks and they come down here to see your sorry ass behind bars. I guarantee you're day is gonna get a whole lot worse!"

"Brian," the soft voice said again and there was a nudge to his arm. The dream world fragmented away and Brian Thorn's mind swam back to consciousness. The bedroom was dark, even with the blinds partway open. The hand nudged him again and he was wide awake.

"Brian, wake up," Maryanne Thorn said in her soft whisper of a voice.

"I'm awake," Brian said, sitting up and turning on the light.

"I think it's time, Brian," she said.

"Time for your medicine? No, Maryanne, it's late, it's the middle of the night," Brian said, looking first to the clock, then to her.

"No, my love... I think it's *time*," Maryanne looked at him, her eyes were clearer than he often saw them these days, between the drugs and her depression. She smiled the same warm, bright smile he fell in love with twenty-seven years earlier, when he had finally screwed up the courage to ask her out at the town fair. Maryanne Drummond had said yes and smiled that same beautiful smile. In that moment, Brian Thorn told himself he'd be in heaven if he could marry her someday.

"No," Brian said, the horror of what she was saying chilling him to his core. "No, Maryanne, you've got a lot of time left..." But he trailed off as her expression, still smiling, still open, changed now, the truth of the moment laid bare.

"Brian," her voice was weaker now and he knew she was right. He couldn't think. Tears rolled down his cheeks and he didn't notice.

"Promise me you'll stop drinking so much after I'm gone," she said.

"I promise," Brian hoped he could keep the promise but he had strong doubts. "Maryanne, I love you. I won't be able to go on when you..." His voice cracked and failed.

"You will. You're strong. My strong, handsome love," Maryanne closed her eyes and Brian cried out. She opened them again and smiled.

"I'm sorry I couldn't give you a son," she said.

"We tried. We tried a bunch, didn't we?" Brian was smiling through his tears, thinking this was going to be the last time he'd ever smile. After today, there'd be no reason to smile, no joy at all.

"Yes, we did," Maryanne said. "Thank you for being my true love, Brian Thorn."

Brian wanted to say everything he was feeling, tell her of every precious memory he had of her, but the words wouldn't come. He choked in a few breaths and squeezed her hand. At last he blubbered out, "Maryanne, I love you. Don't go!"

"I love you, too," she whispered and was gone.

Brian Thorn held her hand in the soft lamp light for what felt like an eternity. His mind had stopped working. Time had no meaning. He cried, gasping for air and trying to hold on to this moment. He held her hand as if doing so meant she was still there. The pain came in waves, bigger each time. When it was too much, he let out an agonized, primitive howl that hurt his throat, but he didn't care. Then he put her hand down, got up from the bed horribly numb, devoid of anything like an emotion, and left the room. He was halfway down the stairs when another great wave of agony tore through him. He curled up on the stairs and cried out again. He lay there for either hours or minutes, it was impossible for him to tell. He got up again after it passed and made it downstairs. Not caring that he was wearing only his skivvies and an old undershirt, Brian went out onto the front porch.

Outside, the sky grew lighter. The air was fresh and Brian took a few deep breaths. It would be a beautiful late spring day, practically summer now, and Brian Thorn didn't care. If it had suddenly started snowing, it wouldn't matter. Nothing mattered. Everything that had once mattered, the only thing that had mattered, was gone. Her earthly vessel laid empty upstairs. Brian would tend to it soon, make the calls that needed making, because that's what he was supposed to do, but there would be no emotion in it. The funeral plans had been arranged long ago, him and Maryanne pouring over every detail. He remembered most of that discussion, despite having been rather lubricated at the time. The funeral home had a copy of the arrangements, so it didn't matter if Brian Thorn remembered any of it.

He took another deep breath, not because he wanted to smell the sweet spring air of Orchard Bend, but because his lungs said breathe and he was quite content to let them do the deciding right now. There was a package at his feet and he couldn't recall if he'd seen it when he came out of the house a moment ago. It didn't matter if he did or not. He picked it up. It was wrapped in newspaper and twine, with '*Sheriff Thorn. Important*' written on it. The Sheriff looked at it. It felt like a book inside. He turned, went into the house and tossed the package into the small study off the main hall, where it landed with a dull *thump* on the hardwood floor. Brian continued to the kitchen to use the phone there, not thinking about the package anymore the moment it left his hand.

Not caring at all.

17

August 17, 1879
Sutter Grove

Emery Dale sat by her small campfire on the outskirts of the riverside town as the sun set. The high point of land afforded her a view of farm country to the west, including the small cluster of buildings at the water's edge which made up the downtown core of Sutter Grove. She had been down there a few hours before, running an errand for Maxwell McCabe. Nothing too serious, nothing deadly, just greasing a few palms on behalf of her employer. A few well-placed bills kept Maxwell McCabe informed not just in these parts, but also about what happened in towns along the river. The bargemen passed news along faster than the newspapers did much of the time.

At the fireside, as the bone scraps of her meal burned, Dale wasn't thinking about the network of contacts McCabe had. She was testing a theory and it was proving true, though what it meant still eluded her. The theory was simple: something was pulling her back to Orchard Bend.

It all started with a visit from Maxwell McCabe.

After discovering the grove of aspens and the mysterious signal, Dale took up residence in the once-abandoned McCormack cabin in the ravine, not far from the bridge and the river. She couldn't explain it, but it seemed right to be near the grove and the symbol carved into the tree. One morning, coffee in hand, Dale watched McCabe and Burke make their way to her new home on foot, down the path along the bank of the river. She didn't expect trouble, but took one of the guns from its holster just in case. The gunbelts hung from a peg by the door, with the harness and her knives hanging next to it on one side and her sword in its scabbard on the other.

When McCabe knocked, Dale opened the door to find him smiling.

"Top of the mornin', Miss Dale," Maxwell said. "I've come on business and ask if we could speak inside."

"No," Dale said, "but we can talk out here. I need to get some water from the river, anyway. I'll just be a moment."

"At your leisure," McCabe said, tipping his hat. "I'll wait out here."

Dale tucked the gun in the back of her pants. She took a bucket from the corner nook she thought of as her kitchen, put on her boots and went outside. McCabe and Burke were waiting for her and Burke stepped forward, reaching for the bucket.

"Allow me, ma'am, it's the least I can do," Burke said.

"It will afford us the opportunity to speak with fewer distractions," McCabe said.

"Very well, Mr Burke. Thank you," Dale replied. "The best spot to get water is a small pool about twenty yards down river."

Burke took the bucket and left his boss and Dale to talk.

"How is Mrs McCabe?" Emery asked.

"She sends her greetings," McCabe replied.

"And the children?"

"Healthy and full of God's joy," McCabe said. "Allow me to get straight to the point, Miss Dale. I'm here to extend another offer of employment."

"Your family needs my protection again?" Dale asked.

"This is work of a different, longer-term sort," McCabe explained. "I own a respectable amount of land in Orchard Bend and the surrounding county. I also have business interests extending as far afield as Sutter Grove and Yellow Creek, for example. The death of Mr Miller has left a void in my business operations, one I'd like you to fill."

"What does the job entail?"

"It is two-fold. First, you would act as landlady to the tenant farmers and sharecroppers on land I own in and around the county." McCabe said. "There are contracts specific to each, so you would need to acquaint yourself with the particulars, but the bottom line is that they need supervising and some delinquent payments need collecting. The other tasks involve errands I would have you run from time to time," McCabe went on. "I have business partners and contacts, people who keep me informed, that sort of thing."

"And I expect there are individuals whose intentions may be at cross-purposes to your own," Dale said.

"An unfortunate reality of some business dealings," McCabe said. "It might interest you to know that Marshal Saunders was the son of one such partner."

Dale looked at McCabe, but as was often the case the man knew how to mask his feelings behind an exterior of brazen confidence.

"I did some checking," McCabe said. "His father was one of several men who invested in land with me in Sutter Grove. The deal did not play out to everyone's favour and it seems they came to blame me, probably because I fared better. The elder Saunders ended his life when he lost it all. Had I known things were that dire, I would of course have offered to help the man secure a loan or some other means of support. The entire situation escalated beyond any rational sense, with Saunders and this other man Henderson seeking some sort of vengeance."

McCabe threw up his hands and let them fall to his side, letting out a heavy sigh.

"My point, Miss Dale, is that I want to avoid such *dramatics* in the future," McCabe rubbed his chin as he spoke, then smoothed out his moustache. "Maybe I'm partly to blame for not seeing the risks in that deal. It almost cost me my family, so I have reason enough to shore up my affairs so we don't have a repeat of the Saunders mess."

"I understand," Dale said. "I accept your offer, though I'll need a bit of time to learn to ride a horse and to get up to speed on your tenants' contracts."

Burke came back up the path, in his hand the bucket dripped water.

"Certainly. I anticipated as much, as least as far as the contracts go," McCabe said.

"You can leave that by the door, Mr Burke," Dale said. Burke grunted and put the bucket down as instructed.

"Burke can go over those contracts with you and the Statlers can set you up with both a horse and riding lessons in the meantime," McCabe said. He extended his hand and Dale shook it. "It was a pleasure visiting you today, Miss Dale. Gertrude wanted me to pass on an open invitation to tea with her, at a date of your convenience."

"That would be most agreeable, thank you," Dale said.

McCabe and Burke took their leave and Dale brought the bucket of water inside. She placed it on the counter next to the wash basin and walked across the room to the rear window. On the sill was her watch, charging its solar-powered battery in the sunlight. It was warm when she picked it up and turned it on. She scrolled to the message and stared at the screen.

1 New Message
Device Clearance Recognized
Maj. E. A. Dale
Enter GvSci Passcode

— — — —

"Someday," Dale said.

* * *

The pulling sensation, the subtle but distinct feeling within her that she should turn around and go back to Orchard Bend came during Dale's first trek out to inspect some of the tenant farms. She was at last feeling comfortable on a horse after more than a week of lessons with the Statlers.

At the third farm she visited, at the edge of the county, that pulling sensation in the pit of her stomach felt like a knot tightening. It grew in intensity the farther away from the town she travelled. At first she put it down to the general disconnect she felt everyday, amplified by the new job and her role enforcing McCabe's contracts. At the third farm was a family, the Nobles, whose crops had been much less than predicted, who owed money and couldn't pay. Dale was under orders to issue an eviction notice.

"Tenants are apt to lay on you a tale of woe," Burke had told her. "A sick grandmother or a bad crop. It's all very moving and all beside the point. This is something you best steel yourself to, Miss Dale. The land can produce only if farmed good and proper. Some folks come out here looking to start a life, but they get in way over their heads. We give them chances and chances, reasonable by any reckoning, but the time may come when we have to sever ties, lest Mr McCabe start losing money."

And when Dale arrived at his farm, Winston Noble had tried to explain the bad crop. Dale felt for him, but didn't let it show. Noble pointed to his family standing at the small farmhouse door and then to the grave under the tree nearby, the final resting place of his dearly departed mother. What money they had went to her medicine, Noble tried to explain, so couldn't Mr McCabe see his way to making an exception? The next crop was bound to cover what they owed. The knot in Emery Dale's stomach was not putting her much in the talking mood and even if she wanted to, she was in no position to negotiate. McCabe's position was clear. Dale served the eviction notice, which at least gave the Nobles a month to pick up stakes. Once the eviction notice was in Winston's hands, the man stopped protesting and bargaining, his shoulders seemed to deflate and he stood looking at the paper for a long time. Dale waited for him to start trying to negotiate with her again, or maybe get violent, but all he did was look at her, broken, and turned back to his family. They went inside without a word. Dale told herself it was just a job, she was only the messenger. She mounted her horse and rode away without looking back at the farm. Her thoughts were on the family and her mood was dark, but she noticed the pulling sensation from the knot in her stomach lessened as she returned to town.

A month later, Dale rode out to the Noble farm to see if they either had the money they owed or had vacated the farm. They had done the latter. The house was locked up tight, but of course Dale had a key. Inside, it was empty of their possessions. The eviction notice sat on the mantle. Dale took the folded document with her as she walked out, locking the door behind her. The gravestone of Winston Noble's mother caught the afternoon light as a cloud rolled away from the sun in the deep blue sky. The wind picked up, blowing Dale's cloak about her as she walked over to the elder Noble's grave. There was a bouquet of wildflowers resting against the stone, dead and drying, but still with some colour. It hadn't been very long since the Nobles had left. Dale wondered where they had gone and hoped they'd prosper wherever they put down roots next. Guilt felt like a cold hand on her back and she stood up angry.

It's not my fault they couldn't pay, Dale told herself. *They signed a contract. They had their chances, pretty reasonable ones all things considered. I just delivered the bad news. It's a tough old world, it—*

The migraine came without warning. Dale dropped to her knee, her hand found purchase on the edge of Margaret Noble's gravestone and she steadied herself. It was bright, searing pain, but for a moment there was something else there, an image of a family. It was not the Nobles, but a family in scarves, rags, shawls and dirty cloths. They stood against a wall. Then they were splattered with red and all collapsed.

The memory cut off, but it was enough. Dale was certain it was a memory, a genuine recollection. The migraine was dizzying, but it eased into a steady pounding, the sharpness faded. Her heart raced with excitement, though; a memory, little more than a fragment, but a real memory. While the horrific image of a family being shot had no context, she was certain these people had been a family. But why now, she wondered?

Her eyes fell to Margaret Noble's grave.

Wife, Mother, Grandmother, Sister, Aunt.
R.I.P.

Emery Dale looked at the words for a long time and though she had wondered often who she had been in her old life, she now had reason to wonder if she really wanted to know.

I may not like the answer if I find out, Dale mused.

She got up and left the farm again. The knot, the *pulling*, began to loosen in her stomach on the way back to Orchard Bend. It was gone when she walked into Sully's. Irene Sullivan served Dale a few shots and Dale decided that the next day she would ride out in the other direction to explore the outer reaches of Orchard Bend, something she'd been meaning to do, to learn as much about the area around the town as she could.

The next day she'd taken off early, feeling more content and alert, thoughts of the Nobles not far from her mind, but not pressing down on her anymore either. By the time she reached the outskirts, the knot was back and she was acutely aware of it. Something that she could only described as a *pull* wanted to direct her back to town. This impulse got harder to resist the further she travelled and Dale wrestled with it, trying to understand it. The sensation wasn't an emotion exactly, this knot, this *pulling*, it was like tension, like a fishhook in her belly tugging at her.

Why did she need to turn around?

Dale didn't know, there was no immediate business there. This pull just seemed to *want* her back there.

The feeling was strong, but not overpowering. Not yet, anyway. Dale felt she could go on if she needed to, though, further from town. The pull wasn't so strong as to prevent her leaving.

Now in Sutter Grove, Dale was testing the distance. She was somewhat correct that the knot *did* tighten as she travelled and the pull back to Orchard Bend became stronger, but only to a point. It was now a nagging sensation, but had not grown in intensity since before passing over the eastern river.

If I just kept going east would the knot stay there in the pit of my stomach day after day, imploring me to go back to Orchard Bend? Dale wondered. *Will it let me sleep tonight?*

Before Dale turned in for the night, wrapping herself in her blanket under the stars, she decided that if the pulling was a sign of anything, it was that she was meant to stay in Orchard Bend.

Closing her eyes, she thought about the Nobles again, then of the memory of the unnamed family being shot. Dale pushed the scene from her mind. Then Rose Adelaide came to her thoughts. Dale's mind relaxed as she recalled seeing Rose return to teaching, her arm in a sling, its mobility limited as it healed. Rose had smiled when Emery raised her hand to her on the street. It was an open, guileless smile.

She was really happy to see me, Dale thought. That had been the day after she had served the Nobles the eviction notice. If ever there'd been a day Dale needed a smile like that, from someone pleased to see her, it was right then.

Emery hoped she'd see that smile again when she returned to Orchard Bend the next day.

18

September 1, 1882
Orchard Bend

Ellie Picton's favourite place in the whole world was the large pond shared between her family's property and that of the Langfords. For as long as Ellie could remember, she loved sitting on the grassy hill under the line of trees as the sun set behind her, mesmerized by sway of the reeds in the water. Across the pool, the golden light glowed on the farms' crops and on the tall oaks which grew on a wedge of land owned by the railroad. The light was something to behold all year round. After a fresh snowfall Ellie would sometimes bundle up and make her way out to the pond to see the evening light on the winter landscape, stunning yellows and oranges and blue shadows.

She heard the familiar footfalls behind her and turned to see David Langford approaching. They had been neighbours their whole lives, but these days the sight of him gave Ellie a good case of butterflies in her stomach. She hoped she wasn't blushing, but thought she probably was.

"Why, Ellie Picton, aren't you a vision today?" David said in that pretty way of his.

Ellie grinned wide and looked at her hands on her lap, "You do know how to go on so with such foolish talk, David Langford."

"Would you grace me with a walk around the pond, Ellie?" David asked.

"I do believe I will," Ellie said.

It was a path they used to run along as children, him once chasing her with a worm in his hand as she shrieked in both fright and glee. That was not so long ago, but they weren't children anymore. David had grown tall and handsome. The height came from his father and his looks surprisingly from his mother. The thin face and round eyes giving him noble, honest features. For her part, she was becoming a woman and the boys around her age were beginning to notice. She'd catch boys like Sam O'Toole and Reggie Pine giving her a good long look. It was most flattering, but David Langford was the one she wanted as her beau and she hoped someday to marry him.

They walked in silence at first and that was fine. Ellie knew David would be tired from a day's work in the field with his father and brothers. It had been a long summer of fair weather, the crop prospects were good overall, though there had been lingering fears of prices dropping abroad. Ellie's father followed the agricultural news like it was a second religion.

"I'm not goin' back to school this year," David said at last. Ellie stopped and David was a stride past her when he turned to look at her.

"Why not?" she asked, but she had already guessed the answer.

"Time's come I start making my way in the world," he said. Ellie could hear David's father's words coming out of the young man's mouth. "After the crop's harvested, there's a job awaitin' me at the mill. The money is good and it'll be *mine*."

"But your schooling? You're one of the smartest boys in the class," Ellie said, unable to mask her disappointment.

"Remember that delivery I made to the Blue Creek mine with Mr Statler in July? It paid right well. When he handed me my pay, it was more money than I had ever held at one time, Ellie," David said. "I felt like a man's supposed to feel."

"So it's the money?"

"No. No, it's not," David said, "It's about setting my sights ahead. I reckon I save my money, buy myself a plot in a few years."

It made sense and as sad as it made her to see David leave his book learning behind, it really wasn't much of a surprise.

160

He'd stayed in Miss Adelaide's school a few years longer than most boys his age and was now one of the last. The rest had left to work their family's farms and find jobs.

Ellie started walking again and David fell in step next to her. Again, they said little. They crossed the tree line at the edge of the Picton property and continued into the corner of railroad land. The path led well into the trees and undergrowth. It wasn't as easy going there. The terrain was full of dips and little hills, with craggy outcroppings of old, dead trees. If they'd ventured further in, as they'd done as children, they'd reach a spot overlooking the tracks, where they could see the trains go by.

Today, however, they stopped just a few feet into the wooded land, the sight of a dead rabbit taking them by surprise. It wasn't that the animal was dead that surprised them, it was that the animal's head was cut off and lay a few from the rest of its body. Ellie had seen a few slaughtered animals in her life, so it was not the gore of the scene which bothered her, but the fact that there was no reason to do such a thing. There was a snare on the rabbit's foot, meaning someone meant to do this, but this was not the way to skin a rabbit. And why leave the kill out here? The flies had not yet gathered, so this was done earlier that day. Ellie's eyes scanned the trees and undergrowth around them.

"A mind unwell did this," Ellie said.

David took her hand and she looked to him. He wore an intense expression now and it was unlike anything she had seen from him before.

"David...?" Ellie smiled.

"Eloise Picton, I want you to be my wife," David said. "I mean to ask your father for your hand. I'm fixin' to make my own way and if I'm independent and standing on my own two feet in a couple years, which I mean to be, I want you there beside me."

"David, I... Why, of course!" Ellie stammered, her mind running so fast she could hardly form a coherent thought. She took a long breath and added, "It won't be right away, Heavens no, you're right. He'll expect you to be able to provide. But I know he'll agree to your plan, I just know he will!"

The dead rabbit lay forgotten by both of them, for they never gave it another thought after David's proposal was made that day in the sunset by the pond.

* * *

July 29, 1884
Orchard Bend

The summer air was heavy and fragrant as the stagecoach clattered into town. Rose Adelaide's eyes were shut and she was almost dozing, the vehicle's lone passenger. As it slowed, she opened her eyes and watched as the dirt road curved into Main Street. The trees gave way to the tall, false-front buildings. She picked out a few new businesses where there had once been only vacant lots.

"How quickly this town is growing now," she said under her breath.

The coach came to a halt across the street from Sully's. A few doors down, Rose saw Edmond Reed sweeping the boardwalk in front of his general store. The coachman climbed down from his driver's seat and opened the door for Rose. Adjusting her hat and taking the driver's hand, Rose stepped out of the coach.

"Miss Adelaide!"

Rose turned and saw Irene Sullivan hurrying to her, smiling.

"Irene, how are you?" Rose asked.

"Keeping well. How was your trip? I mean, under the circumstances," Irene blushed and looked at her feet. "I'm sorry for your loss and all, Miss."

Rose's smile was warm.

"The funeral was lovely, thank you," Rose said. "The journey was long and I'm happy to be back."

"I'm sorry I have to get going, Miss Adelaide, but my mother's waiting for me," Irene said, taking the schoolteacher's hand. "Again, I'm sorry about your father."

"Yes, do run along. And thank you, again," Rose said, and Irene dashed off to the saloon.

The coach driver set the schoolteacher's bags down on the boardwalk and tipped his hat to her.

"If that will be all, ma'am?" he said.

"Thank you," Rose said, and the driver wasted no time crossing the street to Sully's. Rose took a bag in each hand and started along the boardwalk toward Reed's store. She stopped as the ache in her shoulder became too much. She massaged the joint and tried to ease the pain by rolling her arm.

A dozen yards ahead, Gertrude McCabe and her son, Owen, crossed the street hand in hand. Edmond Reed stopped sweeping and greeted them. The two adults stood talking as Owen reached for Reed's broom. Reed smiled and handed it to the boy. It was much too big for him, but Owen balanced the long broom handle in the crook of his neck. With his whole body, he swept at the boardwalk. Reed and Mrs McCabe laughed.

The ache having dulled, Rose picked up her bags again and continued down the street. Up ahead, Reed said something funny and Gertrude laughed. She put her hand on Edmond's shoulder and looked away for just a moment. Owen kept sweeping, but started walking away from the adults.

The Statler stable was between Rose and Owen. Atop a ladder above the stable door was Herman Statler, pounding nails into a new sign. Owen swept and swept in a steady rhythm and Rose spotted the danger in an instant. She dropped her bags and rushed to the little boy. He was humming a tune and sweeping with all his heart, unaware that he was in front of the stable and about to pass under the ladder.

"Owen!" came Gertrude's voice from down the street as she realized her son had ventured off. Owen either didn't hear or ignored his mother's call as he stepped off the boardwalk futilely sweeping the dirt. He reached the ladder and was a sweep away from connecting with it when Rose scooped the startled boy up in her arms. She brought him away from the ladder and he squirmed in the stranger's grip.

"I was *sweeping!*" Owen protested.

Rose put him down on the boardwalk as Gertrude and Edmond rushed up.

"Thank you, Miss Adelaide!" Gertrude said and knelt to her son "Owen, don't you ever walk away from me!"

"I was sweeping!" Owen said again, wide-eyed and afraid.

"How many times have I told you to stay by my side when we're in town?" Gertrude scolded him.

"I'm sorry," Owen pouted.

"Give Mr Reed back his broom," Gertrude said. "We're going home."

Edmond took the broom from the boy and looked at Rose, who was massaging her shoulder again.

"Are you alright, Miss Adelaide?" he asked.

"Yes, I'll be fine," Rose said, but she grimaced and knew lifting the boy had been too much for her shoulder.

"My heavens, did you exasperate your shoulder fetching Owen? Oh, you *did!*" Gertrude said. "You must go see Dr Shaw immediately and send us the bill for anything he prescribes for the pain, Miss Adelaide!"

"No, no, really, it's alright," Rose said. "I just need some rest and it will be fine."

Gertrude took her hand and said, "If you need anything, you let me know."

"Yes, I will," said Rose.

"I'll see to your bags, Miss Adelaide," Edmond said.

"Hey," called Herman Statler from atop his ladder, "Everything okay down there?"

"Herman Statler! You should pay more attention to where you put your ladder!" Gertrude said.

Herman looked around, confused, and went back to working on the sign.

As Gertrude led Owen away, Edmond picked up the bags from where Rose had dropped them. He brought them to her and said, "I'll carry these to your cottage, Miss Adelaide."

"Thank you, Mr Reed, but I planned to see about shopping at your store before I returned home," Rose said. "After being gone several weeks, I believe I'm in need of fresh food."

"Very well, then," Reed said. "Let me know what you need and I'll see it's delivered to your home this very afternoon."

Mr Reed led the way into the General Store and put her bags down by the counter. Sarah Reed was showing Mrs McManus some new cloth at the back of the store. Rose followed Edmond to the counter where he opened his log book.

"And what would you be needing, Miss Adelaide?" Reed asked.

"A dozen eggs, milk…" Rose listed the groceries as she rubbed her shoulder, which still smarted and throbbed. As she finished the list, the bell above the door jingled. Spurred boots clicked on the wood floor and Rose turned to see Emery Dale stride in. Emery's clothes were dusty. Fatigue all but wore on her. When she scanned the room and saw Rose, she brightened.

"Rose, welcome back!" Emery said. "My condolences on the passing of your father. I was out of town on business when you left. I heard only after you'd gone."

"It's quite alright, truly," Rose said. "And thank you."

"Ms Dale, how can I help you today?" asked Sarah Reed as she approached them down the aisle.

Emery cast an uncertain look at Rose, then turned back to Mrs Reed and said, "I've come to buy some candles, matches and lantern oil."

"I see," said Mrs Reed. "Edmond will bring those right to you."

"I'm helping Miss Adelaide, Sarah," Reed said.

"I'm afraid our stock of lantern oil is in the storehouse out back, Ms Dale," Mrs Reed said. "You can meet Edmond out back and he'll take care of you."

"I see," said Emery. "However, am I correct in pointing out the box of lamp oil on that shelf over your shoulder?"

Mrs Reed didn't turn around to see the box Emery gestured to, but said, "That box is just for show."

Emery nodded and said, "I understand. I'll meet Mr Reed out back, shall I?"

"I'll see to your supplies, Ms Dale," Edmond said with genuine good cheer, ducking out to the back door.

Mrs Reed held her smile until Emery left. When she was gone, the smile vanished from the shopkeeper's face as Mrs Reed let out a world-weary sigh.

"That woman. Truly," Mrs Reed said.

Mrs McManus was at Mrs Reed's side as they watched Emery pass the window walking away from the shop.

"The woman doesn't attend Sunday services," Mrs McManus said with acidy contempt. "She struts about town like a... a cattle rustler, or worse, with those guns and that attire."

"Hardly a shred of decency," Mrs Reed said.

"She should never have come to this town," Mrs McManus.

"Had she not, Mrs McManus," Rose said, her voice bringing a chill to the room, "I would certainly be in a grave. No doubt one in the cemetery next to the church you condemn her for not attending,"

"Miss Adelaide, you misunderstand—" Mrs McManus started, only to be cut off by the teacher.

"No, I do not think I misunderstand at all," Rose said.

"Miss Adelaide, you're tired from you're journey," said Mrs Reed. "You should go home and rest."

"You're afraid of her, Mrs McManus," Rose said with quiet disgust. "I see that now. Good day, ladies."

Rose walked out of the store, fully aware her bags were still at the counter. She walked around the side of the building to the storehouse in back, hoping to find Mr Reed with Emery Dale. Neither was there. Rose shook her head and leaned against the side of the store in the shade, collecting herself. Her shoulder throbbed, but adrenalin soothed it. She knew she shouldn't have given Roberta McManus what for, but it infuriated her to hear Emery disparaged like that. Sarah Reed wasn't much better and the truth was Rose already knew the two could cluck gossip like a pair of hens. It probably was fatigue that gave Rose such a short fuse. As for getting her luggage from the store, she hoped Edmond Reed would send it over to her cottage with her groceries.

Satisfied she felt more in control, Rose returned to the boardwalk, only wanting now to have a hot bath at her cottage.

"Forget something, Miss Adelaide?"

166

Emery stood in front of the general store with Rose's bags at her feet.

"I left in a hurry, I..." Rose stammered in surprise.

"I heard," Emery said. "Or rather I was present at the aftermath. Mr Reed insisted I come inside to pay for my goods. Mrs Reed and McManus are inside extolling your virtues in hushed tones as we speak."

"Oh, are they now?" Rose said, a giddiness overtaking her.

"If I had to measure by their response, I'd say you gave them a tongue lashing they probably deserved," Emery said. She picked up Rose's bags and the two crossed the street.

"They did deserve it. God forgive me that I didn't turn the other cheek, but the things they said..." Rose sighed.

"I can't imagine anyone would have a quarrel with you," Emery said.

"*I* was not the target of their lack of charity," Rose said.

"Who then?" Emery asked.

They reached the boardwalk across the street and Rose stopped, uncertain, regretting she had said anything. She didn't want to hurt Emery's feelings now. Rose looked back at the general store.

"They are of small minds and low opinion, Emery," Rose said, starting again toward her cottage. "We should pay them no mind."

"We?" Emery said. "Was I in some way the subject of their unkind words?"

"It pains me to say you were," Rose said.

Emery frowned.

"You are my friend, Emery Dale," Rose said. "If anyone in Orchard Bend tarnishes your good name in my presence, I will not hold my tongue."

Emery looked at her.

"Thank you for that," she said. "I count you among the few friends I have here."

Emery spoke in a pragmatic tone that saddened Rose. She wanted to say it shouldn't be like that, that Emery had a lot to offer Orchard Bend and the townsfolk like Mrs McManus should be grateful this woman was among them. But Emery was not wrong, what *should* be very often didn't align with what *was*.

They walked in silence the rest of the way to Rose's cottage.

* * *

June 12, 1953
Orchard Bend

On the hardwood floor of Sheriff Thorn's study laid the forgotten package, Owen McCabe's ledger, stolen hours before by Tyler Brand. Amongst the newspaper clippings contained within, one read:

Orchard Herald
November 3, 1885

LOCAL MERCHANT DEAD IN STOREHOUSE FIRE
Tragedy befell Orchard Bend as prominent businessman Edmond Reed was killed in a fire on Saturday last, October 31. Mr. Reed and his wife, Sarah, own and operate the Orchard Bend General Store & Feed and were attending Hallowe'en festivities at the home of Mr. & Mrs. Maxwell McCabe earlier that evening. The storehouse was located behind the General Store & Feed, housing much of the Reed's inventory and stock.

No other person was harmed in the fire and due to rain and the quick actions of local residents, more property and businesses were spared. The cause of the fire is said by Sheriff Anderson to have been a lantern igniting the contents of the storehouse.

Below this clipping, from the *About Town* column of the *Herald*, same date:

Mr. & Mrs. Maxwell McCabe and young Masters Henry and Owen McCabe welcomed guests to their home Saturday last on the occasion of Hallowe'en. Guests included Dr. Alfred Shaw, Mr. & Mrs Earl McManus, Mr. Martin Griesbach, Ms. Rose

Adelaide, Ms. Emery Dale, Mr. Edgar Allman, Mr & Mrs. Edmond Reed, Mr. & Mrs. Thomas Wilson (family friends of the McCabe's visiting from Sutter Grove), among others.

Masquerade was the order of the night and a delightful evening was had by all.

Below this second clipping, in Owen's cursive handwriting was the caption: "Reed storehouse - Henry's doing."

* * *

October 31, 1885
Orchard Bend

"What Orchard Bend needs is a proper Town Hall," announced Maxwell McCabe to a small group of guests, including Earl McManus, the local blacksmith, Edgar Allman, the undertaker, and other aldermen. "These meetings at the church have served our needs since the town's founding all those years ago, but I feel the building just isn't equipped to be our center of government anymore."

There were nods of agreement. At the back of the group, notepad out, was Thomas Buchanan, owner and editor of the Orchard Herald. Buchanan was a large man with wide shoulders and a thick moustache, who to Emery Dale had a high voice that didn't seem to match his build. He raised his pencil as he spoke to McCabe, his other hand holding the masquerade mask by its handle and balancing his notepad at the same time.

"With the population of the town currently witnessing a state of increased growth, do you see merit in expanding the town's government? Formalizing such things as having a mayor? And would you yourself contemplate occupying said position?" Buchanan asked in a way that almost rambled, as if he felt he had to get the questions out before someone cut him off.

"Thomas, you are an astute man," McCabe said, pointing at the editor with his own mask. "Orchard Bend is growing, we all of us here have seen it. A new Town Hall would declare we are

169

not just some boom town like Blue Creek, a company town owned and run by a mining consortium. There are no company stores here. Nor is there railroad police like they have in Ashleyville, a law practically unto themselves."

There were nods and words of agreement. Buchanan jotted as fast as he could on his notepad. Dale watched this business while leaning against the doorframe of the study as the Hallowe'en party went on about her. McCabe continued his impromptu speech.

"*Maxwell McCabe for mayor*, Thomas? As always you ask those pointed questions that I'm sure occupy the thoughts of my fellow Orchard Bend citizens, but no. I'm afraid, sir, I'd decline such a nomination. I'm a businessman, as are we all here, not a politician. Oh, I serve with my fellow alderman, but in so doing I am one voice among many. The mantle of mayor-hood should fall to a gentleman better suited to be the face of Orchard Bend, while I continue my role as..."

Puppet master, pulling the strings? Dale thought with a smile.

"...as humble barber, grooming our citizens young and old," McCabe finished and there were more words of agreement.

Edgar Allman spoke up, saying, "Just the other day, Edmond Reed and I were discussing the matter of elections in Orchard Bend and what it would mean."

Dale picked Allman out as the youngest man in the group, in his early-thirties if he was a day, and despite his occupation, was known to turn a few of the ladies' heads when about town.

"Say, where is Reed?" Earl McManus asked.

"I expect he's topping up on the punch!" said Wayne Statler. The men laughed. Wayne had taught Dale how to ride a horse all those years ago, after she'd arrived in Orchard Bend. A shadow crossed her smile as she thought, *Has it been six years already?*

Her right hand tapped the grip of the pistol on her hip, one of the pair she wore that night and most every day. Dale was the only woman at the party not wearing a dress, a point underlined by the glances of some of the other guests. They were quick, fleeting looks, but they held on her an extra moment or two. Dale noticed them and knew what they meant. They were uneasy looks, nervous looks. Six years and she was still an anomaly, an unknown, and in a lot of ways unknowable.

Six years and the basic question remained: Who was she?

"Folks are apt to think you have an itch to use that, the way you tap it so" said Rose Adelaide in a hushed voice behind Emery. Emery let out a laugh, letting her hand drop away from the pistol's grip. She turned and smiled at the schoolteacher.

"It would liven up this soiree, to be sure," Emery said.

"Such a deed might make the front page of the Orchard Herald," Rose said in a mock conspiratorial tone.

"Do you reckon it would be newsworthy enough?" Emery asked. "Granted, such a display would no doubt startle our fellow guests, but if the news were to occupy the front page, it would deny loyal Orchard Bend readers the opportunity to learn about *Dr Hollenbach's Fantastical Elixir* and the sale the Reeds are having on yards of cloth. It would seem a crime to overshadow such vital information."

"Yes. Quite right," Rose agreed. "Do refrain from gunplay this evening if at all possible, Ms Dale."

Emery let out an exaggerated sigh and said, "Very well."

"I believe I require more punch," Rose said, looking at her empty glass. "And it appears you are likewise without potation, Ms Dale."

"That I am."

"I shall be nary a minute, if you wish to meet me on the front porch for some air," Rose said as she slipped away to find the punch bowl.

Outside, the air was cool and the wind had picked up. Rain would come before long. In the distant west, there was lightning, but Dale suspected that much of that storm would pass Orchard Bend by as it headed south.

Much closer, the lantern lights of the town glittered and Dale reflected on how correct McCabe was, that the town was growing. In her six years, the population had almost doubled. The center of town back then had been little more than a crossroads cluster of buildings. Now there were several distinct

171

streets intersecting. Sully's still offered room and board in the saloon, but a proper hotel had opened a few years ago, *The Harvest Moon*, owned and operated by Martin Griesbach, catering to travellers of more means. Other businesses had arrived, including a photography studio and a tailor, and a few existing ones had expanded, including the Orchard Herald's offices.

Rose came outside with two cups of hot apple cider instead of punch and Dale wrapped her fingers around her drink to warm them up.

"Mr McCabe is still going on about building a new town hall," Rose said. "When I suggested a proper schoolhouse would also be in the town's best interest, he congratulated me on my 'fine use of limited resources,' citing it as an example of the pioneering spirit."

"His children are tutored by Gertrude here at home, so there's no direct benefit to his supporting a school beyond what the town already allocates you," Emery said and took a sip of her cider. Rose held hers and wisps of steam floated from it.

"What the town allocates is hardly enough," Rose said. "I have books in tatters and all were an edition old when I began teaching here."

Emery didn't need to ask how long that had been. Rose had been teaching in Orchard Bend for two years before Dale's arrival the day she saved her life.

"Surely the other aldermen see the issue plain as day," Emery said. "The Reeds' children are among your students..."

Rose was shaking her head.

"I've spoken to them," she said, "they offered their sympathies, but the 'town's priorities are clear,' Mr Reed informed me. I had to bite my tongue to correct him on the point of *whose* priorities are paramount in Orchard Bend."

Rose looked at her cider, which had stopped steaming in the cool air, and poured it over the side of the porch with a jerk of her arm. Emery set her own cup down and the two women watched the lightning storm in the west for a few minutes before Rose spoke again.

"I believe I wish to retire from this masquerade, though it might take some convincing of Dr Shaw to escort me home early," Rose said.

"I expect so," Emery agreed. "I last saw him singing ballads with Brian Faraday and Jim Speck at the piano. That being said, if you're intent on leaving, *I* could escort you. I think I've had my fill of cider and punch this evening."

"If it wouldn't be too much trouble, Emery," Rose said.

"None at all. Just give me a moment to bid our hosts goodbye," Emery replied.

"Yes, I should take my leave of them, as well," Rose said as they crossed the porch to the door.

The two split off once inside and Dale searched around for Gertrude McCabe without success. She was not upstairs as far as Dale could see, but she did not look in either of the boys' rooms for fear of waking them up. Downstairs she went to the kitchen, finding only the cook and her two daughters. The girls were cleaning dishes and their mother sat near the bottle of whiskey used in the punch, supervising.

Dale went out the back door. The wind had picked up a good deal. It would be wise to get going, she knew. The trees groaned as they swayed and a sharp gust made the barn door across the yard clatter. The various buggies and horses were corralled next to the barn, but unless someone was out here, the door ought to be shut.

Thinking it was probably nothing, that maybe the door had broken loose by the wind, Dale crossed the grass to the barn. The door was unbroken and she was planning on closing it when she heard voices. The wind drowned out much of it, but there were two people having a conversation in the barn.

Curiosity got the better of Dale. She stood in the darkness outside the barn and listened, catching only snippets. It was a man and a woman speaking.

"...but he doesn't love you," the man said, "I told you that."

"And you do? You would abandon her for..." and the wind and creaking of the barn made the rest of her words indecipherable. Dale strained to pick up fragments of the conversation amid the noise around her.

"...go on like this everyday," the man said.

"It has gone too far already," the woman replied, "What of our children? I'd not desert mine and not for a man who would consider doing so to his."

"No, no, you misunderstand. I just... I simply want us to be happy," the man said.

"It would be unwise to consider any option beyond this arrangement," she replied, "and as it stands, I feel we have been too foolhardy thus far."

The wind gusted and a tree creaked at the far end of the yard, causing a few of the horses to whiny and become restless. Inside the barn, the voices fell silent and Dale heard the crunching and shuffling of footsteps coming to the door. She backed away and slipped into the shadows of the corral.

A man appeared at the door and Dale recognized him as Edmond Reed. Reed checked that no one was outside, turned and said something to the other occupant. Then he walked back to the house. After a few seconds, the woman stepped out of the barn, visibly hesitant.

It was Gertrude McCabe.

Dale watched her friend leave the barn and return to the house, entering through the kitchen.

* * *

Henry McCabe was about to come out from darkness at the side of the barn when he saw Emery Dale step out of the corral. She looked at the barn, then back to the house, and then stood with her head down, deep in thought. Henry didn't move. Dale turned and walked back to the house. When she went inside, Henry started across the lawn in the direction of his family's apple orchard.

He knew what had to be done.

* * *

Emery was aware that she hadn't spoken since she and Rose set out from the McCabes' back to town. She looked to Rose,

174

ready to say something, but no words came to her. She would not speak of what she saw at the barn, of Gertrude and Reed, but felt she ought to fill the tense night with *some* conversation. Each time she made to speak, Rose looked at her expectantly, and each time Emery failed to say anything, turning her attention back to the dark road ahead of them. The schoolteacher did likewise. And so it went for the duration of the journey.

Rose Adelaide's rented cottage was not far from the church that doubled as her schoolhouse. The wind no longer gusted, but had become a continuous gale. The distinct smell of rain filled the air, though it had yet to fall. Emery hoped she could make it back to her little cabin on the western side of town before it hit.

As if reading her mind, Rose spoke up as she stepped down from the buggy.

"Emery, you'll not make it home in advance of the storm," Rose said. "Stay here tonight, I have a good amount of room."

An irrational urge to decline sprang up in Emery and she almost did just that. The wind bit at her duster. The flat, wide brim of her hat caught the air and was almost pulled from her head. Only the stampede string under her chin kept it on.

"Thank you, Rose, I believe staying the night would be wise," Emery said and she dismounted.

* * *

It took Henry an hour to reach the center of town. He crossed first through his family's orchard and then along the road, without even starlight or a moon to guide him. At one point, two people came up behind him and he dashed into the brush at the side of the road. It was the Dale woman and the schoolteacher, Adelaide. They went past him without pausing and when they were a good distance away, Henry climbed back onto the road and kept walking.

Henry saw that not many folks were out that night. A storm was on its way. Doors and shutters were closed. Moving from shadow to shadow, Henry made his way to the Reed's General Store & Feed.

The Prisoner was why he was here.

Through the Prisoner, Henry learned to control death.

Ever since that night six years ago when the bad men attacked, the Prisoner had looked out for Henry, told him things and kept him safe. The Prisoner was in the barn when the bad man Saunders wanted him dead. He'd never met Saunders, but Saunders gibbered and cried about Henry's father. Revenge was to be his, Saunders said. McCabe had killed Saunders' father, so Saunders was going to kill Henry. Henry saw in his eyes that the bad man wasn't lying. Henry cried and tried to get away, but the Prisoner came and stayed with him until the Dale woman arrived. It was hard, but the noisy voice was somehow soothing.

The Dale woman had come, but it never occurred to Henry once to credit her with saving him. The Prisoner had been there the whole time with him, keeping him calm, keeping him alive until she came and cut off Saunders' head. And afterwards, it had been the Prisoner who had befriended Henry, who had helped keep the nightmares away, not the Dale woman. The Prisoner told him that killing things was the way to control the bouts of fear and anger that seemed to burst up in him like a volcano. There had been mice around the house and in the barn. Their deaths had been for the sake of his peace of mind, as Henry found he could control life and death now and no longer needed to fear it. The nightmares became more infrequent.

A stray cat arrived one summer day, a few years ago, and Henry knew it needed to be sacrificed, too. He fed the cat, earned its trust and when the day came, everything was perfect. Henry lined a box in the barn with an open bag, because cats like boxes. The cat curled up in it and started to doze. The time was right and Henry sprung the trap, closing the bag. The cat hissed and writhed and a claw caught Henry's hand, digging in and drawing blood. Henry dropped the bag and the cat bolted. Henry waited days for it to come back, but it never did. Henry went looking for it, one day walking to the eastern edge of the McCabe property, near the railroad land. He thought about the relaxing days watching the train go by. He walked and walked, through the thickets and trees. The sounds of a quiet summer day calmed him. He closed his eyes and felt the breeze on his face. When he opened his eyes he saw the rabbit. It was ten feet away and looking at him. Henry wanted it dead, but knew it couldn't be now. The next day he set snares around the area, even as far as by the pond near the Picton farm. Mr Miller had taught Henry about snares and Henry felt it was fitting to use one to do this deed, for Mr Miller had been shot dead by Saunders the night this whole dark journey began. Henry checked the snares every day until at last he found the rabbit caught. Unlike the cat, the rabbit didn't escape and Henry decapitated it. Peace filled him and he left the rabbit for whatever animals might want it. He walked with contentment back to his house, unaware that hours later the dead rabbit was discovered by the young couple of Eloise Picton and David Langford.

However, things had begun to change between Henry and the Prisoner, who insisted that Henry no longer needed to kill the animals, that it would draw too much attention one day. If Henry were ever caught, there would be questions. At first Henry listened and did as the Prisoner suggested, but the dark need proved too much. Over the next few years, several more rabbits and a few squirrels fell victim to Henry McCabe. The Prisoner came to him less often, stopped telling him things and sharing secrets. Henry didn't mind, though, for he knew he'd learned much about the power of death. In his heart, Maxwell and Gertrude's eldest son knew he could deal out death as he saw fit.

On this night, the night of the Hallowe'en party, Henry and Owen had been dismissed early, having been presented to the guests in their animal masks. Henry's was a rabbit. He tried to sleep as the party wore on, but sleep wouldn't come. Sneaking out of the house, Henry had come upon his mother and Mr Reed in the barn, kissing and in each other's embrace. Henry spied on them from outside. The anger was both seething and black and it drove Henry to the General Store & Feed that night.

Tonight, Mr Reed was going to die.

* * *

Emery could sense Rose watching her as she undid the gunbelts from her waist and placed them on the low table next to the sofa. She took off the leather harness that held her cherrywood-gripped knives and set it next to the gun belts. Rose was looking at her through the open kitchen doorway as the schoolteacher made them some hot cocoa. For an unexpected moment, Emery felt naked and exposed now that she was unarmed. Emery took a deep breath and turned as Rose brought the serving tray out to the small parlour. Only a few candles were lit and the space was warm and welcoming.

"Do sit, Emery," Rose said and Emery did, reaching for her drink. Like with the cider earlier, it was warm through the porcelain. There was no fireplace in the cottage, but the lit wood stove radiated heat. The fire glowed through the thick glass window.

"This is delicious, Rose," Emery said. "Thank you."

Rose was about to answer when the gentle drumming of rain on the roof cut her off. It was sudden and a blast of wind followed. It made the cottage shudder.

The two looked at each other and laughed.

"Fear not," Rose said, "this cottage will not blow away in the storm. It has seen its share of harsh weather."

Emery winced. An image came to her on the tail of a stabbing headache. It came just as suddenly as the rain had, but the pain was not crippling. The image was of a book and an illustration: A house blown into the air on a cyclone. Emery knew there was a little girl inside, even though the girl was not in the illustration itself. She didn't know how she knew, but she was certain. The pain subsided after a few seconds and was replaced with uneasy certainty. She'd found another memory.

Rose saw the sudden furrowing of Emery's brow and the far away expression that overtook her friend. The teacher leaned forward and touched Emery's arm.

"What is it?" Rose asked.

"A memory," Emery said.

"You seem... haunted," Rose said. "Was it something unpleasant?"

Emery turned to her with a hint of a smile.

"No, quite the contrary," Emery said. "It was something pleasant. Something I'd long forgotten. I thought it was gone forever."

There were a dozen or more questions Emery could see behind Rose's eyes, but the schoolteacher did not ask them. Instead she said with a simple smile, "I hope more pleasant memories come out of hiding for you."

Emery grinned, nodding as she spoke.

"Yes," Emery said, "that would be most agreeable."

Rose raised her cup to sip her hot cocoa and Emery caught a flash of pain as it crossed her friend's face. As Rose lowered her cup her right hand trembled.

"Your shoulder still bothers you?" Emery asked.

Rose shifted on her seat.

"Yes, from time to time a phantom ache possesses it," Rose replied. "Considering the alternative, it is something I accept."

Emery put her drink down and reached for the gun in the right-hand holster resting on the coffee table. Rose watched her, inquisitive and a little afraid. Emery could tell by the way Rose sat up and held her breath, her body tense. Emery unloaded the rounds from the cylinder, closed it and presented it to her friend.

Rose only looked at it, then to Emery, not understanding.

Emery clarified, her voice soft.

"This is the gun that shot you," Emery said.

Rose drew in a breath as her hand went to her mouth, but then she relaxed and looked at the weapon with deep curiosity.

"Take it," Emery said. "Hold it. I bought it from the marshals who came to clean up the mess. You and I didn't know each other then and I was planning to move on from Orchard Bend anyway."

Rose turned the gun over in her hands, almost caressing the metal and wood. She held it tight and touched the shoulder where a bullet fired from this gun had struck her.

"A painful reminder of our first meeting," Emery said, looking at the glowing firelight in the wood stove.

"I don't choose to see it that way," Rose said, putting the gun down and leaning forward. Again she put her hand on Emery's arm. "We met when I awoke in Dr Shaw's office, safe and rescued by you. Not a day goes by that I don't thank the Lord for sending you to save me and Sam O'Toole."

"Was it God's doing?" Emery had her doubts.

"His will is not for us to know, but you were there and I don't think it was an accident," Rose was squeezing Emery's arm. It was a pleasant touch and Emery smiled again. She wanted to ask Rose where freewill came into this. She wanted to ask Rose if it was God's will that she not remember who she was before waking up by the bridge six years ago. Why only a few fragmented memories of her old life had surfaced in all that time. She wanted to ask Rose if she would ever come to remember who she was and if she would ever get home again. Emery blinked a tear from her eye. It glinted in the candlelight as it rolled down her cheek.

"I feel safe when you are around, Emery Ann Dale," Rose continued. Her hand moved up to Emery's shoulder as she said this. Emery turned to her again, took the hand from her shoulder and held it. Their fingers interlocked. The eyes of the woman she had saved six year previous were now wide and a little wet. Emery kissed her and Rose pulled away.

"Wait, no—" Rose stammered.

Emery held her gaze, but stopped.

Rose looked down at the gun on her lap.

Emery stood up.

"I should go," Emery said.

Rose was still holding her hand.

"Please don't," Rose said and put Emery's hand to her breast. Emery leaned in and kissed Rose and this time Rose did not pull away.

* * *

Things did not go as planned for Henry McCabe that Hallowe'en night.

Rain poured as the Reeds returned home. Henry waited in the shadows by the storehouse, picking his moment. It came when Mrs Reed went inside their home, located at the back of the store. Outside, Mr Reed tended to their team of horses. When he came out of the stable carrying a lantern, Henry acted, throwing a rock and smashing one of the windows of the storehouse. Reed heard it and went to investigate. With another rock, Henry clubbed Reed on the head. The merchant collapsed in a heap, unconscious, but still breathing. The lantern went out as it landed on its side in a deep puddle. Henry dragged Reed to the door of the storehouse, thankful for the cover of darkness, but cursing the rain that made it harder to move the unconscious man. With Reed's key, Henry unlocked the storehouse door and dragged the man inside.

That's when the plan began to fall apart.

If Reed had stayed unconscious, Henry knew everything would have gone smoothly. When Reed awoke and struggled, real fear took hold of Henry. If Reed had been fifteen years younger, he might have been able to fight off the young man, but with the help of an ax handle, one of many in the storehouse's inventory, Henry clubbed Reed back into unconsciousness. He stood up and thought good and hard despite the panic in his guts. His sole purpose in coming here was to cut Reed's head off, but he'd taken too much time already. Mrs Reed was probably already wondering where her husband was.

Henry peeked out the storehouse door to the Reeds' house at the back of the General Store & Feed. The upstairs light was on, but no one was looking out. Henry dashed outside, grabbed the lantern from the puddle and slipped back into the

181

storehouse. The need to hurry was strong now. Henry found the matches in Reed's pocket, lit the lantern and dropped it carefully next to Reed. The glass broke and the flame danced in the open air. Henry toppled a stack of dry, wooden crates onto the lantern and the unconscious Reed. He heard the soft *whuff* as the wood caught fire. Just to be sure, Henry used the matches to ignite a stack of books before tossing the unlit matches next to Reed as the storehouse filled with smoke.

Henry fled the scene, ducking into the shadows of an alley across the street. There, he kept vigil on the storehouse, which at first only glowed from the inside. Henry feared he'd see Reed stumble out of the building at any moment or that Mrs Reed or someone else would investigate the glow and save the man, but it didn't happen.

It took only minutes for the storehouse to go up in flames. For Henry, they were long, tense minutes. When the flames broke through the roof and the windows, the first onlookers appeared on the street. It didn't take long for them to rally to stop the fire from spreading, but Henry didn't stay to see their efforts. It was going to be a long walk back home in the rain.

Things did not go as planned for Henry McCabe that night, but he could live with the results.

19

June 12, 1953
Orchard Bend

"That detective! Tom Fucking Reed," Owen McCabe said, the words coming out like spit. He sat at his desk in his study fuming. "He stole it. He must have stolen it. That piece of shit son of a bitch! He broke in here last night while I slept and—"

The police don't have the ledger, the Prisoner said.

"Who does then?!" Owen snapped. He didn't question how the Prisoner knew this. The Prisoner knew things and those things were always correct.

The ledger is not important.

"*Everything is in there!*" Owen yelled, standing up so fast the wheeled chair rolled back and hit the shelves behind him. The study was a mess, with shelves emptied and books and papers strewn everywhere.

Owen McCabe had awoken at dawn and it had not taken long for him to discover the ledger was missing. He was certain he had brought it upstairs with him and put it in the nightstand next to the bed. Thinking he might simply have had a lapse of memory, he checked under the sheets, under the bed, in the bathroom. With growing concern, Owen moved faster than his legs had in years. He shuffled down the stairs to the study, the last place he'd been before going to bed. He assured himself it would be on the desk, left where he used to leave it years ago. It had just been a lapse, something not uncommon at his age (though until now, Owen thought, his memory had not diminished much with old age). The ledger wasn't on the desk. Or under it. Or on the shelves.

That's when fear came, which Owen responded to with tempered anger. Giving in to fear was what cowards did. They panic, lose focus and things only go down hill from there.

"That ain't me," Owen said. "Pull your goddamn self together, McCabe, and square this shit up."

He thought about the night before, recalling his every movement. He'd sat at the desk, reading the newspaper clippings of the bitch Gabby's death. He'd had a drink of brandy. The bottle and the tumbler were still on the desk. He had gotten up, taken the ledger and left the study, locking it behind him. He had climbed the stairs to his bedroom and locked the door behind him.

Standing amongst the mess of books and papers, Owen froze, the fear churning a little inside him.

He'd locked the door behind him.

But the study door had not been locked. In his rush to find the ledger, Owen had simply opened the unlocked door.

Someone had been in this room.

And that person must have gone into his bedroom.

That person had stolen the ledger.

Owen felt weak in his legs and collapsed in his chair. His mind reeled.

It had to be Reed, that pissant cop who had been poking around Emery Dale's remains. McCabe had ears in the Sheriff's Department and Reed had not been happy when the Dale evidence from the hunter's cabin disappeared. Of course he'd strike back.

But now the Prisoner was denying this was the case. Reed didn't have the ledger.

Who then?

The Prisoner was silent now after Owen's outburst. The Prisoner was waiting for him to calm down. After so many years, Owen could read the moods. Owen took a few deep breaths. There was something else there, too. Owen sensed the Prisoner might be distracted.

"Okay," Owen said. "I'm calm as a summer's fucking day now."

There's a package waiting for you on your porch, the Prisoner said.

Owen retrieved it and returned to his desk in the study. He poured himself a drink, not caring that it wasn't even 8 AM. He unwrapped the newspaper and looked at the device. Owen wanted to ask how it had gotten here, who had delivered it, but knew the Prisoner would tell him if it was important for him to know.

The other traveller from the Breach has at last come to Orchard Bend, the Prisoner said. *You will find her for me.*

"You know she's here, but you can't find her yourself?" Owen asked.

No reply.

Owen picked up the device. "What do I do with this?"

Nothing, until you find her.

"Then answer my question!" Owen said.

In the long pause, Owen didn't think the Prisoner would respond, but the noise-filled voice said, *It's difficult to see travellers once they leave the Breach, but they leave echoes. I perceive her echoes in Orchard Bend. You were told she was coming, now find this woman so we can end this!*

* * *

Cal Watson didn't know that he needn't have worried about the Sheriff that morning, that he wasn't going to be hassled again. Unaware that Sheriff Thorn's wife had passed away only hours earlier, Cal looked over his shoulder every so often as he crossed the park in front of the Town Hall. He arrived at the bench where he'd met the Sheriff the day before and looked around. It was also the bench where he'd seen the woman, when the headaches and the grey visions had started. His gut told him there was a connection between her and what was happening to him. With nothing else to go on, Cal listened to it.

After fleeing the Shadow and the Ghost the night before, Cal had laid in bed thinking about the grey visions, the smoky, translucent world he had seen twice. He questioned his sanity, but decided that if he were crazy, none of this meant anything and someday they might lock him up and throw away the key. But if it *did* mean something, if this ability was something that would recur, he would be doing himself a big favor learning about it.

The Shadow worried him. Cal didn't want to think about what it would do if it caught him last night.

And the Ghost, he wondered, what of her?

She led the Shadow away on purpose, so I could escape. Why did she do that?

Cal wondered if she could communicate, if somehow they could converse.

The park was quiet that morning. With school out for the summer, there were no teenagers rushing to class. Adults hurried to their jobs and a good number of elderly citizens came and went from Ed's Diner. In the evenings it would be the kids' hang out, but in the morning it was almost exclusively retirees. Cal sat on the bench. He knew it was a long shot waiting on the slim chance the mystery woman would happen by.

And if she did, then what?

Cal didn't know. Assuming she didn't tell him to scram, how would he bring up the subject of the grey visions? Cal decided he'd find her first and worry about that conversation after.

"Cal Watson, as I live and breathe," said a female voice behind him. It was Grace Pine and Cal stumbled to his feet.

"Grace! Hi," Cal said. "What are you doing here?"

Grace leaned in and said in a stage whisper, "Believe it or not, I *live* in Orchard Bend!"

Cal smiled.

"No," he said, "I mean what are you doing *here*, at the park?"

"Starting my summer job," Grace said, looking at the Town Hall. "I'm working in the Sheriff's Office. My dad's the lieutenant and arranged for me to work there. I'm going to be filing and typing and getting coffee and lots of other things."

As she spoke, she pointed to the Town Hall, where Cal saw a man in uniform at the main door watching them, waiting for Grace.

"Wow! Okay," Cal said. "Hey, sorry for what happened last night."

"It wasn't your fault," Grace said, "Terry and I are splitsville, but he's having trouble getting that through his thick head."

Grace's father was walking toward them now.

"You should get going," Cal said. "You don't want to be late for your first day."

"Cal Watson, your wisdom knows no bounds," Grace said, walking away. "I'll be taking my lunch around one. How about I meet you here?"

"Swell," Cal said. He wanted to say more as she gave a wave and turned away, but nothing came to mind. Cal watched her say something to her father as they walked into the Town Hall together.

* * *

News of Maryanne Thorn's death spread quickly through the Sheriff's Office and the mood was sombre. The Emery Dale case, which for Reed had occupied much of his thoughts over the past few weeks, was set aside as he processed the news. Before the cancer, Mrs Thorn was a regular face around the Office. She'd made a point to remember everyone's name and to ask after their families, recalling the smallest detail. She hadn't set foot in the building in so long Reed couldn't remember the last time he'd seen her in person. The thought that she'd never walk through the Office doors to visit or to drop off the Sheriff's lunch left Reed feeling more empty than he expected. And even though he was aware of how sick she was, Tom Reed deep down had held out hope that she'd somehow go into remission and Sheriff Thorn would climb out of the bottle he was hiding in.

Now, though, with his wife gone, Reed could only guess how the man was doing.

187

"Okay, everyone," Lieutenant Pine said, standing in the middle of the Office, "Many of us have heard the sad news, but if any of you haven't been briefed, here it is: Maryanne Thorn, the wife of our own Sheriff Thorn, passed away this morning after a long, courageous battle with cancer. Many of us knew Mrs Thorn personally and her death hits close to home. In this Office, she was family."

There were murmurs of agreement throughout the room.

"Funeral details will be posted on the relevant bulletin boards," Pine continued. "The Sheriff's Office will of course send flowers. Shelly is taking care of those arrangements. Thank you, Shelly."

Shelly Dickson waved a hand in acknowledgment as she dabbed her eyes at the reception desk by the door.

"Sheriff Thorn is on leave," Pine went on. "We don't have a date for his return, but we wish him the best in this difficult time. In the meantime, I'll be filling his duties as they pertain to the day-to-day operations of the Office. So, that's it. Everyone knows their job and the best thing we can do for Sheriff Thorn right now is to keep things running smoothly and to stay safe. Thanks, everyone."

"Lieutenant, you have a call on line one," Shelly said.

"Thank you, I'll take it in my office," Pine said.

Reed watched Shelly show Pine's daughter, Grace, how to transfer a call. In his hand he anxiously turned over and over the stone he'd picked up at the ravine. The *Jane Doe #13* case file was on his desk. He looked at the clock.

9:32 AM, Reed thought. *Still early. Peter should be calling around a quarter to ten.*

Reed tapped the stone on his desk, sipped his coffee, and waited.

Lieutenant Pine came out of his office and went to the radio room, sticking his head in the door. Ruby Pressman was working dispatch that morning.

"Ruby, radio for Officer Clarke to meet me at the home of Tyler Brand, give him the address and tell him to wait for me there. I'm on my way," Pine said.

Reed sat up and as Pine passed his desk he asked, "Lieutenant, what's going on with Tyler Brand?"

"We have reason to think he was involved with a burglary," Pine said. "We're going to investigate."

"A burglary?" Reed asked. "Where? Of who?"

"Don't you have cases to work on, Tom?" Pine asked in a tone that told Reed that he'd be wise to drop the subject right now. Pine walked out of the Office leaving Reed to stew at his desk.

Okay, calm down, Reed told himself. *Does Pine think Ty broke in to the Museum office? Or is something else going on? If not the Museum, what?*

Reed picked up the phone and called Peter Howard's office. He waited as the phone rang and no one picked up. He caught sight of Shelly standing up from her desk across the room, her purse in her hand. Reed knew she was leaving the office to have her morning cigarette. She tried to keep it a secret, but Reed had figured it out long ago. Grace Pine sat at the desk alone now. Reed hung up the phone and went to her.

"Grace, keeping busy on your first day?" Reed smiled.

"Detective! Why yes I am," Grace smiled back. "Thank you for asking."

"I had a question for your father, but I don't know when he'll be back," Reed said. "I heard something about a burglary. Do you happen to know who called just now?"

Grace looked around, uncertain.

"No. No, I don't know," Grace said. "Should I have asked? Mrs Dickson didn't say anything about that."

"Sometimes people identify themselves when they call the police, that's all," Reed said with a shrug. "It could've been a prank call. We get kids calling in with false reports sometimes."

"Oh, it wasn't a kid!" Grace said. "It sounded like an older gentlemen. He was very stern."

Reed nodded.

"Okay," Reed said. "I guess my question for your dad will have to wait till he comes back. It wasn't all that important, anyway."

"Sorry I couldn't help more, Detective," Grace said.

"You're doing a great job, Grace," Reed said, walking back to his desk. "Glad to have you on the team."

Before he finished his sentence, the phone next to Grace rang and she answered it.

"Orchard Bend Sheriff's Office," she said.

Reed waited. Grace listened to the caller, nodding. After a moment, she looked up at Reed, replying to the caller, "Of course, Mr Howard. I'll put you through to him."

Reed pointed to himself and Grace nodded. She looked away to the small switchboard in front of her and Reed rushed to his desk. This was the call he was waiting for.

"Transferring the call now, Detective!" Grace called out.

His phone rang and he resisted picking up immediately. He took a breath and answered it.

"Detective Reed here," he said.

"Tom! It's Peter Howard,' said the caller. "Someone broke into the museum last night!"

* * *

The Prisoner may have told him not to worry about the ledger, but there was no way Owen was going to let the matter drop. He'd find the woman the Prisoner was after, but McCabe also intended to hunt down whoever broke into his house.

Someone violated his home and robbed him, but when the initial shock of it wore off, Owen began to consider who could have done this. Despite the Prisoner saying the Sheriff's Office didn't have the ledger, Owen wasn't about to cross Reed off the list entirely. Though such a crime seemed too bold for the detective, it would also be counter-productive if he intended to charge McCabe with anything. The fact that he broke in and stole the evidence would nullify it in court. McCabe didn't need to be a lawyer to understand that rule.

So if not Tom Reed, then who?

Owen tried to picture the crime, the intruder creeping about his house. They'd unlocked the study, but failed to find the ledger there. And Owen was certain the ledger had been their goal, not just because it was missing, but because there were plenty of heirlooms, antiques and expensive items in the house a burglar could have stolen, but hadn't. Likewise, there were documents and records in the study, which could have damaged Owen's business affairs and banking if they'd been taken, but they too had been left alone. So it had to be the ledger. And since it wasn't in the study, the intruder must have guessed it had to be upstairs with Owen himself.

So why steal the ledger and not just kill the old man in his sleep? The pearl-handled six-shooter that had once belonged to a US Marshal named Saunders was sitting untouched in its box in the desk drawer. The intruder could have simply shot him and made it look like a suicide. Maybe the intruder didn't have the guts to take a life. Or maybe killing Owen wasn't the endgame. The ledger was damning, would at best ruin him and at worst also land him on death row. If that was the intruder's intention, to not just kill Owen McCabe but to destroy him, it put Reed back on the top of the list, unless there was someone else.

Gabby had tried to steal his money and the Prisoner had seen to her...

Owen sat still in his chair as he realized who was now acting against him.

Ty Brand.

It made perfect sense and even though he would have counted Brand as one of his loyal employees, Owen was sharp enough and callous enough to know no man's loyalty was absolute. Was Brand trying to avenge Gabby? That must be it. Had Brand been playing him all along, all these years, all this time working in secret with his granddaughter? It made sense and maybe Brand had Gabby's keys, which would explain how he'd unlocked the doors and waltzed right in. But in the words of the Prisoner, that didn't matter. Gabby was gone and soon Brand would be gone.

That's when Owen reached for his address book and the phone on his desk and called Lieutenant Pine at the Sheriff's Office.

Pine was still trustworthy and this job didn't involve any dirty work. Owen smiled in spite of the severity of the situation. There would be no need to kill Ty Brand, at least not yet, because if he had the ledger it was stolen property. Pine could be counted on to disregard its contents, because there were details in the ledger which incriminated the lieutenant. And McCabe paid him well. His daughter, Grace, was heading to a fine college before long and that was not on a county lieutenant's pay. No, Pine would arrest Brand and return the ledger, no questions asked.

* * *

Tom Reed pretended to look closely at the broken pane of glass in the window of the Orchard Bend Museum. In truth he remembered just how it felt to drive his elbow into it the night before. It had taken several tries and his elbow still smarted.

"They broke the glass, undid the latch and climbed right in!" Peter said behind him. "I knew it as soon as I saw the window!"

Peter stood in the middle of the room, hands on his hips, looking at the overturned chairs, framed photos on the floor and artefacts lying about.

"Is anything broken," Reed asked, "besides this window."

"It doesn't look like it," Peter said. "They could've caused a lot of destruction, but they didn't."

Reed nodded and jotted in his notebook. Of course, during this very break-in, Tom had been careful to create a scene of burglary, but with none of the vandalism. He had to make it look authentic, but didn't want to actually destroy anything. If McCabe had decided to send one of his one goons to steal the Emery Dale archives, they probably wouldn't have been so accommodating.

"Anything stolen?" Reed asked.

"Yes, as a matter of fact," Peter said with a deep sigh. "You're not going to like it, Tom. They took the Emery Dale material. Everything. It was in a box. The Eloise Langford 78s, the photo, the newspaper articles, all of it. They took a couple of boxes, including the one where I kept all that archived. It's all gone, Tom. It was a priceless collection."

Peter stood dejected, looking at the floor.

192

Tom went to his friend and put his hand on his shoulder.

"I'm going to make this right, Peter," Reed said. "Please believe me. I'm going to do everything I can to get back what was stolen."

"I don't get it," Peter said, looking around the room. "The things in *here* are much more valuable to collectors than what was in those boxes. Why would anyone steal that stuff and not an antique chair? Or this oil lamp? It doesn't make a lot of sense. All I can figure is maybe it was connected to your case. Remember when you asked me all about Emery Dale? Maybe your case is connected with this. You might want to look into that."

It broke his heart to see Peter this way. The Museum was more than his job, it was his life's work, and it had been ransacked. Tom knew the missing boxes were safe, but he felt a little ashamed at having to put his friend through this.

Reed replied, "I'm going to follow every lead, Peter. Believe me. Let's go to the Sheriff's Office and write up a report."

* * *

"What was that you were humming?" Grace asked Cal as she sat down on the bench.

"Oh, a tune called 'Dark Was The Night, Cold Was The Ground' by Blind Willie Johnson," Cal said.

"Ah, classical music," Grace said, opening her paper-bagged lunch.

"Yeah, I listen to only the finest composers," Cal said. "Howlin' Wolfgang Mozart, Johann Shifty Bach, Fats Mahler."

"It really is a shame more classical composers didn't have nicknames," Grace said as she took a bite from her sandwich.

"My dad has a rare 78 record of...," and Cal trailed off. For a moment, for a brief happy few seconds he had forgotten what happened to his family. He could picture the 78 record, Barbecue Bob's "Honey You're Going Too Fast." His dad had only ever played it once the day he found it at a yard sale. That hadn't even been a year ago. The plan was to try to copy it onto tape. His dad was going to buy one of those reel to reel tape players and copy all his old 78s and other rare vinyl, but hadn't gotten around to it. All the records were probably still sitting in the living room. Cal could picture them now, under the record player. A lump was forming in his throat and he pushed it down with a great deal of anger and effort.

Grace was watching him. There was sympathy in her expression. Cal knew the questions she wanted to ask. He couldn't bear to explain it to her. Someday maybe, but not now, but he had to tell her something.

"Sorry, Grace, I don't want to ruin your lunch being such a wet blanket," Cal said, his sorrow replaced by embarrassment.

"It's alright, really," Grace said. "I don't know about Blue Creek, but around these parts, no one's said 'wet blanket' since Prohibition."

"Okay, well, you know this town so well, where does a fella find the nearest speakeasy? I need to wet my whistle with some hooch," Cal said with the ghost of a smile.

"Hooch. Hooch, you say?" Grace nodded. "Word around the campfire is that Ed Howell, owner of Ed's Diner, had the finest bathtub gin in the county back when my grandmother danced The Jitterbug. He might have a bottle under the soda fountain if you know the secret password."

"Do you know the password?"

"Cal Watson, what kind of girl do you think I am?" Grace said dramatically. "To think I'd visit an establishment that would serve such refreshments. Shame on you. Shame."

Cal smiled and looked around the park. More people were out now, enjoying the weather. Some teenagers made their way to Ed's Diner. He expected an exodus of the older crowd at any moment.

Grace took another bite of her sandwich. Cal turned back to her and asked, "How are you enjoying the new job?"

"Glad for a break, I can tell you," Grace frowned. "It's a drag today. Sheriff Thorn's wife died this morning, so everyone's in the dumps about that. It's sad and all, I know that, it's just..."
"You don't know what to say or do?" Cal offered.
"Yes! Exactly!"

194

"It's tough, I know," Cal said, looking back at the diner and the elderly couple coming out. Grace had that look on her face again. He could see it out of the corner of his eye. She wanted to ask, but wouldn't. Cal was starting to think, though, that there would come a time when her politeness and decorum would give way to curiosity.

For now, all she did was nod. Cal turned to her, taking in her every feature, thinking how different she was from Debbie. Debbie had been sweet, quiet until you got her excited and then she'd talk your ear off, and every bit a proper young woman. Cal loved her and thinking about her now hurt him inside in ways he couldn't even articulate to himself, but he could see Grace was different. His father would've called her a firecracker or a spitfire. She played at being proper and was so good at it when she needed to be, like at work, Cal guessed, but she smoked and spoke her mind like few girls he'd known. Part of him wanted to know what other vices besides than smoking she had. Debbie had had no vices Cal could remember.

And now Debbie was gone. Mr Bullock from down the street had murdered her.

The scene came again to Cal, clear and intense, of Bullock over her body.

Without warning, not even a dull throb of a headache, the grey, smoke-like world came forward. Cal stood up out of reflex, surprising Grace. He looked around, remembering the Shadow and the Ghost, but he didn't see either right now.

"Cal, what's wrong?" Grace asked.

"Nothing," he said. "It's a gorgeous day, isn't it?"

"Yes," she replied, a little hesitant. "Look, I'm sorry I brought up Mrs Thorn..."

"No," Cal cut in, "no, it's fine."

"I should get back to work," Grace said, packing up the remains of her lunch.

"Yeah, you don't want your dad to send out a search party," Cal said with a convincing smile. Grace stood up and took his hand. Cal felt a pang of guilt, mixed with sudden arousal, as he saw through her dress and the outline of her body beneath her clothes.

She gave him a peck on the cheek, took out a small piece of paper from her pocket and handed it to him, saying, "Call me tonight between 7 and 8!"

On the paper was her phone number.

Cal sat back down on the bench as she hurried to the Town Hall. He watched her, seeing her layered form through the grey vision as she went inside. For a moment he could see her through the doors, disappearing down the hallway. He pressed the sore, healing puncture on his hand and the pain forced the clouded other world of the grey vision to start to pull away. A sensation like a muscle relaxing accompanied the dissipation of the vision. In his mind, he tried to flex it and the greyness returned. He tried to relax it again and the vision began to pull back just a little, but stopped and reasserted itself. Cal jabbed the wound on his hand and concentrated, repeating the process. The grey world pulled back. He flexed that feeling in his mind once more and the grey world returned. He concentrated on relaxing it and the vision pulled back again, the smokiness seeping back into the shadows, but it took a lot of concentration and his head was pounding when his sight returned to normal.

It really is like a muscle, difficult to use if it's out of shape, Cal mused. Then he wondered, *Is this new or did I always have this ability?*

There was no way to know, so he put the question aside, got up from the bench and started walking. Cal thought he might head west, toward the river out that way. Melissa had mentioned once there was a trail that lead in that direction. Maybe today was a good day to find it.

Cal put Grace's phone number in his pocket, repeating it to himself, committing it to memory as he walked toward the west river.

* * *

As Tom Reed typed up the police report of the museum burglary, Peter Howard sat across from him, drumming his fingers on Reed's desk. It was distracting, but Red didn't want

196

to tell his friend to stop. The gloomy expression on Peter's face was like a storm brewing on a distant horizon. He was staring at the wall, sitting sideways to Reed. The man was taking the break-in very much to heart. Tom almost regretted having stolen the boxes himself.

Almost.

Reed stopped typing and looked at his friend.

"We'll get the archives back, Peter," Reed said.

"Did you know that in 1939, one of the WPA-funded projects in Orchard Bend was the renovation and expansion of the Town Hall?" Peter asked, seeming not to hear Reed. "The central feature of the old Town Hall was a grand assembly hall. It also served as a court house as needed. The expansion left very few obvious signs of the original building after it was completed, but if you look closely, you can see it all around. This part we're in with the Sheriff's Office came later, but the big columns in the main hall out there, those are original to the first Town Hall. The assembly hall held town meetings, dances, even the odd theatre production. The big staircase down at the other end is where the stage used to be."

"I didn't know that," Reed said, his gaze following Peter's.

"You should visit the museum more often," Peter replied. "I know I'm just about the only person in town who takes this stuff so seriously, but someone has to. It's too important to let the past fade off into oblivion entirely, don't you think?"

Peter was looking at Reed now and Reed nodded, turning back to him.

"Yes," Reed said. "I agree."

"It's a safe bet she was in the assembly hall during her lifetime," Peter said.

"Who?" Reed asked.

"Emery Dale," Peter said quietly. "Think about that when you walk through that hall. It was bigger back then, wider, but the columns are still as impressive as the day the hall first opened. I found a newspaper piece about that. No one was mentioned by name except Maxwell McCabe, who gave a speech. And the band from out of town that played, they're named, too, The

197

Blue Creek Family Jug Band. They were a big hit according to the article."

Peter went back to staring at the wall and drumming his fingers.

"When I get off work, I'll buy you drink over at Sully's, whaddaya say?" Reed offered.

Before Peter could answer, the Sheriff's Office door burst open. Lieutenant Pine strode into the room and went straight to Ruby Pressman at the radio room.

"Ruby, any responses to the all-point bulletin on Tyler Brand?" Pine asked.

"No, Lieutenant," Ruby replied. "Of course I'll tell you as soon as something comes in. I notified everyone from here to the city, as per your instructions."

"Thank you, Ruby," Pine said. He looked around at the faces watching him and spotted Peter Howard at Reed's desk. Pine marched past Reed's desk and said without looking at him, "Detective, join me in my office, please."

Reed looked at Howard, who was equally perplexed.

"I'll be right be back, Peter," Reed said.

He followed the lieutenant into his office and closed the door.

"What's the story with *him*?" Pine asked, nodding back at Peter.

"A burglary at the museum last night," Reed said. "I'm taking his report, but it seems a few boxes of archive material were stolen."

"Is that so?" Pine said, sitting behind his desk. "This happened last night?"

"Yes, sir," Reed said. "We don't know much beyond that. There's no apparent motive, seeing as valuable items were untouched and mainly documents were stolen. Newspaper clippings, that sort of thing. It'll all be in the report."

"Has Tyler Brand's name come up?" Pine asked.

"No, lieutenant," Reed said. "Do you think Brand broke into the museum, too? And if I may ask, who was the other burglary victim? If the two break-ins are related..."

Pine was deep in thought, leaning back in his chair. Reed waited. After a few long moments, Pine sat up.

"The situation is delicate, Detective," Pine said.

"Delicate? How so?"

"It requires discretion," Pine said. "Type up your report and give it to me. I have reason to suspect the two burglaries *are* related, so I'll take over your case."

"Ty Brand is a reporter," Reed protested. "I can't say I'm convinced he's behind the museum break in."

"Reed, I want your report on my desk by the end of the day," Pine said, looking the detective square in the eye. "Is that clear?"

"Yes, sir."

Pine nodded and Reed left the lieutenant's office. He took a few slow steps to his desk, stopped and hung his head, turning over what Pine had just revealed by mistake.

Brand is onto something, Reed deduced. *And they're after him. And Pine is McCabe's man inside the Sheriff's Office.*

Reed continued to his desk, Peter watching him, aware something was up.

"What's wrong?" Peter asked.

"I'm not sure," Reed lied. He was looking at the closed blinds of the lieutenant's office.

Pine probably also stole the Emery Dale crime scene evidence, Reed thought.

He knew now he had to find Tyler Brand before The Barber did.

20

April 19, 1886
Orchard Bend

Ever since construction began on the new Town Hall, Sheriff Anderson could find no peace at the jailhouse. Eventually, he resolved to spend as little time there as possible. Sully's became his defacto office. Deputy Wilson made he wise-crack that the real reason he'd set himself up there was to have a few drinks. Anderson didn't drink while on the job, except coffee. He ignored the ribbing, but he *did* notice a habit of buying his meals more often than he brought a lunch, so a small toll was taken on his pocketbook. Anderson figured the expense was worth his sanity.

It was quieter than most days that Monday. The sheriff sat at his usual table, a cup of coffee black and hot next to a copy of the Orchard Herald. It was almost redundant for Anderson to read the paper, because he knew so much of the town business before the Herald reported it. Staring down the barrel of sixty years on God's green earth, James Anderson was not lax in his duty and he prided himself on it. Know the patterns of the town. Know the comings, the goings, births, deaths, reaping, sowing and everything in between and you'll better spot trouble coming. Sure, there were wild cards in the deck, like Emery Dale, the Underwood Gang and Marshal Saunders, but they only served as a lesson to stay vigilant and keep a keen eye on anything irregular.

That keen eye was watching a young man in Sully's who was nursing a drink. Something in the man's face was familiar and Anderson was trying to place it. He was no older than twenty years if Anderson had to guess. And he was not from these parts.

The man saw Anderson watching him, smiled and raised his pint.

"Sheriff," the man said, as if to toast him, and took a swallow. Anderson didn't acknowledge the gesture, but still watched the stranger. He noted the dust on the stranger's pants and how he had stretched his legs and adjusted his back, the way a man does after a long ride on a horse. He had no gun belt, but maybe he'd followed the town ordinance and left it at the jailhouse with Wilson.

Maybe.

Anderson eyed the man for a few more moments and then looked down at the newspaper again. Birth notices and death notices spelled out plain before him.

At 9:45 yesterday evening Ms Winifred Bartel was called into the golden hereafter, following a sudden onset of pneumonia four days agone. Dr. Alfred Shaw had previously tended to Ms Bartel and all that could be done was done. In her 79th year, Ms Bartel had not married and is survived by her cousin, Mrs P. Norton.

A boy was born to the wife of Mr. J. McMillan yesterday.

It is with regret that this newspaper offers a late report of the death of Mr. Stephen Campbell on April 16th at twenty minutes to 6 o'clock in the evening, following the unfortunate accidental discharge of his rifle at his home. Witness to the event was his eldest son, Walter. Mr. Campbell succumbed to his fatal injuries less than an hour after the accident. Campbell was predeceased by his wife two years previous and is survived only by young Master Walter.

Anderson had investigated that last one, Campbell shooting himself by accident. The boy, Walter, was broken up and close to incoherence. What Anderson got out of him was that the rifle had been loaded while on the mantle and when the elder

Campbell had taken it down, it had gone off, shooting him in the stomach. The Campbell farm was northwest of town and Walter had tried to drive his father in their wagon to get help, but the man was dead when they reached Dr Shaw. Buchanan had wanted to run an entire story about the incident, but Shaw had pressed him not to. Anderson heard that Shaw threatened to break the Hippocratic Oath and Buchanan's jaw if the Herald editor printed one sensational word of the story. In the end, both parties eventually agreed upon this late report. Young Walter, 15 years old, was staying with the Langfords for the time being.

Anderson looked up from the Herald and watched the man take another sip of his beer, that familiarity tugging harder at him now.

Births and deaths, Anderson thought and sipped his coffee.

The idea came to him to check the Wanted posters and notices. Being sheriff, Anderson tried to keep current on such things and while this man didn't seem to fit any of the current reports, maybe he'd missed something.

Anderson finished his coffee in a single swallow, got up and walked to the door. The man at the bar glanced at him, then went back to his beer. Anderson left Sully's and stepped up his pace to the jailhouse. Wilson was at the sheriff's desk, reading a dime novel. He didn't look up as Anderson came in.

"Boss, you're not gonna believe this book I'm reading," Wilson said. "There's this stage coach driver fella, this guy who everyone knows all up and down the length of California. He's named 'One-Eyed Charlie' and he dies. When the undertaker's preparing the body, it turns out Charlie is a *woman*."

Anderson was looking at the wall of Wanted posters, notices and warrants. He examined each, tuning out Wilson for the most part. Wilson noticed and asked, "What's going on, boss?"

"Maybe something," Anderson said low, "Maybe nothing. Anyone from out of town deposit their gun here today?"

"No," Wilson said, putting the book down and joining Anderson at the poster display. "You think one of these fellas is in Orchard Bend?"

Anderson looked grim, examining one image at a time before moving to the next, sometimes going back to look at a previous face.

"Saw a man lookin' a might familiar," the Sheriff said. "Doesn't look like any of these, though."

"Who is it?" Wilson asked. "I could go take a look. Fresh pair of eyes."

"Not a bad idea," Anderson nodded. "Young man, not a day over twenty, I'd reckon, over at Sully's having a drink. Scruffy, thin beard. If he's still there, you'll spot him. If he's someone we want to keep our eye on, don't let on you're there to have a look-see, got it?"

"Yeah, boss, I got it. Don't spook the squirrel," Wilson said and left the jailhouse.

Anderson stood back, rubbed his eyes and wondered if it was his imagination. Maybe the fella at Sully's was just passing through, looking to have a drink, or maybe he had legitimate business in town. Anderson considered perhaps he was getting a bit old for this job, jumping at shadows. Could be, but the fact remained that this man reminded him of someone, someone Anderson couldn't place, and the sheriff couldn't let that go.

Wilson came back a few minutes later.

"Whoever it was is gone, boss," the deputy said. "Irene said he finished his beer and vacated right after you. Did you get to figuring who he was?"

"No," Anderson said. "I'm gonna go do my rounds and see what there is to see. Take up a chair outside and keep your eyes open."

* * *

Emery Dale rode back to Orchard Bend from the Campbell farm. The thick, grey clouds settled over the county and the wind picked up. Sudden rain storms were frequent this time of year. Dale had dressed for the seasonable chill in her long, black duster. She pulled the stampede string of her hat tight under her chin and slipped on her gloves.

Dale had to check on the Campbell farm, that everything was locked up and that the Montgomerys were tending to the livestock. The Campbells' team of horses were at the Statler livery in town, but the cows, chickens and other animals needed to be fed and cared for. The Montgomery family, whose farm neighboured the Campbells, had agreed to do so. Both the Campbell farm and the Montgomery farm were owned by Maxwell McCabe. So McCabe, in a grand gesture of goodwill, had agreed to pay the Montgomerys a small fee to tend to the Campbell farm. It was a short-term solution. Soon, it would have to be decided what to do with the Campbell farm with no family living there. The boy, Walter, was too young to handle the farm on his own. His future was just as much a question mark right now.

As the town's buildings rose up before her, Dale set her thoughts of the unfortunate situation aside. A home-cooked meal awaited her at Rose's cottage tonight. The thought of an evening with Rose, listening to the soft clatter of rain on the roof, took some of the cold from the air around her.

The grey, almost shadow-less light of the early evening cast an eerie tone on Main Street as Dale arrived in Orchard Bend. The work on the new Town Hall had stopped for the day, but the quiet went deeper than that. Everything told her something was wrong. Dale tied her horse at the Statlers', but couldn't find either brother there. Across the street, a *Closed* sign hung in the Reed's General Store & Feed window. Dale adjusted her gun belts and felt the reassuring weight of the knives harnessed under each arm. She walked past the jailhouse and tried the door. It was locked. She knocked and there was no answer. Peering into the window she saw no one inside. In fact, she'd seen no one since arriving in town.

Dale hastened to Sully's, where raised voices replaced the usual piano-scored rowdiness of the saloon. When she reached the door, she found Deputy Wilson speaking to a group of townsfolk, including the Statlers, Mary Reed and others.

"...going to be fine, that's what Doc Shaw just said, ain't that right, Mrs Reed?" Wilson asked.

"Yes."

"We don't know what business they have with Sheriff Anderson, but there's been no ransom and no demands," Wilson continued. "But we have to find these bandits and bring them to justice. Men, consider yourselves deputized. Mrs Reed, you should go back and tell Doc Shaw that he may have more work to do tonight if the Sheriff is hurt."

"Or if we find those pissants," said a voice from the crowd.

"If we can take them alive, more's the better," Wilson said, "especially if they don't have the sheriff with them. But if they start shooting, you shoot back, got it?"

"You don't need to remind me of that, Wilson," said the same man. Dale saw it was Seamus O'Toole. His son, Sam, stood next to him. At eighteen years old, Sam stood broad-shouldered but nervous, with a shotgun in his hand. There were murmurs of agreement at Seamus's remark and Dale pushed through the group to Wilson.

"What's happening?" Dale asked the deputy.

"The sheriff was onto a fella in town this afternoon. Just after the school let out, the Ramsay boy, Wendell, happens upon three men in the alley behind the picture studio," Wilson explained. "They had the Sheriff bound and gagged, Wendell says. One of them rings the boy's bell good and when he wakes up, the men and the sheriff are gone. No one else has set eyes on them. We're about to send out parties to search the area." Wilson lowered his voice and said, "In all honesty, and in the strictest confidence, I couldn't be happier to see you, Ms Dale. I warrant you have more experience in matters of crisis than I do, so I would value your reckoning of the state of things."

"What time did Wendell see the men with the sheriff?" Dale asked.

"School's out at three o'clock sharp. You could set your watch by Miss Adelaide," Wilson said. Emery knew that to be true. Dale would've smiled if the moment wasn't so urgent. Wilson went on, "I'd figure no more than fifteen minutes after that the boy was knocked unconscious. He came to and Mrs Reed spotted him and took him straight to Dr Shaw. It's now a little after five o'clock and I fear we're losing daylight if we're going to search."

He doesn't realize it, Dale thought, *but Wilson's waiting on my assurance that he's making the right call.*

"And we know nothing about these men?" Dale asked.

"Near as anyone can figure, no. Sheriff Anderson thought he recognized one of them here in the saloon and was looking at the Wanted posts, but this fella wasn't among them," Wilson said.

Dale nodded.

"Send out your search parties, but there's no telling what they'll find, if anything," Dale said.

Wilson's expression told her that she'd just put a voice to his doubts and fears, but he steeled himself and turned to back to men to split them off into search parties.

"...And Seamus and Sammy, you're with me," Wilson finished.

Dale took his arm.

"No, Wilson," Dale said quietly.

"I beg your pardon?" Wilson said.

"You're the Acting Sheriff with Anderson gone, maybe even dead," Dale explained. "You have to stay here to coordinate the search, otherwise there will be chaos and you're unlikely to find him that way."

"But I can't—!"

"You have to, Deputy," Dale said, her voice stern.

I was a major once in my past life, she thought, *I'm sure I gave orders to plenty of men and women.*

Wilson's internal struggle between his duty and his desire to search showed on his face, but he shrugged, turned to the men and sent the search parties out without him. Irene and Sully himself stood behind the bar, his arm around his daughter. Dale couldn't remember the last time the saloon had been so quiet. Wilson went to Mary Reed and told her to stay with Wendell until his parents arrived. That done, Wilson stood alone in the middle of the room, hands on his hips and visibly uncertain what to do next. Dale went to him.

"Okay, Deputy, take me to where the boy saw the men," she said.

When Emery hurried into the cottage, she found Rose at the dining table.

"Emery! My goodness, did you hear?" the school-teacher exclaimed.

"Yes," Emery said, going to her. "I was just with Wilson. They're organizing search parties. I hope you understand that I need to help."

"Yes, most definitely you should," Rose said. She took Emery's hand, squeezing it in both of hers. "Just promise me you'll be careful."

"I will," Dale smiled. Rose's eyes were glistening and worry lined her face. Dale gave her a kiss and turned to leave the cottage, pausing for just a moment at the door.

Outside, Dale's duster flitted in the sharp gusts of wind. She wished she had her sword with her, but it was locked at her cabin by the ravine and there was no time to retrieve it. Over the years she'd gotten out of the habit of carrying it everywhere she went. She was reconsidering the habit now.

Dale made her way back to the alley behind the photography studio. According to Wilson, it was here where the boy saw the men take Sheriff Anderson. There were drops of blood and boot prints. The boy said there were three men and the sheriff bound and gagged. They would not be moving too fast with a captive. Dale did not consider herself much of a tracker, but it was clear they led the Sheriff out of the alley away from Main Street. Wilson had come to the same conclusion. At the far end of the alley, the tracks faded into the general disarray of the traffic on Church Street. After Wilson showed her this, Dale had sent him back to Sully's to oversee the search. She then went to Rose's cottage. Back now, without an anxious deputy hovering over her, Dale could consider the pattern in the dirt with greater attention. The dull, grey light didn't help. It flattened the footprints and made them harder to detect, but Dale could still make them out.

Dale tried to picture what had happened.

One of the men had come up behind the boy, Wendell Ramsay. He fell right here. There are blood drops to mark the spot. And a handprint, too small for a grown man.

While much of the dirt was an almost indecipherable map of prints, Dale picked out more details.

The man who knocked Wendell cold proceeded to step over him, leaving this deep boot print as he did so.

Dale followed that footprint as it joined the others and then saw something unusual.

One of the kidnappers broke off from the group.

The tracks lead to a door, the only door in the alley, and it belonged to Jackson Picture Studio. Dale tested the door of the photography business and found it locked. She looked at the path of the prints on the ground again and there was little doubt in her mind.

One of the kidnappers went inside.

She drew her gun.

This man might be waiting on the other side, with a gun of his own trained on the door. The photographer, Jackson, might even be a hostage.

The door looked sturdy, but Dale knew the real test was the frame. She suspected it would give with a hard enough kick. She took off her hat and let it hang on her back. Drawing a deep breath, she reared back and fired a kick at the door near the handle. It gave way with a sharp crack of splintering wood. Almost in the same motion, Dale pivoted and ducked away from the door in case anyone inside opened fire. No one did. She levelled her gun and had a quick look inside, taking in as much as she could. The room beyond was small, littered with props, drapery and a desk with papers lit by an oil lamp. She entered the office low, gun and eyes scanning for targets. Across the room, open curtains hung in the doorway which separated the office from the shadowy room beyond.

Dale crept forward. As she did, she saw the legs and feet of a body on the floor. Moving closer, Dale saw the body of Jackson himself, two bullet holes in his chest.

One of the kidnappers definitely came through here.

Dale slipped into the room, almost firing on the full-length mirror reflecting her dark form in the corner. Dale grabbed the mirror. Ahead of her was another doorway, this one covered in strings of beads which were drawn open. Dale rolled the mirror forward, positioning it in the corner opposite the open door to the next room. It afforded her a quick glimpse into the full studio beyond. Though the curtains were drawn closed, soft, pale light streamed in. She could see no one, but there was a blind corner. With another deep breath, Dale came around through the door and dropped to a knee, scanning the room.

No one there.

Dale stood up and holstered her weapon.

That's when the blinding flash went off, followed by the cocking of a gun. Dale's hands went to her own guns and drew them. The sharp report of a bullet cut the air near her ear. Dale couldn't see anything. Pulsing white shapes from the flash flooded her sight. She fired four rounds in the direction of her assailant. She heard feet scuffle on her left.

He was hiding in the shadows of the drapes by the window. I couldn't see him!

She cursed herself for being so stupid.

Another round whizzed past her ear and she fired twice more herself. Dale's assailant bolted past her. Still fighting the blurry afterimage of the flash, she fired again at the fleeing man and shattered the mirror in the next room. Her assailant's footfalls told her he was heading out the back to the alley. She followed, but stopped as she reached the rear office. Until her sight improved it would be foolhardy to pursue the man. She reloaded her guns. It felt like precious seconds were passing, but Dale knew she had to let her sight clear. As she slid the last round into the chamber, the flash's afterimage fogging her vision was no more than a faint green and red discolouration. She could wait no longer.

Determining it was clear, Dale followed the fresh tracks toward Church Street. Dale stopped where the alley met the street and wondered if she should go back to Sully's and get help. She weighed the pros and cons. Getting some backup would be helpful, but the trail could run cold. Her assailant would most likely make a mistake as he fled in haste.

She decided to press on after him.

Dale stepped onto the boardwalk. Like Main Street, Church Street was also deserted. Wilson had ordered everyone indoors. Assuming the townsfolk followed his orders, there were fewer places for the kidnappers to hide now.

Dale caught movement from one of the windows of *The Harvest Moon* hotel. Someone was waving at her. It was the hotel's owner, Bartholomew Trask. He pointed down the street, emphatic. Dale thought she understood.

The man she pursued fled that way.

Dale pointed in the same direction and Trask nodded.

Dale nodded back and Trask waved a hand before drawing the blinds closed. Dale guessed Trask was still peering through the blinds, still watching everything happening on the street. She reckoned he probably wasn't the only one.

Trying to stay ready for any sudden move against her, Dale didn't expect to see Sheriff Anderson running in her direction. He came from the narrow alleyway near the millinery. Blood covered his hands and the side of is head. The crimson stained his shirt in an ugly patch that covered most of his shoulder.

"Dale!" he called out, his voice clear and urgent.

Behind him, from the same alley across the street, appeared a man raising a gun. Dale raised hers. Whether the sheriff thought she would shoot him or whether he simply stumbled from the blow to his head she didn't know. As Dale brought her own weapon up to fire, Anderson jerked to his right and blocked her shot. The man in the alley fired and red blood sprayed from the sheriff's stomach. Anderson dropped to his knees looking at the exit hole in his gut as if it wasn't real. Dale fired at the assailant, her line of sight clear as Anderson dropped down. The shot hit the wall inches from the man's body, splintering the wood. His next shot went past Dale and a window shattered behind her. She fired again, missed her target and brought up her second gun, levelling both at him. Before she could fire, a second man appeared next to the first, coming out of the alley and charging towards her. On pure instinct she targeted the charging man, who swore to end the son of a bitch who'd killed his brother. This man fired wild and reckless at Anderson, now crouched and clutching his gut. The charging man seemed to not notice or care about Dale. Dale fired three rounds and two hit their mark. The man fell to the dirt on his back, gasping.

The first man fired again and hit Anderson in the back before disappearing down the alley. The Sheriff jerked upright and looked at Dale.

"He's here for you," Anderson said and fell onto his back, squirming. Dale was at his side in an instant and he grabbed her duster, pulling her close. He uttered one word:

"Underwood."

Blood gushed from his mouth as he gurgled out his death rattle.

Emery Dale rose to her feet under the leaden afternoon sky, a gun in each hand, her duster fluttering in the wind.

* * *

Beyond the alley, past the millinery, Emery Dale came to the building site of Orchard Bend's Town Hall. The foundation and basement were finished and the single ground floor was well under way. Masons had begun laying the brick walls.

There was no tension in Dale now, no anxiety or worry, just efficiency and purpose. She was a killing machine and there was no doubt some killing needed to be done this day.

The body of a man bludgeoned with a hammer lay sprawled on the ground next to the construction site. It wasn't the man Dale was after, nor was it any of the townsfolk she recognized.

Anderson killed him to get away, she thought. *Some of the blood he was covered in belonged to this man.*

Three men now reduced to one.

The dead man's holster was empty and Dale had to assume the last man had it.

A shadow moved inside the Town Hall. The crack of a fired round made Dale duck behind a stack of lumber. She had his position now and could track him, so wasted no time, not even

211

pausing behind the wood. She moved in a crouch away from him, along the length of the lumber pile. She circled around and arrived at the partially completed brick wall. Dale paused and listened. The wind gave a deathly howl through the open, unfinished spaces of the building. After a few seconds it died down. There came a soft creak, the shifting of the hard soles on wood. She moved again, dashing the length of the brick wall. At the door frame, Dale slipped inside.

The smell of sawdust was heavy. Shrieks of wind through the rafters masked her footsteps. Dale was quite aware that the movements of the man she hunted were masked, too. Around her was a jigsaw puzzle of deepening shadows in grey light, cast from the incomplete walls. Frames of the lesser chambers and rooms surrounded the great hall itself, with its massive wooden columns. There was no roof yet, just a canopy of darkening clouds.

Movement to her right.

Dale pivoted around. One of the shadows fired and grazed the wooden support to her left. She ducked and retreated into a dark, unfinished room. A wheelbarrow sat propped against the wooden frame walls. Dale holstered her guns and slipped out of her duster. Two rounds from her opponent hit the barrow, but she was again already moving, sliding between the walls' studs. She unsheathed one of her knives. It felt good in her grip, lighter than her gun, almost an extension of her hand.

In the next room now, Dale saw her target, but instead of striking, she circled him. He saw her approach, but mistook her trajectory. When he fired, the bullet hit the floor behind her.

Then she was on him, driving the knife up and into his back. The man struck out with a wild fist that caught Dale in the cheek and unbalanced her. She hit the floor and rolled, her right hand drawing and shooting from the hip. The man levelled one of his guns at her and they fired at almost the same time. Dale's shot hit the man's shoulder. His shot tore the flesh of her right bicep. She wanted to fire again, but the arm felt both numb and on fire, her fingers no longer responding to orders from her brain. The next second, the arm dropped limp at her side.

The man's wounded shoulder did not slow him. He was taking aim as her left hand went for her other knife. Like the deciding moment seven years before, in the McCabe barn with Saunders, Dale hoped she would be fast enough. The knife left her hand and drove itself into his upper stomach, just below the solar plexus. He fired and her leg burned as the shot grazed it between the holster and her knee.

The man stumbled back against the nearest column and still he took aim. Her wounded arm felt useless. Her grazed leg was on fire, but that pain was distant. Adrenalin poured through her. Dale moved without consciously choosing to, her mind in survival mode to get her out of the line of fire, to kill this man trying to kill her. Even as she moved, her left hand drew her remaining gun. The man fired and missed. So did she. Her movements were staggered and clumsy in her injured state. Dale collapsed sideways onto a stack of wood. She fired again, hitting his leg. She aimed for his heart, the killing shot, and pulled the trigger.

There was only a click.

He was bringing his gun to bear on her and she pulled the trigger again.

Click.

This is it, then, Dale thought. *He'll die from his wounds, but he's taking me with him.*

She was in his sights now and he grinned through the blood and hate on his face.

A thunderous boom exploded. The man's chest shredded as he dropped from the column to the floor.

Dale blinked in surprise.

Voices called her name, but they came from somewhere that seemed far away. She focused on the man lying dead on the floor before her. Dale forced herself up and there was such a mixture of pain from her wounds that she felt close to passing out. The darkness swirled around her vision, but she dropped to her knees next to the kidnapper, her assailant, looking hard at his face.

"Underwood," Dale said, recognizing the man's features.

213

It's almost uncanny, she thought. *He looks so much like Ernest Underwood, only younger. He's got to be Ernest's son. Or maybe his nephew, but probably his son.*

A hand took her shoulder and there were more voices.

"Miss Dale...!"

"Dad, is she alright?"

"Stay back, Sammy. Keep that shotgun on him. Miss Dale, can you hear me?"

She looked up and saw Seamus O'Toole. Past him was Sammy, his shotgun aimed at the body on the floor next to her.

And there was someone else there, some*thing* else.

The dark figure she'd seen in the McCabe study, all those years before, now stood over the body. Dale could make out arms, legs and hands through the swirling smoke of the Prisoner. In the study of the McCabe house, this person had been little more than a shadow, but now it was more distinct, with a face she could almost make out, even with its gaping black holes for eyes.

"I know you," Dale said to the Prisoner.

Major, it's me, the Prisoner said.

Emery Dale lost what little balance she had and sank into darkness herself.

21

June 12, 1953
Orchard Bend

The sun was low in the sky, casting deep shadows as they criss-crossed the dirt path. The disused bridge west of town was overgrown with vegetation. Cal had walked far after his lunch with Grace. He'd been following the road, but turned onto the narrow dirt path until it reached the bridge in the ravine. Cal kept his eyes open for "No Trespassing" signs, but saw none. It was a public road, just one now long out of use.

On the bridge, Cal picked up a stone and tossed it into the rippling water below. He thought of Grace and her roguish smile. He was happy. Cal knew sooner or later he'd have to tell her what happened to his family. The happy feeling fell away with a chill. He picked up a rock. With some anger, he launched one into the trees. It hit with a loud *crack* and landed in the underbrush.

Cal made ready to throw another. He wanted to see how far down the river he could fire it, but screaming pain lit up his hand. A stone had struck it, tearing the flesh. He doubled over in pain as a voice spoke.

"Did you *see* that? A one in a million throw!" Terry said.

Cal looked up to see Grace's ex-boyfriend and two of his buddies walking down the hill toward him. one had brown hair and the other bright, curly red. Cal clutched his bloody, swollen hand.

"And I wasn't even aiming for his hand, imagine that! I thought I'd just graze his stomach or something," Terry laughed, adjust his horn-rimmed glasses.

Cal looked at the three of them, muscled from years of farm work, and knew trying to take them on would be foolish. Trying to reason with Terry seemed a long shot, too. Had Terry followed him here? It seemed likely. Terry might have seen him walking and waited for his chance. Or worse (and Cal didn't put it past the jealous ex), Terry might have seen him having lunch with Grace. How perfect was it that Cal had come to this secluded spot?

Cal looked around.

"No one's here, shit for brains," Terry chided.

Cal looked at him, already feeling dizzy with shock from the pain in his hand. He could feel the blood pouring out of the wound. Cal smiled and Terry stopped, his own grin uncertain.

Cal charged and Terry and his friends backed away, startled. However, Cal wasn't charging *them*. Instead, he made for the edge of the bridge and launched himself from the small lip. When he hit the ground, he landed in the mess of mud, rocks and scrubby brush along the shore below. His bloody hand drove into the cold mud with a surge of pain. One foot landed on a rock jutting out from the earth, but it gave way under his weight. If it hadn't, he knew he'd probably have twisted his ankle. The landing was hard enough, though, and his momentum caused him to roll forward and onto his back. He scrambled up the bank. He saw the wound on his hand was a bloody gash, smaller than he thought it would be, though still pretty ugly.

Terry and his friends were shouting obscenities and moving to pursue him, running to the where the bridge met the land.

Not going to jump after me, huh? Cal thought. *Good. I get a head start.*

He ran along the edge of the water, following what seemed like an old path. He could hear the taunts and heavy footfalls well behind him.

At the stone foundation of a long-gone building, Cal turned and looked back. Terry and his friends were about twenty yards back up the path. Cal ran around the side of the foundation, hoping he could double back if his pursuers ran past him. He ducked down, his legs burning from the sudden work-out. His wounded hand still bled, but not so as bad as before. It was a mixture of every possible pain Cal thought he could feel: throbbing, aching, stinging and sharp jolts that made him want to cry out. He glanced at the path and saw the trio slow down at the clearing. He ducked down, now panicked that he would not get the chance to double back. He cast about for a weapon. Anything would do, a big stick, something to maybe show that what they had in mind for him wasn't worth the effort.

But there was nothing useful around.

Large branches from the storm the month before littered the area, and he considered trying to rip off a length of one, but it would take too much time.

Cal looked back, heard the trio, but couldn't see them. There were clusters of trees and undergrowth and he guessed they were making sure he hadn't continued down the path. If only he could see where they were, he might be able to make a break for it...

Cal almost laughed as he remembered the grey vision, then for an awful moment forgot how to bring that view into focus.

It was like flexing a muscle in my mind, he thought, and then he felt it again. Cal focused and flexed and the world went grey. Through the trees not far from him he saw Terry and the others milling about, looking for him. They'd find him soon if he didn't move on from his hiding place.

Turning from the boys, Cal was so startled by the Ghost watching him that he almost swore out loud.

As before, the Ghost was little more than a swirling form of white against the grey world around them both, but Cal could see her face, her dark hair and the outline of her body. She looked at him with no real expression, but he thought she seemed concerned.

Not knowing what else to do, Cal mouthed the word, "Help."

The Ghost turned and looked toward a grove of aspens up ahead, then turned back to him. Cal nodded in that direction and the Ghost hung there motionless for a few moments before half turning to the grove once more. She gave another nod. Cal fled in that direction. He hoped to find something there to help him. He didn't think she could simply lead Terry's group away as she'd done with the Shadow the night before.

He ran to the grove and after a few yards heard one of Terry's friends call out, "There he is!"

With no real path to follow, Cal dodged and wended his way between the trees, hoping the Ghost was really aiding him somehow. Even with the grey vision, he couldn't see how this route was better than making a run for the road.

When he saw the second Ghost he stopped. Terry and his friends were not far behind, weaving through the aspens. Where the first Ghost had dark hair and was about his height, this second Ghost was taller. Her smoke-like body was thin and willowy, her hair light. She stood next to a tree with a carving in it, that of a flower. This Ghost's expression was impassive, but her eyes were clear and intense.

"Help me!" Cal said to her out loud, breathing hard. He knew he could try running further, but Terry and his friends would catch him. What little ground he had ahead of them was all but gone. He'd make it twenty yards, maybe thirty, but they'd catch him. The blonde Ghost looked at him but made no move to do anything. Cal growled in frustration and looked at his feet for something to fight with. He found a good sized stone and he thought that would have to do. He turned, letting the grey vision fade and his sight returned to normal. Terry was ten feet away and striding slow toward him, his friends spread out, flanking their prey. Cal raised the stone, holding it with his bloody, wounded throwing hand.

"Done running, rabbit?" Terry said.

Cal then noticed the other carving, on the tree opposite the one with the flower. It was the "L" and "P" symbol like on the broach in his pocket.

"What? Got nothin' to say, tough guy?" Terry taunted.

"Thinks he's gonna scare us off with a rock," his friend with the red hair chuckled.

The carving looked like it had been there a long time, almost as long as the weathered tree itself. The symbol made Cal think of his mother. Fear slipped away, replaced with such anger it was a barely tethered rage.

218

Terry was only a few feet from him when he told his buddies, "Grab him."

Cal was about to spin and fire the stone at the red-haired assailant, but there came a sudden movement behind Terry. A harsh, cold voice said, "Stop."

The stranger had a knife to Terry's throat. Terry's friends stopped advancing on Cal and froze in place.

"What were you going to do to this boy?" the stranger asked, sounding very amused. "Beat him to within an inch of his life? Kill him? Hope no one would find his body out here?"

It took a moment for Cal to get over his surprise. It was *her*, the mystery woman he'd seen at the bench and at the train tracks the day before. She was here now, saving him.

"Cat got your tongue, big guy?" the woman asked.

"We, uh, we don't want any trouble," said the brown-haired friend. "We were just messing around with this guy."

"Is that so?" she replied, then asked Terry, "That true? You were just messing with this kid? Giving him a scare?"

Terry grunted, nudging his head only as much as he dared with a knife to his throat.

The woman nodded to Cal and said, "Well, he's a friend of mine, see, and I don't appreciate my friends getting beaten on. I think you can understand that. Do you? You understand what it is I'm telling you?"

Terry nodded again and forced out a gasp of, "Yes. Yes, I understand."

The knife was gone from Terry's throat in an instant and the woman stepped back, shoving him away. His friends backed off, now completely unnerved. Cal still had the stone in his hand, ready to hurl it at one of them.

"Go," the woman ordered.

Terry looked at her, then his buddies, and backed away. He sent a glare of fear and hate at Cal. He and the woman watched the three leave.

"Thank you," Cal said, at last lowering the stone and letting it drop to the ground.

219

"You're welcome," she replied. Cal examined his wounded hand. It was bleeding again. "You'll want a doctor to look at that, but I can field dress it until you get back to town."

She led him the short distance to her camp. It was little more than a cold campfire, a small rolled up sleeping bag and her pack. She produced a first aid kit and set to work.

"Thank you," Cal said again.

"You already thanked me. Once was enough," she said.

"I saw you yesterday," Cal said, "at the park next to the Town Hall. And before that, by the train tracks."

The woman nodded, but took her time treating his hand before replying. She cleaned the wound of the dirt and much of the dried blood.

"I walked here along the tracks," she said. "Why were those boys chasing you?"

"A misunderstanding. I met his ex-girlfriend last night and he's not happy about that," Cal explained. He winced as she wrapped the dressing around the gash. The pain made him think of the broach and its strange symbol, the same one as on the tree. What did it mean? There were so many questions and Cal didn't know where to start nor even how to ask any of them without sounding delusional. The Ghost had pointed him here and this woman had saved him. Cal wondered if the Ghosts were around, so brought the grey vision back to his sight.

The dark-haired Ghost skipped through the aspens nearby. Cal thought of the Shadow and what its relationship was to the Ghosts, if there was one. Did they know each other and if so, how?

The Ghost interrupted her playful dance when she reached the tree with the flower carved in it. She stood motionless for a moment looking at it, head tilted to the side, before continuing her frolic.

It's a rose, I think, Cal thought. *The carving in the tree is of a rose.*

The taller, blonde Ghost approached the campsite and stood over the mystery woman's shoulder. The Ghost looking at her with such intense focus, yet such a dead expression, that Cal was for a moment taken aback, jerking himself away as he did.

The woman looked up at Cal, who was looking past her. She spun around, no doubt expecting to see Terry and his thugs had returned to finish the job. Seeing nothing, she asked, "What is it? What do you see?"

Cal looked at her, seeing her skull and teeth and eyeballs under her skin, but still reading her expression. How could he explain what he was seeing, he wondered?

She then asked, "Is it a ghost?"

Cal stammered, "Yes. She's right behind you. She's looking at you."

"It's this place. Lost souls gather here," the woman said. "I think there might be two of them. I've caught glimpses, quickly and out of the corner of my eye."

"I can see them," Cal said. "I know that sounds utterly nuts, but—!"

"I believe you," she said.

"You do?"

"Yes. I've seen some odd things in my life, so yes, I believe you can see them," the woman said as she bound the dressing.

"But I couldn't see them before yesterday, before I saw you," Cal said. "Did you do something to me? To my sight?"

"No," the woman said. "I don't have any magical powers. *You* might if you can see ghosts, but I don't."

Cal sat disappointed. If this woman wasn't responsible for giving him the grey vision, who or what was? He let his sight transition back to the real world.

She finished dressing his wound, which throbbed and stabbed his hand.

"Don't try to make a fist and avoid using the hand if you can. And go see a doctor. You don't want an infection," she ordered as she stood up. Cal rose and stuck out his good hand.

"Thanks," he said. "My name is Cal. Cal Watson."

She took his hand and gave it a firm shake.

"Good to meet you, Cal. I'm Mara Dale."

* * *

221

July 14, 1946
Orchard Bend

In the ravine that hot summer day, Gabby turned from the odd "L" and "P" carving to see a pale shape of a person standing before her. There was no time even for fear as the smoke-like figure reached out to her. She heard the whisper of a voice in her mind.

I'm not going to hurt you, the woman said. And Gabby was certain this *ghost* was a woman. The voice was soft, gentle, almost delicate, like a strong breeze would carry it away. There was a beauty in it that made Gabby relax.

As the Ghost's hand caressed her cheek, images and thoughts came to her mind. They were fragmented, but one recurred over and over. A face. A woman's face, with plain but pretty features and intelligent eyes.

You loved her, didn't you? Gabby asked.

Another image came, this one clear and distinct.

A rose.

If anyone had seen Gabby in the ravine, they would have witnessed the girl standing motionless. They might have wondered if she was in a trance. If they looked even harder, they would have seen the wispy blonde Ghost next to her. Without looking, Gabby reached into the pocket of her shorts and produced her father's pocket knife. She unfolded it and began to carve the rose into the aspen opposite the one bearing the "L" and "P" symbol. The two images would face each other. The operation took just under two hours and when she was done, Gabby stepped back, not to admire her work, since her conscious thoughts were elsewhere. She folded up the knife, returned it to her pocket, lay on the ground and closed her eyes.

The willowy blonde Ghost watched her do this and knelt next to her.

Thank you, the Ghost said.

Gabby smiled in her sleep.

222

22

Date Unknown
A Ravine

The rain woke Rateliff up. He was lying on his side. His feet and legs were cold. The steady drops of water on his cheek brought his mind out of the black unconsciousness. There had been gunplay, yelling, an explosion of some kind. His sidearm was still in his hand. Rateliff sat up, confused. The setting sun broke through the clouds and lit up the rain around him. It was very pretty, but he didn't pay much attention. He'd been in an underground facility in a city...

Which one, which city?

The name wouldn't come to him, but he could picture it. The streetlights. The traffic. Bright electric signs everywhere. And now he was here, lying on the muddy bank of a river. The rain was warm, but the river water soaking his legs was not. He climb up the bank and stood in the small clearing. The rain had slowed to a light trickle.

"Hello?" Rateliff called out.

There was no answer, only the sound of the breeze moving through the ravine. He holstered his weapon and sat on a large rock.

"Byron Rateliff, Tech Sergeant," he said aloud. "That's my name. I went to Bradshaw High School. I took Suzy Westmore to the prom. Afterwards, we..."

He smiled as he trailed off.

Then more memories came to him.

"The Major told us to fire," he said. He could see it all in his mind's eye, scientists in lab coats ducking behind desks. His team was hand-picked by the Major herself for this job. They fired without hesitation, himself included.

Only that wasn't exact right, was it?

"No," he said. "We weren't shooting at the scientists. We needed them. We were shot at..."

He trailed off again, seeing the rounds from his gun tear into the soldiers assigned to guard the facility. There had been a change, a big one, at the highest levels of the government. The President was dead, assassinated. That had started something, or... or had it just been a symptom? Rateliff couldn't remember exactly. Details were fractured, but he remembered the facility well and why he'd been selected. He was a scientist in his way as well as a soldier. His tech specialty was engineering, power systems and computers.

"The Major needed me to sort through what precisely was set up in the lab and to be able to control it," Rateliff said. The rain had stopped. Sunlight was pouring in over the trees, but the sky above was still full of clouds so dark as to be nearly black. "She said she hoped the people there would surrender without incident, but to be ready if they didn't. And they didn't and we had to fire.

"Then there was the explosion. Some damn fool tried to close the Portal."

Rateliff nodded to himself, fitting the memories together piece by piece. The Portal to the Breach was open when they arrived to take control of the facility. They could simply have closed it, but the scientists must have known the Major's team would figure out how to open it again sooner or later. That's what the yelling was about, that we didn't understand, that *they* didn't even fully understand. So they hoped to blow it up and bury the entire thing, taking everyone with them. No Breach for anyone.

Except those of us who were close to it.

It had felt like an invisible hand had grabbed him by the gut, him and others. To his horror, he watched them pulled into the Portal to the Breach, both his people and their people. Major Dale was one of them. When the invisible hand yanked him in he'd been holding his sidearm and one of the control devices. It was handheld and could open and close the Portal to the Breach. He'd have to unlock the encryption on the device, but that would be more time-consuming than difficult.

Rateliff stood up from the rock in the clearing and rushed back to the riverbank. The device was not there. He climbed down and clawed through the mud. If he could find it, maybe he could open the Portal here. He splashed in the water, hoping maybe it was under the surface, maybe he could dry it out and use it.

It wasn't there. He knew it wasn't there because as he was pulled into the Breach, the device slipped from his grip. It was probably on the floor of the lab under the city whose name he couldn't remember.

Rateliff went back to the rock and sat down again, wondering what to do next.

* * *

March 17, 1802
A River

It worked! was the first thing that came to the Scientist's mind as he awoke. It was soon replaced with the awareness that tree branches were cracking and shattering around him. The wind blasted the trees and they groaned. The air was bitter cold and the Scientist got up. A tree branch fell only a few yards from him in the storm and he knew he had to find to cover. The world around him was shades of blue, grey and black. It was hard to make out anything beyond the ghost-like shapes of the trees around him. He ran in the opposite direction of the fallen branch, manoeuvring through the underbrush until he reached an open area of knee-high grass. The untamed field afforded a view of the sky and the storm clouds. Lightning flashed and rippled, followed by thunder pounding the air.

"Just a storm," the Scientist said. The words were all but drowned out by the wind. He looked to the horizon, hoping to see the light of a building, maybe a town, but there was none.

His hands hurt from the cold and he tucked them under his armpits. The thin material of his pants and shirt provided little protection from the elements. He knew he had to find shelter and get warm. Everything around him, the absence of leaves on the branches, the frigid air, all pointed to late winter. Cold was his enemy.

He took the satchel off his shoulder and put it on the ground. He undid his necktie and wrapped it around his ears like a bandana, then knelt next to the satchel.

I grabbed this when the soldiers arrived, the Scientist remembered. He could remember that, but not his own name. Things happened very fast at the lab facility. There had been very little warning. The captain of the guard told them the President was dead. Facilities and bases were being locked down. There wasn't much time, she said. She expected soldiers from the new regime to arrive at any moment.

The captain took him aside and...

The Scientist struggled to remember. She gave him an order and he refused.

"It was too important, I said. I grabbed the nearest control computer," he said out loud as he opened the satchel in the nearly freezing field. He pulled out what was inside, the very computer he'd taken from the facility, and felt the warmth pouring off it. The bottom where the battery was located was the warmest part and he held it close to his body. Another memory came, the captain and he embracing, long before things went south. "But I couldn't stop you. You did it anyway, didn't you? You set off the charges to close the Portal."

He could see her doing it after the soldiers opened fire on the guards. She set off the charges. The soldiers were under orders to take control of the facility. When the captain, the woman he loved, detonated the explosives, the major watched in horror. Then they were caught in the Breach. Pulled into it. And he woke up here.

The Scientist, warmer now but still in need of shelter, crossed the field and came upon a river. The winds were dying down and the sky above was clearing up. Stars and moonlight peaked through the clouds. He picked out a constellation he couldn't name as he walked.

* * *

It was only a little warmer the next morning. The Scientist awoke on a thin bed of evergreen branches in a small cluster of the trees. He was curled up on his side with the computer under his shirt, his feet in the thick, padded satchel, and using his shoes as a pillow. Despite the computer's warmth, he was shivering. Sleep came in tiny pieces and more than once he thought he might die of hypothermia.

In the morning light his situation didn't look much better. The landscape was trees, hills, grass and the river. He drank from it and decided to follow it west. West seemed the right choice, though he couldn't explain why exactly. Anyway, one direction was as good as another. He hoped to see fish in the river or vegetation on land he could eat. Or better yet, find something like civilization out here.

The day warmed up and walking generated heat, so after a while the Scientist put the computer back in the satchel. He spent a bit of time with it that morning, turning it on and checking out the readouts on the display. It had searched for a signal and found none. The apps worked and he began a relative geo-sync operation to try to see if the computer could determine the date and where he was. He spent the morning entering in variables at its prompting, mostly related to the position of the sun, moon and stars. It would take a few sessions, at least one of them at night, before the computer could even hazard a guess. When he finished entering all the data he could, the Scientist started west along the river.

He saw no fish or food and was getting hungry when he reached the ravine. When he caught the smell of burning meat, he thought at first he was imagining it. He'd seen no sign of anyone since the night before. The smell didn't go away, so he proceeded along the river hoping to find its source. Soon he spotted smoke and hurried along the bank. His stomach growled.

The smoke came from a campfire over which a small animal was mounted on a spit. The flesh was golden brown and the Scientist walked toward it, as if in a trance.

"Hold it, guy," said a voice behind him. There was the telltale cocking of a gun and the Scientist put his hands up.

"I'm not armed," said the Scientist.

"Very slowly take off the satchel and turn around," the voice said.

The Scientist did so. He didn't know what he expected to see when he turned around, but the man before him was not it. Covered in a mixture of furs from a few different animals and the military gear of a soldier, the man with the gun looked like something out of a post-apocalyptic movie. That was startling enough, but more so was in fact that the Scientist recognized the man under his thick beard and unkempt hair.

The man with the gun seemed to come to a similar conclusion.

"You're one of them, one of the scientists," the man said. "Are you real?"

The Scientist didn't quite know how to answer that except to say, "Yes, I'm real."

The man held the gun on him a few uncertain seconds longer, then holstered it, saying, "You can put your hands down."

"You were one of the soldiers who came into the facility to take control of the Portal," the Scientist said.

The man's eyes lit up.

"Yes! Those were our orders," the man said, walking past the Scientist to the cooking animal on the spit. He turned it over and sat on a large rock.

"And like me, you were pulled in and ended up here?" the Scientist asked.

"Yeah, that's right," the man said. "That was so long ago. Three years, maybe four. Been out here by myself, so I'm not sure. A least three years."

"But wait," the Scientist said, "I only arrived here last night. We entered at nearly the same time and came out years apart?"

228

"Not exactly at the same time," the man said. "One by one we were pulled in. Maybe that made a difference. Or not. We're here now, though. Spat us out at the same place."

"I woke up a few hours from here, upriver," said the Scientist. "I walked and then smelled the food. Is it almost done? I'm starving."

"You're hungry, but you ain't starving," the man said. "That feels a whole lot different than hungry."

The man took the animal off the spit and it steamed in the cool air. The Scientist's mouth watered.

The man nodded for the Scientist to join him, saying, "Come on over, guy."

"Thank you!" the Scientist said.

"Here," the man broke off a big piece of the animal's hindquarters and held it out to him. The Scientist took at bite, marvelled at how good it tasted and devoured his portion.

"I'm Rateliff," the man said.

"I, um, I can't remember my name," the Scientist said.

"Is that a fact?" Rateliff mused. "The Breach screws around with your memory. Don't I know it. I'll just call you Doc, then. You were a doctor at the facility, right? A scientist?"

"Yes," the Scientist said.

"The storm last night was unseasonal. I watched the front roll in from the east. It was something else," Rateliff said. "I guess that was you, huh? There was a storm when I arrived, too."

A soft chime came from the satchel. The two men stopped eating and looked at it.

"What do you have in there?" Rateliff asked.

The Scientist reached for the satchel, saying, "Some equipment. May I...?"

"By all means, Doc."

The Scientist opened the satchel and took out the small computer. He looked at Rateliff, who was watching him, his face still.

"It's asking for more information," the Scientist said. "I'm trying to use it to figure out what year it is. Maybe even where we are."

Rateliff's expression hadn't changed. The Scientist wondered if the man had heard him at all.

"Are you okay?" the Scientist asked.

"I know that piece of equipment," Rateliff said. "I was examining one similar to it, but smaller, before we were pulled into the Breach. It was in my hand and I dropped it. You can open a Portal with it, can't you?"

It was the Scientist's turn now to watch this man intently.

"Okay, Doc, how do we get home?" asked Rateliff.

The Scientist had asked himself the same question during his hours of walking.

"Um, we don't," he said to Rateliff.

Rateliff stopped chewing. His eyes first widened, then narrowed. His cheek twitched. He dropped his food and leapt over the campfire at the Scientist.

"Wrong answer, Doc," he said in a whisper that bordered on a growl. "I'm not staying stuck out here, wherever the hell *here* is! Turn that thing on and get us home!"

"I can only open a Portal at a specific spot," the Scientist explained. "The Breach is like a series of fractures, fissures, each spreading out slowly over time. We were just starting to map the fissures. The Portal we were studying was at the tip of just one of the cracks. We tried repeatedly to open a Portal along the length of the Breach and failed. Every time. We could *see* into the Breach, but couldn't venture inside. To go into the Breach, you have to enter from the tip of a fissure. The coordinates have to be precise. We were constantly recalculating. We tried to learn from our mistakes."

Rateliff backed down, returning to his rock and picking up the cooked animal he'd tossed aside.

"What mistakes?" Rateliff asked.

"We thought we'd mapped another fissure completely and a team went out to find the tip so we could try to open a portal," the Scientist said. "We were close, but whether the coordinates were off or the fissure grew suddenly we're not sure. My theory was that trying to force our way in caused that fissure to break open even more. I wasn't there, but I saw the footage. The Portal opened as expected, but in seconds it became unstable.

It consumed the volunteer operating the control module before closing. Until we knew more, we stopped trying to open new Portals. We stuck to the one we'd been studying and even then precautions were stepped up."

"When the computer in that device finishes its geo-sync, we're opening the damn thing up and going home," Rateliff said between chews on the dead animal.

"We don't know where the tip of a fissure is!" the Scientist said.

"Yes, we do."

* * *

The Scientist touched the carving on the aspen in the grove. It looked like a "P" crossed with an "L."

"I marked it after I first got here," Rateliff said.

"How do you know?" the Scientist asked. "We studied the Breach for years. We had computers and specialists..."

Rateliff was pointing to his stomach.

"You said you walked here, from hours in that direction?" Rateliff pointed back the way the Scientist had come. "Something compelled you, didn't it?"

The Scientist said nothing.

"I've been out here for years," Rateliff said. "I've explored and wandered and searched. The farther away I got from this spot, the more I felt that urge to come back. It pulls you. It keeps pulling until you give in. It's the same pull that took us into the Breach, remember? You must have felt it."

"Yeah," the Scientist said. "I felt it. And yes, that might have been what brought me here. But that's a whole lot different from trying to open up the Breach, to actually go *inside*, based on a gut feeling, no matter how *literal* that is."

"You get that thing fired up, mister, and you will see I know what I'm talking about," Rateliff said.

* * *

231

The Scientist sat with the computer on his lap next to the fire. Rateliff spared one of his crude fur coverings for him so he wouldn't freeze. The geo-sync app was requesting information on the night sky and the Scientist tapped the screen to enter the data or ran procedures at the app's prompting to calibrate the positions of things like constellations.

"I'll say this, Doc," Rateliff said after a long period of silently staring at the fire. "It's good to have company again. Ain't seen a soul in years. Man starts getting a little funny in the head after a while being on his own like this."

* * *

The Scientist was dozing when the chime came from the computer again. It was still night and the stars were easily visible in the clear sky overhead. The fire was low and Rateliff was curled up on the other side. Expecting the device was requesting additional data, he sat up and looked at the screen.

Geo-sync Complete
Calendar updated
March 18, 1802

Click HERE for
geographic coordinates

The Scientist stared at it, unable to believe it had determined the date based on his data. What if it was wrong? He clicked the prompt and a map appeared. It was accurate as far as he knew. The river was there, as well as the few landmarks he'd seen. He zoomed out and saw where they were in North America.

"What does it say, Doc?" asked Rateliff. His eyes were open, watching the Scientist.

"It has the date and our location," he replied.

Rateliff rose on his elbow, looking across the fire at the Scientist.

"Then we're going home," Rateliff said, "Right now."

"What if it's wrong? We have no way of corroborating the data!" said the Scientist.

Rateliff stood up and that's when the Scientist saw the gun in his hand.

"Let's get moving, Doc. Chop, chop. Time waits for no man," the Tech Sergeant said.

The Scientist got up. At gunpoint he was marched to the grove of aspens.

"We should test it first," the Scientist said.

"Test it *how*? There's only me and you here," Rateliff said. "We don't have a government facility at our disposal. We turn it on and we go in. Simple as that. If we don't come out exactly where we started, well, anywhere and any time has got to be better than this. Maybe it'll drop us in the '50s and we can see the birth of rock & roll."

They reached the aspen tree with the symbol carved into it, the end-point of the Breach according to Rateliff.

"Know what that symbol is, Doc?" Rateliff asked.

The Scientist didn't know.

"Fort McDaniel, home of The Fighting Dragons," Rateliff explained. "Any soldier who trained there could breathe fire and kick ass, they told us. They were right and that training has kept me alive all these years. I copied the dragon symbol from my tattoo. I know, I know, it hardly looks like anything but a squiggle, but that's part of the point. Simplicity. Keep it simple, stupid. That's what I'm doing now. Keeping it simple. We're going home. Right. Fucking. Now. Give me that thing."

He held out his hand for the computer and the Scientist handed it over. Rateliff balanced it on his arm while keeping the gun pointed at the Scientist. With his free hand, he tapped the screen and called up the app to open the Portal to the Breach.

"We can wait," said the Scientist.

"I'm done waiting," Rateliff said. "You'll thank me on the other side. We'll have a beer and some nachos and laugh about all this. What do you say, Doc?"

The Scientist didn't respond. He remembered the grainy footage of the volunteer who tried to open a new Portal. The

Portal had seemed to gobble him up. *Consume* had been the word the Scientist had used before and it still seemed appropriate. The man had been consumed and soon so would he and Rateliff.

The Tech Sergeant keyed the control computer and the Scientist held his breath.

There was nothing.

Then there was something.

A great wrenching sound erupted around them as deep as thunder and as awful as nails on a chalkboard.

"Time to go home, Doc!" Rateliff yelled.

The Scientist ran.

Rateliff fired his gun and the round missed him, but the Scientist dodged to his left and his foot caught a root. He went down as the world became grey around them. He turned back to see Rateliff holstering his gun.

"I only had the one round left, Doc. I was saving it for myself. I was maybe going to use it, but you showed up and brought me the return ticket," Rateliff said as he walked toward the Scientist. Behind the Tech Sergeant, the Scientist saw some of the grey world peeling away, the way wallpaper peels off the plaster in an old house. Another of the wrenching sounds accompanied it. Rateliff turned around.

"It's pulling me! This is the way out of here, Doc!" Rateliff yelled. He didn't wait for the Scientist now, but ran to the tear in reality. The Tech Sergeant's foot caught either a root or a rock and he stumbled. The computer slipped from his grasp and hit the ground. The green block was replaced by a red circle and the grey world began to fade. The Scientist darted to the computer, picked it up and backed away. Rateliff reached the tear, touched it and screamed. He pounded on it like it was a window. He stepped back, looked around and turned back to the Scientist. As the grey world of the Breach vanished, so too did Rateliff. He cried out to the Scientist again, but there was no sound. The Scientist, realizing what was happening, jabbed at the red circled, which flashed green again for a split second before returning to red. The Scientist tried again as Rateliff, himself little more than a shadow now, reached out to him. It was no use. The Portal wouldn't open. The grey world returned to normal and the shadow that was Rateliff faded into the darkness of the aspen grove.

"I'm sorry," the Scientist said. "If you can hear me, I'm sorry."

23

August 14, 1811
A Field

The wagon train wasn't the first to pass through the area, but it was the first he'd seen stay for any length of time. After the company of settlers had been there a week and showed no sign of leaving, Doc left his quiet, secluded ravine and walked out to meet them. He'd counted five or six families in the group, twenty-five souls in all. It was midday as he walked out across the field. When the settlers saw him, they stopped what they were doing and waited. A few called the children to stop playing and come back to the wagons. He expected the men might open fire or tell him to be off, to go away, but they didn't. The leader came out and stood between the camp and the scientist. Doc raised his hands.

"Greetings," Doc said. "I'm alone, a settler who only seeks the company of others and to get to know your group. I have knowledge of the area I'm happy to share."

"How long have you been out here?" said the camp's leader, a man with a thick Irish accent.

"A good many years," Doc said. "Are you looking to settle or will you be moving on?"

"We have a mind to put down roots," the man replied, pointing around him. "Yonder river would support a mill, me thinks. And back that a-ways to the east I'm thinking of planting an apple orchard, right below that hill there."

"Traffic's been on the upswing of late, so a community would no doubt prosper out here, I expect," Doc said.

"Are you hungry, stranger? We're looking to fix some lunch and I'd be most interested in your knowledge of the land," the man said, gesturing Doc to join him.

"Thank you, sir," Doc smiled. "A home-cooked meal would be grand."

"Liam McCabe's my name," the man said, offering his hand. Doc shook it.

"Good to meet you," Doc said. "They call me Doc. Doc Reed."

* * *

That evening, Doc returned to the ravine and the grove of aspens.

"Reed," he said to himself. "It has a good ring to it."

It was the first time he'd said it to another person, but the last name came to him a few years earlier. He'd come upon a pond and there enjoyed a thin meal of dried meat and berries. The reeds at the water's edge swayed in the breeze and a kind of peace settled upon him at last. He expected he'd sleep that night without having nightmares of Rateliff being lost in the Breach. When he hiked back to the ravine and bedded down, he was correct, his sleep was sound and refreshing.

He had a name now, though not the one he was born with. He wondered if he'd ever come to remember his real name or the name of the captain he loved in his old life. He could almost glimpse her in his shattered memory, but his feelings for her had not diminished. Many of the memories of that life were gone to him, but some of those final moments in the facility were still there and unusually still fresh.

She had been pulled in along with himself, Rateliff and the others. He and Rateliff had re-emerged and Doc knew she would too.

He picked up the control computer, which had been charging its battery in the sun all day, and activated it. In the days and weeks after Rateliff was lost in the Portal, Doc had tried several times to recalibrate it, to try to open the Portal and if Rateliff was inside somewhere, maybe he could save him.

Nothing worked, though. The re-syncs failed and Doc never figured out why. Eventually, he stopped trying and deep down hoped Rateliff was dead. No one deserved to be lost in that place.

He selected the message app and thought about the letter he would leave the captain, hoping against hope that maybe she (or perhaps even one of the others) would find it.

If they're drawn here as I was, as Rateliff was, there's hope, Doc thought.

He'd compose the message and leave the computer here, somewhere safe, and pray it kept transmitting for a good long time to come.

* * *

As Doc Reed began writing his message, a shadow moved behind him. So focused on his work was Doc that he did not notice it. The shadow moved out of the grove. It passed Doc on the bank of the river and left the ravine.

The shadow of the Prisoner Rateliff stopped at the top of the hill. Below, the campfires of the new settlement flickered in the distance.

About The Author

Patrick Lemieux is a Canadian artist and writer based in Toronto. He has exhibited his work internationally and it has featured in magazines and album sleeves.

He is currently working on the sequel to *The Prisoner Of Orchard Bend*. He is also assembling the second volume of his comic book series *Horizon Line*. Future book projects include a second collection of his artwork and a collection of his photography.

You can find him on Facebook and Instagram at *Patrick Lemieux Artist* and on Twitter @MadTheDJ